WREN TAYLOR

Author of the Sapphic Seas Series

Homestead for the Holidays

EPICEA PRESS
TACOMA, WA

Chapter One

"Ugh, I hate it," Katie said, squinting at the quivering laptop screen. She'd forgotten her glasses at home so she already had a headache and the intern's shaking hands weren't making it any easier to see the screen thrust in front of her face. "Whatever, size it for all the socials and send it over to me."

"You hate it? I thought I followed your brief exactly." The intern looked hurt, and Katie felt herself softening.

"The design is fine, it's what I asked for. I just hate the holidays, but that's not your fault." The advertisement was a mess of red and green ribbons curling through gold text pushing a laughable discount on the overpriced mass of shit sitting in the warehouse. And it was her job to get it moved before the new products arrived in January and the cycle started all over again.

"I thought you loved this time of year. You've been talking about it since I started in August."

"I love making money," Katie corrected. And usually the holiday season meant record sales and fat bonuses.

Usually.

She had delivered on her end of the bargain– despite numerous hangups that weren't even her fault along the way– and the C-Suite had been full of laudatory words but quiet about her annual bonus since Black Friday. If she thought about it too much, it really pissed her off. After eight years of busting her ass for them, they still seemed to think she worked for personal gratification instead of a paycheck. As if praise would get her any closer to her dream of leaving it all behind. But that was a spiral she couldn't go down. The intern with the trembling hands was still hovering.

"Let's get this wrapped up so we can get out of here. Send me those files and you can take off for the weekend. Go have fun."

The intern nodded and backed out of Katie's office.

Fun. It sounded like a foreign concept, but the intern was still young and hadn't had all the joy sucked out of her yet. Katie could almost remember when she'd been like that.

She picked up a mug of tepid coffee and stared out the huge floor-to-ceiling windows at the darkening gray outside. The weather certainly wasn't helping her mood. Raindrops splattered against the window pane, distorting the view of Puget Sound peeking between the corridors of high rise buildings. It was only mid-afternoon but the light was already fading. There was only one week left until the shortest day of the year, and it would be pitch black by the time she got home to her empty apartment.

Her email pinged with the files from the intern, and she went through the motions robotically, first double checking that they were the correct files, then uploading them into various email and social media scheduling programs. She dashed out a quick caption, the same regurgitated nonsense she had spewed about the products a thousand times before, then shut her laptop and picked up her phone. Three new notifications begged for her attention, and she swiped to open the dating app and check out her latest matches.

Jenna, 26, Ballard. She clicked on photos and the woman's smiling face filled her screen. Straight, blondish, shoulder-length hair was tucked under a backwards trucker hat, an enamel pin of the pride flag stuck into the mesh. Katie swiped through the rest of the pictures, the typical PNW array of hiking, camping, and craft beers. Meh. Jenna seemed like a walking granola stereotype, and was decidedly not Katie's type.

It wasn't that she was against spending time outside, but she preferred to spend her weekends doing normal weekend things. Not waking up at three in the morning on a Saturday to drive four hours into the wilderness in a futile attempt to beat all the other hikers to the trailhead. She swiped to the next match.

Audrey, 43, Bellevue. Too old for her, and way too Bellevue. Katie didn't have the patience for suburban yuppie types rediscovering themselves after being married to their absent tech guru husbands for twenty years. Too much baggage. Nice house, though. Good for her. Katie hoped Audrey found what she was looking for, but it wasn't going to be with Katie.

She swiped through a few more profiles, but it was more of the same. *Alex, 30, Queen Anne.* Katie paused. Alex looked interesting. No, she didn't, not really. But she had a nice smile, and she was nearby. Ugh. Katie took a screenshot of the profile and texted it to her best friend.

"Thoughts?" she asked, waiting for the three dots to pop up that showed her friend was writing back. None appeared. Of course. Megan was busy. It was dinner time on the east coast and she had a new baby at home that was taking up all her time. Not that Katie blamed her, she wasn't that much of a bitch. But it still hurt to feel so alone, all of the time. She clicked her phone off, and went back to watching the red and white car lights snaking through the Seattle streets below.

Eight years in the city and she still felt like she had yet to find her place. She was friendly enough with her coworkers, but too introverted to put herself out there to make real friends. The few times she had tried, plans had always fallen through. Her ex had given her a social circle, but they were always Jackie's friends first, and disappeared with the breakup.

A knock sounded at her office door, then her boss, Peter, poked his head in. He was like every boss she'd ever had, a brawny white man who thought he knew way more than he did despite having no background or education in marketing, too young for his title and given the job through nepotism. It had cost Katie a promotion she had more than earned, but she had taken it in stride, waiting patiently for her turn even when he proved time and time again that he didn't have a clue what he was doing. Katie groaned internally, wondering which of his messes she was going to have to clean up before she could finally leave for the weekend.

"Got a sec?" he asked, inviting himself in.

"Of course." Katie faked a smile, even though looking at his dumb face made her want to strangle him.

He sat across from her. "Everything scheduled for the next few weeks?"

"Yeah, the first email goes out tomorrow and the social ads are in the approval process, should be cleared soon. I'll check to make sure everything's running smoothly before I fly out."

"Excited for your vacation?"

"You have no idea," Katie said. By Monday, she would be lounging on a beach at a resort in Mexico, trading in the gloom of Seattle winter for sun and sand until the new year. It was exactly the fresh start she needed. "I'll have my phone though, in case you need anything. The resort should have good internet."

Peter looked uncomfortable, his already flushed cheeks turning an even deeper shade of red. Katie's stomach turned with apprehension, wondering what fresh hell he was about to spring on her. Whenever he asked to meet with her, he always had some bombshell of a problem he created to drop in her lap for her to fix and she could sense him dancing around the ask. Whatever it was, it had better not interfere with her vacation.

"This is just not working anymore," he blurted out, so quickly that Katie could barely parse the words. "Today will be your last day with the company. I'm sorry."

His words hit Katie like a bucket of ice water, drenching her with shock. He couldn't be saying what she thought he was saying. It was impossible. "You're..." she trailed off, still trying to compose herself. "You're firing me?"

"Calm down," Peter said in that maddening tone that men used to chastise women when they were perfectly calm to begin with. His ears and neck were turning the same crimson shade as his face. It looked like he was the one who needed to calm down before he had a heart attack. "It's nothing you did, it's just the way the economy is right now. We appreciate everything you've done for us to this point."

"That's bullshit! I made you three million dollars last month."

Peter shrugged. "They want to restructure and bring marketing and creative under the same umbrella. Unfortunately in reorgs, sometimes there isn't room for everyone."

There was no point in protesting. Peter could pretend all he wanted that the decision was out of his hands and passed down from above, but Katie knew it was because she had called him out in a meeting just a few weeks prior. The only crime worse than proving a man wrong was doing it in front of his peers. Whatever. If they wanted to drive their company off a cliff, she was happy to get out of the way and let them do it. Fuck them.

Peter laid a thick stack of papers in front of her. "They're offering you a very generous severance package."

Katie looked down, tears blurring her vision. She wouldn't give him the satisfaction. "I can't sign this right now. I need time." It was too much to think about, and she was smart enough to know she probably needed to consult a lawyer for the mountain of legal-looking documents he pushed at her.

"That's fine," Peter said, though his tone had gone cold and the color was fading rapidly from his cheeks. "They need it by Tuesday or you waive your severance option."

He knew exactly what he was doing, and it was enraging, but what was she supposed to do? The company that had shown themselves to be nothing but bullies was staying true to itself in her final hour. They knew she was leaving on vacation, they knew she would be pressured into signing because of the time crunch. They were completely and utterly inhumane, and they didn't care. Katie blinked, trying to read the paper more clearly.

Eight weeks severance. Pathetic. *Performance issues.* But she had just had a performance review and gotten a near perfect score. *Not eligible for rehire.* Not that Katie ever wanted anything to do with the company again, but seriously? Based on what? The phrases kept jumping out at her, each making her throat constrict with hurt, betrayal, and anger. She had done nothing wrong, but they were pretending it was her fault.

Fuck it. She picked up a pen and scrawled her signature on the first paper. Eight weeks pay was better than nothing and they were forcing her hand. The sooner she was done with them the better. She flipped to the next page. *Equipment return.* She slid the laptop across her desk to Peter, then scrawled her signature again. One by one, she worked through the pages, then pushed the stack back to Peter, glaring at him.

"I'll make you copies of all this while you pack up your things, then I'll walk you out."

Like a criminal, Katie thought. Her only crime was being too outspoken, too unaccepting of the status quo, too tired of a room full of men telling her what they thought women wanted. But they were going to make an example of her anyways, trotting her out of the office on a perp walk for everyone to gawk and gossip about what had happened. Fuck them all.

She had given them everything. She'd moved across the country, away from her friends to take what she thought was her dream job in the city she'd scribbled in the margins of her notebooks over the years. She'd stayed late too many times to count, missing date nights and working holidays, all to show them how much she cared. She never took time off if it wasn't convenient for the company, and had picked up even more job responsibilities since the pandemic when her team was slashed in half. The increased hours had cost her her relationship. If all that wasn't enough for them, it was never going to be.

She didn't have many personal belongings to pack, just a framed quote by Audre Lorde and a cactus Megan had sent her for her birthday with a note joking that it would be impossible for her to kill. Katie had always claimed she kept her office sparse because she liked to keep her professional and personal lives separate. It was easier to believe the lie than confront the truth: she didn't have a personal life.

There had been no time to amass trinkets and photos of loved ones. She was barely on speaking terms with her family, and for nearly a decade, her entire life had revolved around work. And in the span of one casual meeting, it was all ripped away from her. Convenient of him to wait until two days after she had submitted the marketing plan for the first quarter of the new year.

Peter returned to the door, and she refused to meet his eyes. She had nothing left to say to him, or any of them. The elevator ride was awkward and took too long, the doors chiming to open at seemingly every floor before finally spitting her out into the lobby of the building, mere yards away from freedom. She didn't even bother to say goodbye as she hurried to the revolving door, pressed both hands against the glass pane, and spun out into the cold Seattle streets.

Katie made it all the way to the bus stop before the tears forced their way free, trailing alongside the raindrops that pelted her face. If nothing else, she was proud of herself for not crying in front of Peter.

A group of high school students crowded around the benches, completely unperturbed by the rain they had all grown up with, laughing at some inside joke. More commuters pushed under the awning. Some gave her pitying glances as they noticed her distress, but no one offered a word of comfort. Fitting for Seattle, the great bustling city of disconnectedness, so different from the outskirts of DC where she had grown up.

She supposed she preferred the polite, yet cool, interactions over the effusive offers of prayer and endless small talk or the chest puffing of wannabe politicians overly proud of their parentally-subsidized, underpaid jobs on the Hill, but it was lonely and hard for an outsider to break in.

Her phone vibrated with a new text message, and she checked it as she climbed into the bus, snagging a seat by the window before it was completely full.

"She's hot, why not?" Megan's response lit up the screen.

"I just got laid off." Katie's fingers typed the message out quickly, but paused before she hit send. Seeing it written down made it real. It was real, very real, even if it hadn't totally sunk in yet. But she didn't want to burden Megan with that, her friend had enough problems of her own. She deleted the message. "Idk if she's my type. She seems kind of generic." Sent.

"Who cares if she's your type? I thought you were looking for a rebound."

"I am."

"So go out, have fun, get laid, and ghost her. Whatever you do, don't fall in love."

Katie smiled through her tears. Megan's advice may not always have been good, but she always had Katie's back. And she was right. Katie just needed to have a good time and forget about work, forget about Jackie, forget about everything. She liked Megan's message, then switched over to the dating app. *Alex, 30, Queen Anne* stared back at her.

"Hey," Katie typed in the messenger box. "What are you up to tonight?"

Chapter Two

It was still raining, but the sky was a lighter shade of gray that indicated the sun had risen somewhere behind the clouds. For once, Katie didn't mind how dim and drab it was. Her head was pounding, and the deep, painful regret of overconsumption was already setting in. Alex was breathing heavily in the bed beside her, still fast asleep. She looked around the unfamiliar apartment as she tried to piece together what had happened the night before.

Alex had texted her back right away. Happy hour margaritas in Capitol Hill had turned into drinks at a nearby bar, then they'd danced until the early hours of the morning before stumbling upon a taco truck with the best lengua tacos Katie had ever eaten. And then Alex had kissed her, full of passion and alcohol-fueled lust, and taken Katie back to her studio, where they had...

Katie blushed, as though someone else could hear her thoughts. She hadn't indulged in a one night stand in years. The hook up had been fine, nothing world-shattering, but nothing awful. And yet, she felt emptier than ever.

Katie slid out from beneath the blankets, being careful not to disturb Alex's slumber. She retrieved her bra from where it had been discarded near the front door and reclasped it around her ribcage before pulling on the blouse she had worn to work the day before. After quickly checking to make sure she still had her phone, keys, and wallet, she stepped into her rain boots and tiptoed out.

It seemed like all of Seattle had decided to sleep in that Saturday morning. The streets were quiet, devoid of the honking mess of cars that usually clogged the intersections and spit foul-smelling exhaust into the air. The rain that had seemed oppressive in its endlessness the night before was a welcome shower, washing away the mistakes she had made.

Katie pulled out her phone to order a ride back to her place, then decided she would rather walk. It was only a couple miles and would give her time to think while she worked the hangover out of her system. She switched over to the dating app. Alex's eager messages before they met up were still open on the screen. Her finger hovered over the profile picture for a second as Katie felt a pang of guilt. What would Megan do? Katie tapped the button and the notification flashed on the screen. User blocked. She sighed with relief. At least that was done.

There was nothing wrong with Alex, there was just nothing about her that was right for Katie. She'd had fun, or something like it, and it was time to move on. Megan had pushed her to get back into the dating scene, just a few short weeks after Jackie had stormed out for the last time, the day before Thanksgiving. She'd wanted Katie to spend the holiday in the mountains with her family, and couldn't understand why Katie had to work on the most important retail holiday of the year. It wasn't that Katie didn't want to go, but the internet at the cabin would have been too spotty and if something had gone wrong it could have cost the company millions in sales.

Fuck. She was doing it again, thinking about work when she was sure they weren't thinking about her. Peter was probably sleeping in without a care in the world for the life he had just upended. Fuck. She needed to stop thinking about that place. It was dead to her. Dead. None of it had ever mattered, it was just a lie they had made her believe. Her need for approval, to rise in the ranks and make a name for herself, to be a real career woman, the boss bitch in the director's office with her eyes on the C-Suite... it was all a weakness that they had exploited to keep her subservient for far too long.

Katie walked through the quiet neighborhood, passing ornate Craftsman houses decorated with thick, green garlands and multi-colored Christmas lights that blinked mockingly at her through the morning mist. The holidays were hard enough when she still had a girlfriend and a good job. They would be so much worse unemployed and alone. Hot tears pricked at her eyes and she swallowed back her rising anger at the injustice of it all. A dog barked, startling her as its owner mumbled a hasty apology from across the street.

Two more days and she would be on a plane away from it all. Megan had begged her to change her flight and fly out to DC instead after Jackie dumped her, but being an unwilling participant in Megan's family's holiday cheer was the last thing Katie wanted to do. Plus, she would only be intruding. And she didn't really like babies, even if Megan's was one of the cuter ones. Mexico was definitely the better option.

She should have peed before she left Alex's apartment, but she had been in such a rush to leave before Alex woke up that she hadn't even thought of it. Her bladder was beginning to remind her, though, and she cursed her decision to walk home instead of ordering a ride. The scent of coffee filled the air, and Katie followed it to a coffee shop, empty except for the two employees behind the counter. She ordered a latte and rushed to the bathroom while they prepared it, making it there not a moment too soon.

She took a good long look in the mirror while washing her hands, horrified by what she saw. Her mascara had smudged into her eyeliner, giving her the worst raccoon eyes. So much for being waterproof. Her eyes were puffy and bloodshot from drinking a lot and crying even more.

Fuck.

She'd cried in front of Alex, somewhere in between the tacos and the sex. Alex had held her, stroked her hair and told her everything would be alright.

"Katie?" The barista called as she came back out, even though she was the only customer in the shop.

She picked up her latte from the counter and pulled her hood back up, ignoring the pitying glances the baristas gave her as she resumed her walk of shame. Or did they? She was probably reading into it too much. And so what if she was walking home alone in the rain in the morning on a Saturday? As Megan would say, at least she could still get some.

She pulled out her phone and opened the app. She shouldn't have blocked Alex, amazing Alex who was so sweet and bubbly and had mostly been able to get Katie's mind off everything for a little while. What if she was the one? Even if she was so completely different from Katie, at least she was nice and Katie's midnight meltdown hadn't freaked her out too much. Maybe she could build that emotional connection over time. It didn't have to be love at first sight to be worth pursuing. She was too old for that kind of fairy-tale romance anyways. Alex was practical, with a stable job and sane interests.

Unblock profile. Alex's face popped back into view, judging her. *You ran away,* it seemed to say. *Coward. The sex wasn't even that good.* Block profile. No, Megan was right. She needed to slow down, stop rushing into things, let loose, and have a little fun without any strings attached. Which is exactly what Mexico would do for her. She might even extend the trip and stay into the new year. There was nothing holding her back anymore and she could use the time to decompress and figure out what her next move would be.

If the holiday decorations in Queen Anne might have been called tasteful, the ones as she walked towards the more commercialized part of town were downright garish. The city was beginning to wake up, and tourists spilled onto the streets, each vying for the best shot of the Space Needle adorned with its seasonal tree of lights at the top. Christmas carols piped through loudspeakers added aural offense to the visual assault, and her head pounded from her hangover. Finally she arrived at her building and keyed in the code. She stopped at the long wall of mailboxes and emptied hers into the trash without bothering to see if there was anything important among all the junk. There never was.

Her phone buzzed as she took the elevator to the fourth floor. Megan, texting to make sure she had made it home alright. Katie started to type back, then hit call instead.

"Hello?" Megan answered on the first ring.

"What's up?" Katie asked. "Are you busy?"

"Not if you don't mind being on speaker. I'm nursing Quentin. So, how was it?"

"Awful. I cried." Katie laughed, and told her everything.

"Well, I'm still proud of you for putting yourself out there."

"I dunno, maybe I'm just meant to be alone." Katie sighed, looking around the dark apartment. Jackie had taken most of the things that had made it home when she moved out, and their joint lease was up in February, so Katie had already started boxing up the rest of the nonessentials. The result was an apartment that looked half lived-in. Fitting for Katie's half-life she'd been living.

"I'm worried about you, Kitty Kat," Megan said, pulling out Katie's old sorority nickname from what felt like a different lifetime. "You don't seem happy out there."

"I didn't know I was supposed to be happy that my whole fucking life fell apart in less than a month."

"But even before all this happened it seemed like you haven't been yourself."

"I think I just need to unwind, get some sun and sand. Winters are hard here, but Mexico will be good for me."

"Mhmm," Megan hummed. She didn't sound convinced. "Have you ever thought about moving back east? I have this friend from grad school who just relocated here. I think you'd really like her."

"What happened to be single for a while and live it up?"

"Well do that first in Mexico, and then when you're ready to settle down, come home and meet her at least."

"We'll see." Katie had no intention of going back to DC, and Megan knew it, but she still tried every time. "How about you come out here? Maybe this summer when the weather is better?"

"I'd love to, but it's so hard with—"

"—the baby. I know." Katie sighed. "I miss you, Megs." *I miss who you were before you became a mother and forgot about me.* But she would never say that. She was happy, truly, that all of Megan's dreams had come true. They just weren't hers. And even though they had promised nothing would make them grow apart, the distance felt greater than ever.

"Aww, don't make me feel bad. We'll see each other again soon. I gotta run though, Q just spit up all over me. I'm glad you got home safe, though. Love you, miss you, talk to you soon!" The other end of the line went silent.

Katie lay back on the couch and flipped to the weather app. Rain, rain, and more rain. It was nothing unusual, but it did get exhausting after a while. She swiped to the next page, and the sun beamed at her. It was bright and warm in Cozumel, the tiny island crowded with luxury resorts just off the coast of the Yucatan. A notification flashed across the top of the screen. New weather alert. She clicked it.

"The National Weather Service has issued a blizzard warning for the rocky mountain states beginning overnight on Monday. Interstates may be shut down due to hazardous conditions. Roads may become icy without warning, and visibility may be low. Travelers should use extreme caution."

Sucks to be them, she thought, setting the phone down. Luckily she wouldn't have to deal with any of that nonsense. Her flight was leaving Monday afternoon, and she would be sitting on the beach with a margarita as the rest of the nation hunkered down for the storms. The thought of sunshine was motivating enough for her to drag herself off the couch. She chugged a glass of water and felt her headache instantly subside, if only the tiniest bit, then made her way into the bedroom to begin packing.

Chapter Three

"Attention passengers, this is your pilot speaking." The voice crackled over the plane's intercom, startling Katie awake from her nap. She took off her eye mask and squinted in the dim plane lighting. "Due to a medical emergency on board, we will be rerouting through Bozeman." Passengers around her were beginning to mutter to one another. "Our estimated time of arrival in Bozeman is 9:14 PM. We apologize for the inconvenience, and would like to reassure you that our travel agents will be standing by when we land to get you all rebooked and on the way to your final destinations."

The flight had already been delayed leaving Seattle, so of course there was some other issue; that was just the sort of luck Katie had. She almost expected it at that point, and refused to let it phase her. So what if she missed her connecting flight with the short layover in Dallas? The worst that would happen was arriving in Mexico a day late, but she was already planning to stay longer, so it was only a minor inconvenience. After everything else that had happened, she didn't have the energy to be bothered over something as trivial as a flight change.

"Excuse me?" She flagged one of the flight attendants down. "Where was it the pilot said we're landing now?"

"Bozeman, ma'am."

Ew. It always freaked Katie out when people called her ma'am. She was only thirty-two, and she didn't think she looked *that* old yet. "Where is that?" she asked, feeling a little dumb. She knew she had heard of it before, but she just couldn't place the name.

"Montana. We're just about forty minutes out." The flight attendant smiled warily, as if she expected Katie to put up a fight.

She wasn't. Katie was fully in vacation mode, and she refused to let anything get to her. Even Montana, a state she knew almost nothing about except for how they voted in the last presidential election, wasn't going to dull her spirits. She pulled her eye mask back over her eyes and leaned her head against the window, imagining sipping a cocktail from a coconut as palm trees swayed around her.

The next time she opened her eyes, the plane was lurching up and down in the worst turbulence Katie had felt in her life. She gripped the armrests and willed herself not to vomit. She'd never had a problem with motion sickness before, and its sudden onset felt like one more cruel joke from the universe. Another passenger shrieked as the plane jolted again. Katie tightened her seatbelt until it dug into her thighs, wondering how the measly strap was supposed to save her from catapulting to the ground.

"Folks, you may have noticed we're experiencing a bit of turbulence on our descent into Bozeman here. I just need you all to hang tight for about ten more minutes here while we get wheels on the ground."

Katie looked around, meeting the eyes of other travelers who looked as queasy as she felt. She should have listened to Megan and flown to DC. Then she would have been on a safe flight to people and places she knew, not crash landing in some flyover state on a completely misguided journey to somehow find herself again in Mexico like she was the star of some sappy, middle-aged empowerment movie. Really, what had she been thinking?

The plane thudded into the ground, and Katie shut her eyes again. If this was how it was going to end for her, she didn't want to watch. She just hoped it was over quickly. The plane hopped back into the air, tilted to the left, and then thudded into the ground again. She opened one eye to peer out the window as the plane slowed, both wheels finally firmly on the ground, and wondered if they had crashed in a field somewhere. There was nothing but snow as far as the eye could see, on the ground and swirling lightly through the air.

"Welcome to Bozeman, folks," the pilot said cheerfully. "We'll be taxiing into gate 1A, and we ask that you remain seated until paramedics can get our unwell passenger off the plane. We appreciate your flexibility today, and thank you for choosing to fly with us."

It'll be the last time, Katie thought. The plane turned and the smallest airport she had ever seen came into view. It wasn't like she had never traveled before, but this was ridiculous. It looked more like the type of log cabin Jackie's family would rent in the mountains than a bustling hub of travel and tourism. She pulled her phone out of her purse and flipped it out of airplane mode. It buzzed to life, three new text messages.

"Hope you have the best time. Have a safe flight and let me know when you get there!"

Katie snorted. If only Megan knew. It was late on the east coast though, and Katie didn't want to wake her up or make her worry. She would text her back in the morning when everything was sorted out and she was hopefully in Dallas or, even better, Cozumel. She doubted she was getting a flight out that night from the airport that looked like it was used once a week though. Oh well, that was the airline's problem to deal with. She wondered what kind of hotel they would put her up in, what kind of hotel was even available in a place like Bozeman, Montana. As long as it had a hot tub, she would be fine. She could pretend it was Mexico for a night.

People at the front of the plane were standing and retrieving their carry-ons, so it seemed whatever medical emergency had taken place was resolved. When her turn came, she grabbed her bag and nearly sprinted off the plane. There was no need to rush though, everyone on the plane already seemed to be in the line at the single agent's counter.

Her assessment from the plane that the airport looked more like a cabin in the woods than a hub of transit was only amplified once she was inside. Warm wooden beams arched high overhead, and large windows framed what she assumed was a great view, not that she could see it through the pitch black night and swirling snow.

"Welcome to Big Sky Country," proclaimed a large sign. Katie wondered what that was all about. It must have been some brand or local sports team. Who knew what Montana people were into? It was never an area where she had done much market research. The state's population was less than a city like Seattle, and not worth the ad spend or time to figure out what they were into or how to sell to them. Ugh, she was thinking about work again.

"Next in line, please," the tired-looking agent drawled. He looked more like a cowboy than airline support staff, and Katie blinked, wondering if the stress of the long day was making her see things. "Welcome to Bozeman, miss, what can I help you with?" At least he hadn't called her ma'am.

"Yeah, I was on that flight from Seattle that ended up here, and I need to get to Cozumel. In Mexico."

He typed quickly into his computer and frowned. "I can get you on a flight to San Francisco tomorrow afternoon, as long as the weather holds. Then you would change in Mexico City, and get to Cozumel in the evening."

So that would be two days lost. Not ideal. "What other options are there?"

"Everything that leaves earlier would be a longer layover, and there's nothing more direct than that from here."

"Fine, I guess I'll do that then."

"Great." He typed a few more things into his system and then printed a few pages. "This is your new itinerary. Now if anything happens to change, the airline will text this number from your original booking."

"But it won't, right? That's just a thing you have to tell people."

"I can't make any promises, miss. They're saying a storm's comin' but you know how they get those things wrong more often than not. If you're the prayin' sort, you might try that."

"Right. And what am I supposed to do until then?"

He flipped to the next page, which had a large coupon printed on it. "The airline is offering you a $100 hotel voucher. There are a few in town with shuttles from here, and their numbers are listed there for you."

"Aren't you supposed to figure that out for me?"

"If you have any problems using the voucher you can call the airline's corporate helpline here." The man pointed to a tiny number printed at the bottom of the page. "They answer phones 24/7 to assist travelers like yourself."

"Don't bother with the Drive-Inn," a woman behind her in line piped up. "We just booked the last room."

"Is there anything else I can assist you with?" The agent asked.

"I guess not," Katie said, feeling a bit lost.

"I can help the next in line!" the agent called, and Katie gathered the papers and moved off to the side.

The few remaining passengers in line had overheard the conversation, and they were all on their phones. When Katie pulled out hers to try the first number below the Drive-Inn, all she got was a busy signal. Same for the next one. Whatever. She could be patient and wait for everyone else to sort their lodging out. There was a surprising number of hotels on the list, and surely there was plenty to go around. She hadn't seen much of it yet, but she couldn't imagine anyone visiting Bozeman on purpose. It was still early, only 10PM, so she had time to figure it out.

She sat down in one of the uncomfortable airport lobby chairs and scrolled through videos on her phone while she waited for the line to go down. Finally, the last person approached the agent. Instead of looking agitated like everyone else, she sauntered up to the counter casually. Something about her was intriguing, so Katie turned the music blaring through her headphones down so she could eavesdrop on the conversation.

"Welcome back, Lou." The agent's demeanor had completely changed.

It was obvious he knew the woman, and Katie wondered if she was a local or just a frequent traveler. She was wearing jeans and a thick coat, and a black felt cowboy hat covered her head. She radiated masc energy and quiet confidence that immediately pulled Katie in and made her want to know more about her, like who she was and what had driven her to the godforsaken town of Bozeman.

The woman lowered her head in a quick nod. "Good to see you, Marlow. They've got you working late tonight."

"Some flight got diverted from Seattle, caused a whole buncha headaches for a whole lotta people, and they left me here alone to sort it out. I was supposed to be out of here an hour ago. But what can I do for ya?"

"Somehow the people at LAX lost my damned luggage, and I was hoping you might be able to track it down for me."

"I'm sure I can do that for ya, reckon it might be a few days though. Storm's coming in, they're saying it'll shut down everything."

"I heard, but that's alright. Don't have much use for shorts and tank tops up here in December anyways."

"Well, I'll bring it out by the homestead whenever it shows up."

"No need, that's way out of your way. Just send me a text and I'll swing by next time I'm in town."

"You got it, Lou. Now get yourself home before the weather really rolls in."

The woman's round, rosy cheeks lifted with her smile, and she tipped her hat in gratitude, revealing a head of short-cropped hair that Katie found herself longing to touch. "Thanks, Marlow. I'll see you around."

"The last shuttle to the Bozeman Motel is leaving now," the airport's intercom announced as the lights flickered, and Katie realized the airport was shutting down.

Shit. She had been so distracted by her people watching that she hadn't even tried to call any of the hotels on the list. She jumped up and began shoving things back into her purse, then rushed to the doors only to watch the shuttle pull off into the night. Fuck. She pulled out her phone and opened the rideshare app. The map loaded, then refreshed, then refreshed again.

"No cars available. Please try again in a few minutes."

Fuck. Okay, well she would just call the hotels. Beg for them to make an exception, send a shuttle out one more time. After all, none of this was Katie's fault. Surely someone would take pity and help her. Or eventually the app would connect her with a driver.

"Need a ride somewhere?" The question from the woman made Katie jump. She thought she was the only one left at the airport.

"No thanks, I'm fine," she replied quickly, embarrassed that the stranger was able to pick up on her struggle.

"No offense, but you don't look fine." The woman smiled, her blue eyes gleaming playfully in the dim emergency lights. She looked like she was the same age as Katie, maybe a little older. "Unless you wanted to spend the night in the airport? If that's the case I'll leave you to it, but I just had to make sure you were okay."

"Well..." Katie hesitated. Megan would kill her if she hopped in the car with a stranger in the middle of nowhere. That was how people got murdered. But it wasn't like she was running off with some skeezy man. Katie always thought her gaydar was broken, but some women were just so obviously into women that even she couldn't miss it. The woman standing in front of her was one of those women that just screamed "I'm a lesbian!" Her saunter, her smile, her short cropped hair. The loose jeans and thick, tan, no-nonsense jacket. Even her stature, short and strong and stocky. For a brief instant, Katie imagined curling up to her chest, cuddling into her warm curves. She brushed the thought aside. "Yeah, I guess I could use a ride." *On your face.* Her cheeks turned hot. Thank God she hadn't said that out loud. What had gotten into her, anyways? She was probably just delirious from the stress of a long day and a crazy flight. And it didn't help that Lou was insanely attractive.

"Well, come on then. I'm parked out in the back lot. Oh yeah, I'm Lou." The woman stuck her hand out, and Katie shook it, second-guessing her decision already. Lou didn't seem like a serial killer, but then again, none of them did. No. She had to stop thinking like that, it was just the podcasts getting to her.

"Katie," she introduced herself. Her hand was warm where Lou had gripped it, and she missed the feeling as soon as she let go. There was no time to dwell on that, Lou was already striding towards a door marked for employees only. "Oh so, you work here?"

"No, but Marlow lets me park in the back lot so he can keep an eye on my truck when I have to leave town."

"That's nice of him." How small was Bozeman anyways? She'd certainly never known anyone that got airport perks just because they happened to know someone who worked there.

Fluorescent lights flickered overhead as Lou led Katie down a narrow, cinder block hallway through the depths of the airport.

"Brace yourself," Lou said, pausing by a door with a bright red exit sign mounted above it and looking Katie head to toe. "It's pretty cold."

The door clunked as Lou pushed it open, and Katie squealed as the first blast of cool air hit her. Her rain jacket was insulated for the cold Seattle winters, but quickly showed itself to be vastly inadequate for the howling Montana wind that cut through the fabric as if it wasn't even there. Headlights flashed through the snow when Lou clicked her keys, revealing a red truck Katie probably wouldn't have noticed through the snow. It was only a few feet away, but Katie hesitated in the doorway. The distance felt impossibly long.

"Here, let me get that for you." Lou took Katie's suitcase and tossed it in the back of the truck cab, then opened the passenger door for Katie.

She climbed up into the enormous cab, feeling tiny and out of place perched on the wide bench that towered over the snow-covered parking lot. Katie wasn't the type of person that did pickup truck things. She didn't even own a car. But the truck seemed clean enough, and she was thankful to be out of the biting wind, even if there was a faint animal aroma permeating the air. Not bad, necessarily, sort of grassy and musky at the same time, but definitely present.

The engine hummed and heat finally began to pour out of the vents as the car warmed up while Lou brushed snow from the windows. Katie wondered if she was making a huge mistake. She'd learned to listen to her gut instinct a long time ago, but no alarm bells were sounding for Lou. Instead, Katie felt oddly safe in her presence– considering they had just met– and more relaxed than she'd felt in weeks.

"So which hotel are you at?" Lou asked, kicking the snow off her boots before she climbed behind the wheel.

"I actually didn't get a room yet so you can just drop me off at any of them, whatever is easiest for you, and I'll make it work from there."

"Well, there's only a few in town and they're pretty much all clustered together, so we'll just drive over there and see what they've got left." The faintest trace of a frown appeared between Lou's eyebrows, as though she doubted Katie's ability to figure it out on her own.

Katie brushed it aside. She was used to people underestimating her, it had been happening her whole life. They saw her carefully manicured exterior and assumed she was helpless and incompetent because she knew how to do her makeup and what to wear to turn heads. She was a lot smarter and stronger than anyone gave her credit for, and it gave her great satisfaction to prove them wrong.

Katie opened her mouth to ask Lou if she knew of any hotels with hot tubs, then decided that was probably a dream she needed to let go of. She would just settle for a hot shower and a bed at that point. Snow crunched beneath the truck's tires as they rolled slowly through a town that looked like a modern scene from an old western movie. There was a pawn shop and a bank, both closed for the night. A neon sign cut through the snow to advertise that the bar was also closed. Movie theater, closed. Restaurant, closed.

"Is Bozeman always this dead?" Katie asked.

"It's a Monday night in the middle of winter in the middle of nowhere," Lou laughed and the corners of her eyes crinkled. "What did you expect?"

"Not to be in Bozeman," Katie said, smiling. Lou's laughter was contagious, and she couldn't help but relax a little more. Her relief was short-lived though, ending when they arrived at a cluster of chain motels, just as Lou had promised.

"Sorry, we're fully booked," the receptionist at the first motel apologized, not looking very sorry at all.

"I don't have anything until next week, after the game," was the response from the second. "I'd be surprised if you could find anything for sixty miles, between that and the flights that got canceled."

"Please, you have to have something. Even like a shitty room with a broken sink or something? I'll only be here one night." Katie wasn't above begging.

"Sorry, I can't help you."

Ugh. Katie sank down onto one of the plasticky couches in the lobby. She was sure Lou, her last lifeline to anything, was long gone back to a warm house and probably a wife waiting for her with open arms. At least the motel lobby was sheltered from the elements, and she could just hang out for a while until the airport opened back up. The couch wasn't that uncomfortable, and she might even be able to doze awhile. There was even a coffee machine, and maybe the receptionist would take pity on her and make a fresh pot.

"Ma'am, I'm real sorry, but the lobby is for paying motel guests only. You need to leave the premises."

If Katie heard the word sorry one more time, she thought she would probably scream. She would walk back over to the first motel, where the receptionist seemed nicer and less likely to let her freeze to death out in the snow. Trudging back outside, she was nearly blinded by the truck's headlights.

Lou leaned out the window. "No rooms there either?"

Katie shook her head, surprised and relieved Lou was still there. "But it's alright, I don't want to keep you waiting any longer." *Please don't leave me,* she begged silently. She didn't have a backup plan or anyone to call for help. She'd never felt so alone.

"Well, hop on in, before all the hot air gets out. You can stay at my place tonight, and I'll drop you back off at the airport tomorrow. Need to head back over there anyways, damn airline left my bags behind in L.A."

Fuck it. Katie was exhausted and out of options. She had nothing left to lose– well, except her life– but she would rather risk it with Lou than against the cold, winter night. She climbed back into the cab of the truck.

"I'm really sorry to inconvenience you like this," she said.

"Shit happens." Lou shrugged. "Couldn't leave you there, could I?"

Lou had already extended far more generosity than Katie would have, but that was just because things were different in cities. Blindly helping people was a quick way to get taken advantage of. It wasn't that she didn't care for her fellow humans, she just preferred her help to be more monetary and anonymous and less actual shirt off her back. She gave generously to charities that had good ratings, where she was sure the money would be put to good use. But inviting a stranger into her home? That was unthinkable.

"So do you live here in town?" Katie asked, partly to make small talk and partly to figure out where Lou was taking her. She should probably text Megan. No, that would definitely only make her freak out, and what was she going to do from DC? Katie was going to have to trust her gut, and her gut said Lou was harmless.

"Not exactly in town, but Bozeman is the closest real city. I'm about thirty miles out. Oh, and I hope you don't mind animals. I've got a few."

"Oh, what kind?" Katie asked. She wasn't surprised Lou was an animal lover, everything else about her had been wholesome so far.

"In the house, just the dogs. But I've got chickens, goats, horses, and a very grouchy cat out in the barn."

"You're a farmer, then?" Katie's interest was fully piqued. It had always sounded like such a romantic lifestyle, away from the hustle and bustle, at one with nature. She'd spent hours watching videos of millennial homesteaders online, jealous and intrigued by their bucolic self-sufficiency. One of her favorite escapist daydreams was imagining what it might be like to grow her own food and flowers away from it all.

Until she remembered she liked living in the city, she liked her career, she liked all the things a farm couldn't provide like having two top-tier sushi restaurants within walking distance of her apartment or touring Broadway shows passing through. But more power to Lou if she was making it work, even more so if she was doing it alone. Katie glanced at the hands guiding the steering wheel, but they were covered in thick gloves. If Lou was wearing a wedding ring, there was no way to tell.

"I suppose you could call me a farmer, among other things." Lou said. "It's not about making the land turn a profit, though. I'm happy with what I have. I just want to live as close to nature as possible, as sustainably as possible. I'm not some big rancher like some of my neighbors are."

"Are you married? Do you have kids?" *Shut up, Katie, stop interrogating the poor woman.* She really wanted to know, though, before her attraction to Lou grew any stronger. If there was a wife or kids in the picture, she wanted no part of it. She wasn't a homewrecker. But if there was no one else in Lou's romantic life, Katie could all too easily imagine where things might lead.

"No," Lou said simply, leaving it at that. The easy smile was gone from her face, and her eyes glittered a little less brightly. "But enough about me. Tell me something about you."

Katie sensed there was a story there and immediately wanted to know why Lou was so eager to change the subject, but it would be rude to pry. Especially since she just met Lou. "Well, I work in marketing. Worked, I guess, I just got laid off."

"Right before Christmas? That's shitty."

"Very. But oh well, on to bigger and better, right?"

"Is that what you want?"

"Gotta make money somehow. Rent isn't cheap."

"Nothing in life is." Another flicker of sadness crossed Lou's face.

"Where are you from originally?"

"All over. I was an Army brat, lived in five places before high school. But Montana was the first place that really felt like home. When I had the chance to put down permanent roots of my own here, I jumped on it. What about you?"

"Washington, twice over." Sensing Lou's confusion, Katie explained, "I was born and raised in Washington D.C., went to school there, and then moved to Seattle a few years after college. I've been there ever since. Sorry, can I turn the heat down a smidge?" She didn't know if it was the hot air blasting from the radiator or the heat of her attraction to Lou, but Katie was starting to sweat. Thank god she'd remembered to put on a fresh swipe of deodorant before the flight. She hoped it could hang on just a little longer. She wished she'd thought to touch up her makeup when she got off the plane, but she hadn't expected to run into her dream woman in the middle of nowhere, either.

"Of course," Lou said, reaching to turn the dial herself. "But we're almost there. The house is just up this drive, and it looks like Jason left the lights on for us."

"Your roommate?" Katie questioned, trying to stay calm. Lou hadn't mentioned anyone named Jason before, but Katie wished she would have warned her. She might have thought again about going along with a stranger into a snowy night. She was definitely going to text Megan now, as soon as she figured out an address for the house in the middle of nowhere.

"Neighbor," Lou explained, and Katie felt herself relax again. "He comes by while I'm gone to feed and water the animals, and I give him a few jars of my prize-winning huckleberry honey and all the eggs he can collect for the favor." She parked the truck in front of a small log cabin that looked like it belonged in a fairy tale.

Brightly colored Christmas lights twinkled from the gutters where they had been strung, casting a stained glass pattern into the snow piled high on the roof. The windows glowed warmly with electric candlelight, and a huge evergreen wreath adorned the red door. It would have been a cozy scene if Katie was into that sort of thing. But she wasn't, so she rolled her eyes internally. Even in the wilderness of Montana, she couldn't escape the constant reminder of the holiday just ahead. One night. That's all it was. One night, and then she'd be on her way to Mexico, and this would be a silly adventure she could look back and laugh on.

"It's unlocked," Lou said. "Go on in and make yourself at home. Bathroom's down the hall and to the right, bedroom's on the left. You can put your stuff there, I'll take the couch tonight. The sheets are clean, I washed them before I left. I'm just going to check on the animals, I'll be back in a few. Don't mind the dogs, they might try to give you kisses but they're friendly."

Alright, then. Katie hopped down from the cab, and Lou reversed down the driveway back towards the shadow of a barn they had passed on the way in. She tried the doorknob gingerly, and was surprised when it opened even though Lou had already told her it was unlocked. Katie couldn't imagine going off for however long Lou had been gone and just leaving the house open like that for anyone to walk in. Montana was different, that was for sure.

Two big labradors came skittering around the corner, their nails clicking on the hardwood floor. Katie braced herself to be jumped on, but they both screeched to a halt and sat in front of her, wagging their tails.

"Good dogs," she said, reaching out to pat one gingerly on the head. That was enough to gain their trust, and they trotted off happily back into the kitchen. She set her bags down and looked around.

There were none of the guns or hunted animals mounted on the walls that she had expected from a home deep in the country. In fact, Katie was mildly surprised at how normal it all seemed. There was a living room with a big, comfortable-looking sectional sofa and a TV that took up most of one wall. Flannel blankets were draped neatly over the back of the couch, and a tall bookshelf was tucked into a corner next to a wood-burning stove that was cold. Katie wandered over to it. A person's taste in books said a lot about them, and she was curious to see what Lou kept on her shelves.

Volumes on every topic of organic gardening imaginable filled the top shelves. Katie skimmed past those, they made sense for Lou but were of little interest to her. A few dog-eared fantasy novels from a series that had been made into a popular show were stacked next to a pile of lesbian smut. Now that was interesting. And all but confirmed what Katie already suspected. She grabbed one that looked particularly salacious to read if she was having trouble falling asleep later, and was about to go put her things in the bedroom when one last book caught her eye, shoved in the corner of the bottom shelf.

Reclaim Your Life After Loss. Very interesting, and considering the rest of Lou's reading material, very out of place. Katie pulled the book from the shelf and flipped it over to read the back cover. *Whether you are recovering from the loss of a spouse, a parent, a child, or a friend, these ten actionable steps will help you navigate your grieving process.* Morbid curiosity pushed her to open the book to see what kind of advice it offered, even if she didn't need it. An inscription at the front caught her eye.

Louisa, I hope someday you'll see that this isn't the end of your path. Maybe this will help you find your way back to it. Love always, Mom.

Katie shut the book guiltily, painfully aware that her snooping had gone too far and she had seen something she wasn't meant to see. But since she had already seen it, what more harm could be done by looking again? It wasn't like she was going to interrogate Lou about it, her manners were better than that. She flipped the book open to chapter one.

Change of Scenery.

Being around things and places that remind us of our loss can hinder our progress moving forward. Sometimes, when the grief is overwhelming, the best course of action is a change of scenery. Getting away from the things that cause us pain can help us distance ourselves from it, and begin our healing process...

Typical self-help nonsense. Katie always wondered if the authors of those things actually followed their own advice, or if they were just preying on hurt people to make a quick buck. The author probably wasn't even a real therapist. She rifled through the pages until she got to the second chapter.

Honor Their Memory

It may initially seem counterintuitive to do and seek out things that remind you of your loved one who has passed on, especially after the advice offered in the first chapter of this book. But in doing those things, we can honor their memory in a positive way and on our own terms...

Tires crunched through the snow in the driveway, and Katie slammed the book shut, shoving it back on the shelf just as Lou opened the door.

"I was just looking at your books," Katie explained, even though Lou hadn't asked. "Is it okay if I borrow this one tonight?" She held up the romance novel.

"Of course. Sorry I don't have a better selection."

"This is perfect," Katie said. A nice, low-effort romance would take her mind off things. "Exactly what I need."

"Well, that works out, then." Lou looked away. Was she blushing, or were her cheeks just rosy from the chill outside?

"Are you sure you don't mind me taking the bed? I don't want to impose on you more than I already have." *We could share it.* She couldn't think of anything hotter than spending a passionate night with a stranger because of a messed up flight. It would be just like one of those sappy books, only without the happily ever after part. Just one hot night. And that was fine by Katie.

"I don't mind." Lou winked. "Don't ever let anyone tell you chivalry is dead. It's alive and well in Montana. We treat our guests right around here." She took off her coat and hung it on a sturdy wooden rack by the door. Underneath it, she wore a thick flannel shirt that made her look every inch a mountain woman. It was pretty hot, and Katie's mind started to wander again, imagining Lou's soft curves revealed if she were to strip the shirt away. "But if you don't mind, I'd like to turn in. I've had a long day of travel and mornings come early on the homestead."

"Of course," Katie said quickly, snapped out of her reverie. She was ridiculous for having had the thought in the first place. There was no way she was Lou's type, and what was she even thinking, fantasizing about a woman who was clearly just trying to be a good person. She was terrible for even considering it.

But an hour later, Katie was still up, eight chapters deep into the romance novel while Lou snored lightly from the next room. When the heroine of the book went down on her lover in their first sex scene, Katie's fingers trailed down to her own mound, fingering and rubbing herself to an unsatisfying orgasm. It was better than nothing, which seemed to be the theme of the night. That was okay, she reassured herself as she drifted off to sleep, her luck would turn around in the morning.

Chapter Four

Katie woke to the smell of coffee and rolled over to check her phone, equal parts relieved she hadn't been murdered in the night and disappointed she'd had to spend it alone when Lou, who was probably the most perfect woman she'd ever met, was sleeping in the next room. No new messages from Megan. That seemed weird— until Katie noticed she had no service. She knew Lou's farm was remote, but she hadn't realized it was *that* cut off from the rest of civilization. Oh well, Megan would just have to deal for a few more hours until she got back to the airport.

She poked one leg out from under the covers and quickly yanked it back under. Jesus, it was cold. The smell of coffee was too enticing, though, so she braced herself for the chill and threw the blankets off. She peeked out the door, relieved when Lou was nowhere to be seen. Good. She had time to make herself presentable. Grabbing her makeup bag, she darted across the hall and into the bathroom. The mirror was still fogged with steam, it hadn't been long since Lou had been in there showering.

Katie used the corner of a hand towel to wipe it clear, resisting the urge to inspect everything in the bathroom. She was too nosy for her own good, and wanted to know everything about Lou. What brand of shampoo she used, whether she ever wore makeup, if she was a body wash or bar of soap kind of woman. One peek wouldn't hurt. She opened the medicine cabinet.

Neat rows of toiletries lined the shelves, almost all of them the generic store brand. That made sense with what Katie knew about Lou, she was no frills and no-nonsense. One orange pill bottle stood out from the rest of the over-the-counter painkillers and cough syrup. She shouldn't. It was none of her business.

She couldn't help herself. She picked it up.

Take one pill every eight hours as needed for anxiety.

Oh. Katie put the bottle back in its place, making sure it was aligned exactly the way she found it as pangs of guilt echoed in her stomach. She was prying too far, intruding on poor Lou's life like it was some gossip tabloid to discover. And it didn't matter. It wasn't like Lou was hiding anything from her, she didn't even know what she had been looking for in the first place. She shut the cabinet and looked at herself in the mirror, ashamed of herself for stooping so low in her hunt to find more clues about her mysterious host.

"Morning, Seattle," Lou said when she stepped out of the bathroom.

Kate melted at the nickname, even if it wasn't one she would have picked for herself. It was perfect coming from Lou's lips, her slow drawl elongating each syllable of the word into something special and unique. Or maybe Lou had just forgotten her name.

"Morning, Lou."

"Did you sleep alright?"

"Like a rock." *Dreaming of you.* The lewd scenes flooded back, and Kate felt a tingle deep in her core. Maybe it was the cold, or the vulnerable damsel-in-distress position she was in. Or maybe Lou was just that hot, but all she wanted was for Lou to cross the room and press her lips against Katie's and pull her into the bedroom and... "Sorry, I hate to impose more, but do you have Wi-Fi? I just need to check on my flight and let my friend know I'm okay." The new, uninhibited Katie could wait for Mexico. Reserved, organized Katie still needed to get her out of this ordeal and get there.

"No need to apologize, the password is on the router. Normally we get cell service out here but the storm must be messing with it." Lou pointed across the living room to a desk in the corner, the router a blinking beacon underneath it. "Want some coffee?"

"I'd love some coffee," Katie said, going over to type in the password.

"Cream and sugar?"

"Just a little cream, please." Her phone connected to the internet and began vibrating violently in her hand as the messages started streaming in.

"KATIE!?"

"!?!?!?!?"

"Where are you? I'm getting worried."

"If you got kidnapped already I'm going to kill you."

"You better call me or I'm calling the cops."

A text from an unknown number broke through Megan's onslaught. "AIRLINE NOTIFICATION: Flight canceled"

"Bitch answer me, I'm starting to freak out for real." That one was sent just three minutes before Katie got online.

Whoa. Wait, what? Flight canceled? No. No, no, no. It wasn't possible. They must have sent her the wrong message, or maybe it was talking about her flight the night before. Okay. First things first. She needed to let Megan know she was still alive.

"Chill out Megs, I'm fine. Had a bit of a flight situation and wound up in Montana but it's all good. Headed on to Mexico later today."

"WHAT??? Call me right now." The response was instant. Megan must have been waiting by her phone to hear back. Katie felt a pang of guilt for letting her worry that long.

"Sorry, can't. No service here, just figured out internet and it's pretty spotty. But I'm safe. I'll call as soon as I can. Love you."

Katie swiped to the message from the airline, closing her eyes to manifest good news before she looked at it. When she opened them, she got her confirmation that the universe still wasn't on her side. All flights out of Bozeman were canceled due to the blizzard, and they had no estimate for when they would resume service.

"Here you go, I hope that's enough cream for you." Lou appeared behind Katie holding a steaming mug of coffee. "How's the flight look?"

"Canceled because of the weather," Katie said. "I guess just take me back to the airport and I'll wait around there for them to start running again."

"I figured," Lou said, smiling wryly as she pulled back the curtain to reveal the fresh snowfall. At least another foot had accumulated overnight, more than Katie would have thought possible in the few short hours she was asleep. "Don't think I'll be taking you back anywhere today, not til the plows make it out. Don't you worry though, you're welcome to stay as long as you'd like."

"That's too kind of you, Lou," Katie said. "Really, you've done too much for me already."

"It's nothing," she insisted. "Just the Big Sky way."

"What does that even mean?" Katie asked. "I saw it at the airport, too."

"Big Sky?" Lou looked outside again. "It's a Montana thing. Maybe I'll get a chance to show you before you get out of here, but not while the storm's still rollin' through." Snow whirled around in every direction, so thick Katie could barely even see the truck parked just out front. "Where was it you were headed anyways? Home for the holidays? You should still make it before Christmas."

Katie laughed. "The total opposite, actually. Mexico, and running away from them. I hate the holidays."

"Oh. Sorry. Bad memories?"

"Not really," Katie lied. She didn't want to dump her trauma on someone she'd just met, especially someone going out of their way to help her. And it wasn't something she wanted to think about. Lou raised an eyebrow, prompting Katie to elaborate more. "I just never got into it all, even when I was a kid. I guess you could say I never experienced that Christmas magic everyone talks about. Now I just see it for what it is- an excuse to get people to spend lots of money. Now the holiday season just means more work. And I'm not into the whole religion thing either, so why bother?" The lie of omission had enough truth woven into it to be casual, but believable.

"Interesting perspective from someone who has designer rain boots sitting by my front door," Lou said.

"I had cheap ones that started leaking after a month. Then I got those and have worn them for five years."

"I'm just teasing you, Seattle." Lou smiled warmly. "I don't give a fuck what kind of boots you wear."

Katie took a sip of coffee, worried she had made it awkward. "Holy shit."

"Is it okay?"

"It's the best coffee I've had in my life. What roaster is this from?"

Lou chuckled, the sound husky and rich. "Whatever the store brand is. The secret is the cream. It just came out of the cow."

"Really?" Katie asked, peering into her cup. It looked completely normal, but she wondered how safe it was. Didn't milk have to be treated or something before people could drink it? But Lou certainly seemed healthy enough, and more importantly than that, Katie felt like she could trust her.

"Really. And you can meet her later, if you'd like. She's a big sweetheart." Lou bent to toss another log on the fire crackling in the wood burning stove that was blasting heat out into the room. "Come on, I was just about to scramble some eggs up."

Katie followed her into the kitchen. "Let me cook breakfast for you. It's the least I can do."

Lou shrugged, and took a seat at the kitchen table. "If you insist." She opened a book of crossword puzzles and sipped her coffee. "Eggs are on the counter, and there's milk and butter in the fridge."

Katie found the basket of eggs, still warm from the chickens. Once she got over how gross it was that she was holding something that had just come out of a chicken's butt, she realized it was kind of cool to be eating food that came from just a few feet away from where she was standing. Everyone in Seattle loved to talk about eating local, but in the city that still meant food trucked in from farms mostly on the other side of the state. Eating an egg that was just laid that morning, that felt different. She cracked it into a large glass mixing bowl.

"Um, Lou? Is it possible this egg is bad?"

"Oh, did you get a fertilized one? I'll take care of it." She came to stand by Katie, then looked at her, puzzled. "Looks fine to me."

"It's so orange, though. Is that normal?"

"More than normal, that's how they should be. Means the chickens are eating good, not like that factory farm shit they sell in stores. Never had a real egg before?"

"I guess not," Katie said. Nothing else about the egg seemed off except the color, so she was just going to have to trust Lou again. She cracked a few more eggs into the bowl, then added milk and started melting butter in a cast iron pan.

"Hey Seattle, what's a six letter word for destiny? It probably starts with 'k.'"

"Kismet, maybe?" Katie said, stirring the eggs.

"It must be." Lou scribbled it into the book, then set her pencil down and came to stand by Katie at the counter, their elbows just brushing against each other.

Katie felt a flutter in her stomach that was more than hunger from the delicious smells filling the kitchen. Maybe it was fate that she had wound up there.

Lou sliced a loaf of bread that looked homemade, then got two plates from the cupboard and laid them out on the table. It was weird, when Katie was with Jackie she couldn't stand cooking together. They were always getting in each other's way and it usually ended in an argument. But it was different with Lou. They moved around each other easily, as though cooking breakfast together was a routine they had done for years. It was comfortable being around Lou, safe and cozy like an old pair of sweats she had worn a hundred times before. For the first time since getting into the truck with her, Katie was actually afraid. Not that Lou would do anything to hurt her, but of how easy it would be to fall in love with her. And *that*, Katie worried, might be more pain than she would be able to bear when the time came to say goodbye.

"Is this all from the farm?" She asked to distract herself as they sat down to eat. The smart thing to do would be to keep her distance.

"The eggs, milk and butter are, and so is the honey. Jason's wife made the bread from wheat our other neighbors grew just up the road."

"This honey is amazing. You made it?" Katie was stunned.

"The bees did most of the work, but yes, I filtered it and jarred it up." Lou smiled, and Katie could tell she was proud.

"You really do have everything you need here, don't you?"

"For the most part. There's still things we can't grow or raise ourselves though, not in this climate. Like chocolate. And coffee."

"It's still pretty cool. You're really lucky to have all this."

"Something like that." Lou grimaced and looked away. "Lots of work though. Speaking of..." She stood and started to clear the table.

Katie wondered what she had said wrong to cause the sudden shift in mood. She'd thought they were connecting, and then something in Lou's expression shifted. Maybe she should apologize, but for what? Was it because she'd said Lou was lucky? She didn't doubt Lou worked hard, but someone her age usually wouldn't be able to afford a house– let alone a ranch– without luck. But still, some people took offense at the implication that it usually took more than skill to be so fortunate. "Let me help," she said instead, moving to join Lou at the sink.

"No need, I've got it." Lou waved her off. "You're my guest, and you're supposed to be on vacation."

"But I feel bad," Katie protested.

"Don't," Lou said, smiling tersely as she left no room for Katie to argue further. "Just go relax."

Was it just the light, or were those tears Katie noticed glinting in Lou's eyes? She didn't dare ask, she had apparently done enough damage already. She went back into the living room and curled up on the couch under one of the big flannel blankets with her book and her mug of coffee. One of black labs hopped up beside her and nosed her book to the side, plopping his big blocky head in her lap and staring up at her with doleful brown eyes.

"Aww, you just need a little bit of attention, don't you?" Katie cooed, putting the book aside and scratching him behind the ears. *Just like your mama.* She would never voice the opinion out loud, not with Lou in earshot, but she had to be lonely all by herself on a farm in the middle of nowhere all the time. And Katie knew a thing or two about loneliness, so it was easy to recognize in Lou. The dog's eyebrows pricked up and his tail thumped happily against the leather couch. He wriggled in even closer and sighed in contentment. "Alright, I guess you can stay," Katie said, as if she had any choice in the matter, and picked her book back up.

"I see you made a friend." Lou came into the living room and swapped Katie's mug of coffee with a fresh one.

"More like he picked me," Katie said, accepting the coffee gratefully. "Thanks."

"How's the book?"

"Just getting good."

"I'm glad. Well, like I said, make yourself at home. I've got to get some work done, but just holler if you need anything."

"I can help," Katie offered. "I'd love to go see the other animals." Not to mention how eager she was to spend more time with Lou.

"I already went out this morning, before you woke up. The rest of the morning is just business shit, accounting and tax stuff I need to finish to close out the year." Lou sat at her desk across the open living room and opened a laptop, her back to Katie.

Katie watched her for a moment, marveling again at how comfortable she felt around Lou and how completely normal the cozy, snowed-in morning felt, then turned back to her book. The pages turned quickly, and before she knew it, the steamiest scene of the book yet was unfolding in the pages. Katie had always prided herself for her ability to read smut with a straight face, but reading it sitting just a few feet away from one of the most arousing women she had ever been around was another story.

She took a deep breath to try to calm the ache growing inside her, the throbs intensifying as she read each salacious word on the page. Her nipples hardened under her bra, and she glanced over her shoulder to see if Lou had noticed her quickened breath. Smut didn't normally get Katie so worked up, but the warmth of the fire made it all too easy to imagine the story's heat and place herself in the heroine's shoes with Lou across from her to rescue her and save the day.

Desire nagged at Katie like an itch that there was only one way to scratch, and she thought of the tiny bullet vibrator tucked away in a hidden pocket of her luggage. She'd just excuse herself for a quick nap and go take care of it. No, she couldn't. It was so quiet in the little cabin, and what if Lou heard? She probably wouldn't. Katie didn't think the buzzing would be that loud. But what if she did? Maybe she would join. Maybe Katie would ask her to join.

No, that was a terrible idea. She'd only known Lou for less than a day, but she could already tell Lou wasn't the casual hookup, vacation fling type. She deserved so much better than anything Katie could offer her, and Katie needed to get her mind out of the gutter and remember where she was. That Lou was a real person whose feelings mattered, too. Besides, the airport would open back up soon and she would be on a flight far the fuck away from the frozen hellscape of Montana and she'd probably never see Lou again. What she really needed to do was take a walk to clear her head.

She went over to the door and pulled her rain jacket on. She should have packed a hat and gloves, or maybe her actual winter coat, but she could have never imagined she was headed to Montana. That was okay, it couldn't be that cold and she wouldn't be out long.

"Where do you think you're going?" Lou looked up at her in surprise.

"Just a little walk for some fresh air."

"Not gonna happen, Seattle. It's too dangerous right now."

"I've seen snow before, you know." Neither Seattle nor DC got tons of snow in winter, but she'd been to Aspen on a spring break ski trip with her sorority back in college and she was sure she could handle a lap or two around the house.

"Sure, but I bet you've never been out in a blizzard like this. There is no visibility. You could get hopelessly lost thirty feet from the house and you'd never even know it. Can't let you go out in that."

"So we're just stuck here?"

"Pretty much."

"Doesn't it make you crazy after a while?"

"Not really. We don't see blizzards like this that often, where you can't leave the house at all. And I'm thankful for the downtime in winter, because come summer there's none at all. I can get a lot of the less fun work done, and spend more time reading and crafting. It's a season of rest."

"But don't you get lonely?" Katie regretted the question as soon as she asked it. It was too personal, too soon. She didn't want to upset Lou again.

Lou sighed and ran a hand over her bristly hair. "Honestly? Yes. Sometimes. But I have the animals, and good neighbors. It's enough. In a lot of ways I was lonelier back when I lived in the city. People everywhere, but none of 'em give a shit about each other. I'm sure it's different for you, though."

"What makes you say that?"

"I mean, look at you. Hair, makeup, designer clothes... all perfect, even late at night after a flight. You probably have tons of friends, your big corporate career, you fit in everywhere you go."

Lou thought she looked perfect? Katie's heart fluttered. "I get lonely, too. You never know who's actually a friend and who just wants something from you. Seattle is full of tech bros, and they're insufferable. And I work with some of the douchiest people on the planet. Worked with. And probably will again wherever I end up."

"So why marketing? Everything you've said so far makes it sound like you would hate something like that."

"It's just a way to make money, and I happen to be good at it. When I really stop to think about it, it disgusts me. I never imagined I'd end up pushing products that no one needs for people who worship the dollar above everything. But that's capitalism."

"There are other ways to make a living," Lou said. "Not all of them involve selling your soul."

"I liked the challenge of it. Setting new records and hitting stretch goals. It made me feel like I was really accomplishing something. But I'm starting to wish I could do something for the greater good, not against it. And I'm tired of being treated like I'm disposable."

"No one should ever make you feel that way." Lou laid her hand between Katie's shoulder blades, steering her back to the couch. "All I've heard you talk about is that damn job, though. Who is Katie, when she's not working?"

"I don't think I know anymore," she said, and tears she had been fighting back for days broke loose again. "I gave them everything. All of me. And they just cut me loose like I was nothing. I don't even know if I'm good at it anymore. I thought I was, but then they said it was performance related, and I don't even know. Maybe I did fuck up somehow. And I know how stupid it sounds, but I was going to Mexico to find myself again. And then all this happened, so I guess I'm just supposed to stay lost forever. The universe hates me or something."

"Oh, Katie." Lou sat beside her, giving her a one-armed hug. "Somehow I think you're exactly where you're supposed to be."

Katie sank into her softness, hoping she would never forget the comforting feeling of Lou's strong arms wrapped around her. She sobbed into her shoulder for who knows how long, crying for everything: her lost job, her lost relationship with

Jackie, and the chance she would never have with Lou. Lou stroked her hair and held her, murmuring comforting words as Katie let it all out.

"I'm sorry," Katie blubbered. "I'm not normally like this. I didn't mean to dump all that on you."

"The only thing you need to apologize for is saying sorry so damn much," Lou said. "You're gonna be okay. I've got you."

Chapter Five

Katie finished the romance novel and its sequel before night fell, and the blizzard continued to rage on outside. She was starting to have serious doubts that the airport would be anywhere close to operational by morning, and it looked like she was going to get at least one more day on the homestead. The thought was less upsetting than it would have been just twenty four hours earlier, but the longer she spent in Lou's company, the less anxious she was to leave.

"You sure you want to come? You definitely don't have the right clothes for it." Lou raised an eyebrow and opened the front door. A blast of cold air rushed in with a whirl of snowflakes that melted as soon as they hit the floor, leaving little droplets in their wake.

"Maybe I'll just stay here and get dinner started. But, are you sure it's safe for you to go? What if you get lost out there?" Katie asked worriedly, remembering Lou's warning from earlier.

"I'll be fine, I've done this a hundred times before. Plus, I'm taking the dogs. They always find their way back."

"If you say so."

"Use whatever you like in the pantry or fridge for dinner. I'll be back in an hour or so. I'm excited to see what you come up with."

Katie hovered by the window, watching as Lou and the dogs disappeared into the storm of snow. As worried as she was for them, she had to admit Lou's calm confidence was pretty fucking sexy. She loved a woman who was capable of taking care of things, and Lou made her feel so safe, physically and emotionally. It wasn't fair she lived all the way out in Montana. Where were the women like that in Seattle?

She reached for her phone, then realized it wasn't in her pocket. In fact, she hadn't touched it all day, a first in who knew how long. It was kind of nice to have a day filled with reading and deep conversations and cuddling dogs completely cut off from the world. But she needed her best friend to tell her what to do.

She found her phone sitting on the coffee table where she had set it hours earlier. There was still no service, but the internet was strong so she pulled open the messenger app and tapped the icon to open a video call.

"Fucking finally." Megan answered on the first ring and her pixelated face appeared on the screen, speaking out of sync with the sound of her words. Maybe the internet connection wasn't so great after all. "I have been waiting for you to call me all day. Hold on, I'm just changing Q's diaper before he goes down for the night so you have to look at the ceiling for a minute. But Tell. Me. Everything."

"Ok, so—"

"Ooh, I can already tell this is going to be good."

"Are you gonna let me talk, or what?"

"Yes, you did a big poopie!" Megan cooed to Quentin in the background. "Yes, I'm listening. Talk."

Katie rolled her eyes. Undivided attention was a thing of the past. "So the flight, there was a medical emergency—"

"Oh my God, did someone die?"

Katie could practically hear Megan grinning through the phone. She'd always had a morbid streak. "No, Megan— Jesus! Well, at least I don't think they died, I actually have no idea. It's not like they would tell us, right? But that's not the point."

"Right, sorry. But imagine if they did. Where would they put the body? You know, I was listening to this podcast, and apparently they have morgues on cruise ships and when people die they just– nope, nevermind. This is about you. Continue."

Katie walked into the kitchen and started rummaging through the pantry, cradling the phone between her ear and her shoulder. "So anyways, my flight got diverted, right? To fucking Bozeman, Montana. And then there were no flights out and no hotel rooms because of this blizzard and some football game and then this amazing, stunning woman offered to let me stay at her place for the night—"

"Katie, you did not go with her!"

"I did. I mean, we didn't hook up or anything, but what other choice did I have? I needed a place to stay." Katie pushed aside a bag of pasta and found three potatoes, fat and lumpy and still covered with a thin layer of dirt. Perfect. She set them on the counter and went back to rummaging.

"Wait, so where are you now?"

"At her house. In her kitchen. Getting ready to cook her dinner." A can of beef broth would work just fine to make a gravy.

"Shut up, you are not."

"Swear to God I am." Katie walked over to the fridge to see what else she could add to the meal.

"Why are you still there? Hold on. Rob, you need to finish putting Q to bed, Katie is in an emergency situation." Megan sounded downright gleeful, and Katie heard shuffling in the background as she handed the baby off to her husband.

Katie opened the freezer and pulled out a hunk of meat. *Elk-Ground.* She'd never had it, but it couldn't be that different from beef, right? Elk were sort of like deer and deer were sort of like cows. Okay, maybe it was a stretch, but she had to work with what she had. "We're completely snowed in here. There's nowhere else I could go, even if I wanted to. All the flights are canceled." She put the meat on a plate and popped it in the microwave to defrost.

"Okay, but what if she's an ax murderer and this is just a setup?"

"You think she staged a blizzard and then welcomed me into her home so she could murder me?"

"No, but that's what they do, right? It's called a crime of opportunity. I sent you that podcast. The husband-wife duo that used the wife to gain the trust of that poor woman with the flat tire so they could lure her back and eat her liver? Spoiler alert, she ended up very dead."

"Well, you don't have to worry about that. Lou is definitely not straight, and she's single, so I'm pretty sure there's no husband to worry about." Katie walked back to the pantry and grabbed an onion to dice.

"Wow, homophobic much? I'm pretty sure lesbians can be murderers, too. You can be anything you set your little heart to."

"I appreciate your support, but I'll pass."

Megan laughed. "But wait, you found probably the only single lesbian in Montana and she rescued you from a blizzard and you didn't have sex with her last night yet somehow you're still cooking her dinner? Explain."

"Oh my God, I want to have sex with her. I so want to, but I can't. She's different, not hook-up material."

"What do you mean? I've never heard of more perfect hook-up material. Your knight in shining armor that you never have to see again. What could be better? You basically have to sleep with her. The universe is demanding it."

"No, I totally would, but I don't think she's into me. Or casual things. I don't know, she's so mysterious. All strong and tough and capable of anything, but wounded. I feel like sleeping with her would just be taking advantage, and I can't do that to her. Taking it slow feels right."

"Wait, so you actually like her?"

"I think I love her." Katie opened and closed drawers, looking for a potato peeler.

"Shut up, you always do this. You haven't even known her a full day and you think you're in love already?"

"When you know, you know, and she's basically perfect. Just the right mix of assertive and teddy bear. But it doesn't matter, it's not like this is going anywhere."

"That's what you said about Jackie right before you moved in with her. Three fucking weeks after you met her. And look how that turned out." A cork popped free from a bottle in the background and Megan sighed. "I'm just worried about you, I don't want you to get hurt."

"Our leases were both up and it just made sense. It was the practical decision, Seattle's expensive. Plus, we stayed together four years after that."

"About three years longer than you should have. She was terrible for you, but you have to admit you have a tendency to get attached to anyone who is the bare minimum of nice to you."

"Lou is nothing like Jackie, and come on, Megs— it's not like I'm going to move to Montana. Can you even imagine?" Katie tossed the potatoes into a pot of boiling water. "It's just a harmless crush. Nothing is even going to come of it, because I'm pretty sure she's not interested." Not completely sure, though. Lou did say she looked perfect. And her eyes seemed to have an extra twinkle when she looked at Katie, and sometimes her gaze lingered a little long.

"We'll see about that. Just be careful. After all, if she's so wonderful, why is she single?"

"Well, Montana, I assume. But I think she was married before, or had a partner or something. She got weird when I asked her about it and then I found this book about moving on from grief."

"Are there pictures of her with anyone?"

"Not that I've seen." The microwave dinged, and Katie pulled the meat out, adding it to a pan where onions and garlic were softening in a pool of butter.

"Hmm. And you don't think that's weird? If Rob died, I would definitely still have pictures of him everywhere. Unless I murdered him."

"God, you're so ridiculous. She's not a murderer, and I'm not trying to pry into her personal life." Except she already had. "If she wants to tell me, she'll tell me."

"Or she's just waiting for the right moment to murd—"

"Megan, I gotta go, I'm trying to cook dinner. Please don't worry about me, I'm a big girl. I'm not going to get murdered, and no one is going to eat my liver. I'll talk to you soon."

"Okay, okay, I'll let you go. Just be careful. Stick one of those knives under your pillow or something, just in case."

"You're such a psycho. Tell Rob I said hi."

"Love you, lunatic. Text me tomorrow if you're still alive."

"Love you, too," Katie replied, laughing, but the screen had already gone black.

She checked the call log to see how much time had passed, then set her phone on the table and turned to focus on dinner. Thirty-eight minutes on the phone, which left her about twenty minutes to get everything ready before Lou came back from her evening chores. She made a quick roux by adding flour to the onions, garlic, and elk meat, then poured the can of broth over it. It thickened almost instantly into a rich gravy, and she cracked a little black pepper in. The potatoes were soft, so she drained them and added milk and butter, whipping them until they were fluffy. She spread them over the meat and gravy, and topped it with a handful of shredded cheese, then stuck the whole thing in the oven to bake. She checked the time again. Ten minutes.

Katie wandered into the living room to look out the front window for Lou's footprints in the snow. It was so dark that she couldn't see anything to indicate there was even a world beyond the little cabin. How was Lou ever going to find her way back? At what point should Katie go out to look for her? The night hadn't seemed so endless when they'd arrived at the house, and suddenly Katie realized the difference.

All the Christmas lights outside were turned off, and the little plastic candles that had lit every window were missing. She felt a pang of guilt. Lou had taken them down for her.

Katie would never be able to live with herself if that was the reason she got lost.

Ugh. She was being silly. Lou knew what she was doing, much more than Katie did. And anyways, what if Megan was right after all? Maybe she was a murderer who hung around the airport looking for wayward travelers to tempt back to her lair with the promise of kindness and a warm bed. Could 911 even help her if she had no service to call them? And even if they wanted to, would they be able to make it out in a blizzard to save her in time?

The door banged open, caught by a gust of wind, and Katie jumped at the sudden, loud noise. She glanced up and saw a figure in the corner of her eyes, then screamed when she realized the hulking silhouette was carrying an ax slung over one shoulder.

"It's okay, Seattle, it's just me," the figure said, stepping into the light and leaning the ax against the doorframe. It was Lou. "I didn't mean to scare you. I just wanted to see how much time there is until dinner, I was going to finish splitting some logs around back."

Oh, so she chopped wood, too? Of course she did. Katie was beginning to believe there was nothing Lou couldn't do. The rush of adrenaline was fading into the all-too-familiar longing between her legs, and Katie wondered what other skills Lou had with her hands.

Get a grip, she scolded herself. "It's almost ready, just needs another ten, maybe fifteen in the oven."

"Okay, just holler if you need me."

"I will," Katie said, entranced by Lou's crooked smile and lumbering grace as she picked up the ax again. Katie resisted the urge to follow her out into the snow like a dog in heat, even though there was nothing more she wanted to do than watch Lou work in her element.

I could get used to this housewife thing.

The thought came out of nowhere, and it frightened her because it was one that had never occurred to her before. Yet, somehow the day she had spent on Lou's farm just seemed to make sense. It was simple and unhurried to face the needs of each hour as they came, with time to prepare food from scratch and savor it. With time to breathe again and relax.

No, she was being ridiculous, reading too many romance books and letting her head drift off into the clouds. She was a feminist, and a boss. She was meant to be in the corner office, putting out fires and making a name for herself. Even if the window to make a "30 under 30" list was gone, there was still "40 under 40." Giving in to days reading in front of a fire, cooking meals for someone she loved, all that was just the vacation mindset talking. That was giving up. She was in love with the novelty of it all, but she'd never actually want to live on a homestead, or as a housewife. Right?

The timer dinged in the kitchen just as Lou swept into the house a second time, stomping snow from her boots and hanging her scarf and coat on the rack by the door. She was everything all at the same time- beautiful but handsome, masculine but feminine, hard and soft, warm and distant and vulnerable and reserved. She was stunning. Snowflakes glittered in her eyelashes, melting in the cabin heat, and Katie longed to go to her and brush them gently away. But that would be a terrible idea, because if she touched Lou, she didn't trust herself to stop.

"Dinner's ready," she whispered, choking on the over-whelming rush of desire that was spreading from her center and lighting her nerve endings on fire.

"Smells great," Lou said. Was it just Katie's imagination or did her voice sound huskier, sultrier, too? No, she was probably just hoarse from being out in the cold. They walked into the kitchen. "Looks great, too. Shepherd's Pie?"

"My grandma's recipe," Katie confirmed. The one person she'd had growing up to love her unconditionally. "Well, she always used ground beef instead of elk. Where do you even get elk meat, anyways?"

"Jason hunts it, he gives me anything that won't fit in his family's freezers." Lou pulled out a chair for Katie, then took off her hat and set it on the counter before sitting down herself.

"Nice neighbor," Katie remarked. It seemed quaint, like the idea of asking a neighbor for a cup of sugar. Stuff she thought that only happened in old TV shows. "I don't even know my neighbors' names. Even though we literally live on top of each other, people seem a lot closer out here."

"We have to be. We keep an eye on each other and have each others' backs. When one of his dairy cows is struggling through a breech birth and he needs an extra pair of hands— well, the nearest vet's about an hour away, assuming they're not helping someone else that's an hour in the other direction. I can be there in 10 minutes."

"Makes sense," Katie said. "But still, I'd never know who to trust."

"Differences don't matter as much when you need each other to get by." Lou motioned for Katie to serve herself first. "Don't get me wrong, there's bigots everywhere, but the ones here usually have the sense to keep their mouth shut about it. And I know Jason isn't like that." She piled a heaping portion onto her own plate and took a bite before it even stopped steaming. "This is amazing."

"Oh good, did it turn out okay? I've never cooked with elk before, I didn't know if it would work or not–"

Lou put her hand over Katie's, stunning her into silence. Her heart skipped a beat, and then another. "Just try it."

Katie turned her hand over and laced her fingers between Lou's, forgetting to breathe as their palms met, hands clasped across the table. Lou was warm and rough, her hand calloused from physical labor but gentle with its grip. Her eyes were locked on Katie's, the iciest, most intense blue Katie had ever seen, full of questions. Katie felt around for her fork, not willing to be the first to break the gaze. She lifted a bite to her mouth, and–

"Oh wow, that is good," she said in shock. She'd thought Lou was just being nice, but the shepherd's pie was hot and savory and bursting with unfamiliar flavor. The elk meat was rich and lean, meaty and wild-tasting, and Katie scarfed it down quickly, as though it might confer some of that uninhibited nature onto her. "The elk is amazing in this."

"All credit to the chef. You must cook a lot." Lou leaned even closer, her thumb tracing across the back of Katie's hand and setting it on fire.

"Almost never. I get takeout most nights." Katie was ashamed to admit it, especially to someone like Lou. She'd loved cooking when she'd had someone to cook for and time to do it, but that— like everything else— had taken a backseat to her career.

They pulled apart, the moment broken, and ate too quickly for conversation in a silence that wasn't quite comfortable, though not far from it. As soon as their forks scraped empty plates, Katie jumped up to clear the table before Lou could. She'd worked all day, and she deserved to rest. Her eagerness to do the chore surprised her. Housework had always been a constant battle between her and Jackie, but with Lou, Katie found herself wanting to do more to ease that burden for her partner. Except Lou wasn't her partner, even if it felt like she could be.

"I saw you took down the Christmas lights," she said, hoping the water rinsing over the plates drowned out the hitch in her voice. "You didn't have to do that."

"I know." Lou smiled gently. "But I know this is the last place you want to be, so the least I can do is make it a little more comfortable for you for a day or two."

Katie set down the dish she was drying as she felt tears welling up. "No one has ever done something that considerate for me."

"That's the Big Sky way," Lou said, taking the towel from her to finish drying the dishes. "Manners, being considerate, all that stuff still matters out here."

"How long have you been out here, anyways? I know you said you lived all over, but the way you talk, it seems like you were born and raised here."

"My dad was stationed here when I was a teenager, and I fell in love with everything about it. The mountains, the sky, the people, the way time moves a little bit slower and no one is in as much of a rush. And I fell in love with..." Lou hesitated, and Katie saw her chest rise, then fall, as she took a deep breath. "My wife."

"You don't have to tell me any more," Katie said quickly as her heart plummeted into her stomach. "I'm sorry for prying."

"You weren't prying, and there's no reason not to talk about her. She existed. My therapist said it's good to talk about her." Lou sounded like she was trying to convince herself. She sighed again, then motioned for Katie to follow her into the living room. "I'll just show you. It's easier."

Katie curled up in the corner of the couch and pulled the blanket up to her chin, sensing she needed its protection. Lou went to her desk and opened the bottom drawer, then came to sit beside Katie on the couch. She was holding a photo album, the plastic-covered cutout on the front displaying a happy couple on their wedding day. Katie recognized Lou on the left, looking dapper in a black tuxedo that had been perfectly tailored for her, a sprig of white flowers pinned to the lapel. Beside her was a radiant woman in a flowing wedding gown. Instead of looking at the camera, they beamed at each other, the moment of absolute bliss frozen forever.

"You look so young," Katie said. "So happy."

"We were." Lou opened the album to the first page. A slightly faded picture of Lou, holding the girl in her arms on a stage, both grinning triumphantly. "We met in high school and I knew she was special. She lit up every room she walked into. She was popular, pretty, and for some reason, she chose me." She pointed at the photo. "That was after the spring play our senior year. She talked me into joining drama club, even though I was too shy to ever get on stage. I just worked the curtain, but she was a star." Lou's finger trailed down the plastic, stopping at the next picture. "That was us at graduation." She turned the page. The two girls stood by a fully packed station wagon, the roof piled high with bungeed-down totes. Their arms were wrapped around each others' waists as they both flashed a peace sign to the camera. "That was the day we moved to LA. Three weeks after we graduated, the day after she turned 18. That was always Rachel's dream. She wanted to get out of Montana, make it big as an actress. And I would have followed her anywhere." Lou flipped through more pages, each plastic sleeve filled with selfies of the happy couple kissing in front of the Hollywood sign, posing on the beach in front of a sunset, slurping ramen and riding horses in the Santa Monica mountains. A newspaper clipping featured them in a full color photograph, their hands clasped together overhead triumphantly as they marched in a Pride parade. Lou paused again when she got to a full-page close up of Rachel peeking out from beneath a veil. "She bought her dress before I even proposed, and the day after it became legal, we got married. We were so scared they were going to take it back, and it felt like we had already been waiting our whole lives for it. We were only twenty, but I knew I wanted to spend forever with her." Lou's voice cracked.

Tears welled in Katie's eyes and broke free to cascade down her cheeks. She wiped them away and reached for Lou's hand. Lou squeezed it as though she was hanging on for dear life. "What happened?"

Lou flipped past empty photo sleeves, each blank space a heartbreaking monument to a life ended before the album could be finished. The very last page was thick with newspaper clippings tucked into the sleeves, and Lou pulled them out and unfolded one before handing it to Katie to read.

Woman, 23, Killed in High Speed Accident

A 23-year-old woman lost her life when a vehicle traveling at speeds well over the limit collided with her vehicle. Responders arrived and attempted life saving measures, but she was pro-

nounced dead on the scene. One other driver was transported to the hospital with minor injuries. Authorities are currently investigating the cause of the accident and are asking anyone with additional information to come forward.

Katie's breath caught in her throat. "Oh, Lou. I'm so sorry. She was so young."

"It was our third anniversary. She was driving to meet me for dinner. She'd just had an audition, she was on speakerphone telling me about when it happened. I heard–" Lou took a shuddery breath. "I heard her scream, and then the crash, and then she stopped answering me." She covered her face and bent over, her shoulders heaving with silent sobs.

Katie rubbed her back, feeling awkward as she tried to console Lou. She couldn't imagine how traumatic it must have been for Lou. How heartbreaking. It was horrifying. There were no words she could say that would offer any comfort, so she just sat and let Lou cry as the tears streamed down her own face. Finally Lou stood up and walked to the bathroom. Katie heard her blow her nose, and then heard the sink running. Lou came back out, eyes red and puffy, her face damp.

"This place was her last gift to me," she said with a rueful smile. "After the accident, I couldn't be in LA anymore. Everything reminded me of her. Of her dreams. When I finally got her phone back from the police, there was a voicemail from her agent. The studio wanted to offer her the role." Lou sat back down beside Katie and kicked her feet up on the ottoman. "I needed a change of pace, a change of scenery. I needed to come home. As soon as the insurance payout hit my account, I put in an offer on this place and never looked back." She took her feet off the ottoman and stood back up. "Do you want a drink?"

"Why not?" Katie said, watching as Lou walked into the kitchen and climbed on a stepstool to get in the cabinet above the fridge. She pulled out a green bottle of whiskey and two shot glasses from a cabinet over the fridge, then came back and poured them each a shot. "To Rachel," Katie said softly.

"To Rachel," Lou said, tapping the glass on the wooden coffee table before throwing it back. They sat in silence for a moment, letting the whiskey work its magic before Lou changed the subject. "The storm should finally blow over tonight. They might get the roads clear enough by tomorrow."

So they were back to talking about the weather. "That's good news," Katie said half-heartedly. She felt like she had just gotten there, like she was just getting to know Lou for real. She wasn't ready to leave. "But I still want to see the rest of the farm before I go."

"I'm sure that can be arranged. But for now..." Lou yawned and Katie took the hint.

"I know, mornings come early. Wake me up when you get up, though, I want to help with the chores."

Lou raised an eyebrow. "You sure about that? It's going to be early."

"Certain. I want to see what real farm life is like."

"Okay," Lou chuckled. "If you say so."

"Goodnight, Lou." The whiskey made her bold, so she leaned in for a kiss before turning away at the last second. What was she thinking? She wasn't. Lou didn't seem to notice, so Katie rushed into the bedroom and closed the door before Lou could see her burning cheeks.

She didn't need to change into her pajamas because she had never changed out of them. Katie couldn't remember the last time she had allowed herself such a lazy day, doing nothing but reading and talking and cooking. It was a nice change of pace. She flipped off the light switch and crawled into bed.

Maybe even too restful, because even though it was late, Katie couldn't sleep. No matter how hard she tried. Her mind raced with everything Lou had shared with her, trying to process the trauma and heartbreak that had been laid before her. Had she done the right things? Said the right things? Lou was so hard to read, retreating into herself and her glass of whiskey and shutting Katie out.

If nothing else, hearing her story had only made Katie fall for her harder. She knew it was twisted, but seeing the full capacity of Lou's love and devotion only made it clear how much of it had been lacking with Jackie. From both sides. The painful realization made it clear how much she craved a connection like that. But she knew she couldn't push Lou into anything she wasn't ready for, and it definitely didn't seem like Lou was done grieving Rachel. Yet on the other hand, Lou had reached out for Katie first at dinner, and the look in her eyes said she was open to... something.

It was all so confusing.

The room seemed colder than it had the night before, and the vast darkness seemed to stretch into infinity beyond the window. Katie lay in the dark and stared at the ceiling, wondering what had changed. It took her a few minutes before she realized it was the Christmas lights again. They had cast the room in a warm glow from the window outside, making the cabin feel a little less remote, a little less alone in the dark. Weird as it was to admit after decades of being a devout Christmas hater, she kind of missed them.

Chapter Six

K atie awoke to blinding sunlight streaming in the window. She jumped out of bed and ran to the window, wincing as her bare feet touched the cold hardwood floor. As she gazed out, her mouth dropped in awe. Lou's homestead was the most beautiful, picture-perfect, Christmas card-worthy scene she had ever seen, better than she had ever imagined it might look when the pelting snow and clouds cleared. She could scarcely believe it was real.

Snow covered fields rolled into forests of evergreen trees that were so picturesque it looked like they'd been painted there. Mountains rose up sharply in every direction, bathed in pink light from the rising sun and so close Katie felt like she could reach out and touch them. Their jagged peaks of ice pierced through a clear blue sky that seemed to stretch forever. Frost gathered in the corners of the window pane, framing the scene perfectly. It looked like an artist's imagination set free to play, a painting unmarred from the horrors of the real world beyond the valley.

It was too pretty to look at alone, so Katie ran into the living room to wake Lou. To her surprise, the blankets were neatly folded over the back of the couch and Lou's boots and jacket were gone from their place by the door. So were the dogs. Katie walked over to the front window and was greeted with an equally stunning view, this time with a pair of footprints stamped into the snow leading out towards the barn. Fuck. Lou had already gone down without her.

It felt like a rejection, and it stung. Did Lou just not want to spend time with her? Had Katie crossed some unknown line in their conversation the night before? Broken Montana etiquette somewhere along the way? Katie had tried to be respectful, and comforting, but maybe Lou had perceived it differently. Or maybe she just wasn't interested in entertaining a stranded traveler any longer and was trying to get back to her life the way it was before Katie came along to disrupt it.

Katie thought about getting dressed and following her, then decided the warmth of the cabin was too good to give up– especially if Lou wanted space. She went into the kitchen instead, and started preparing breakfast. First, she started a pot of coffee, filling the kitchen with the mouth-watering aroma of the roasted beans. Next up were eggs, found easily in their basket on the counter. The rest of the loaf of bread had gone stale, so Katie cut it into thick slices and soaked it in eggs, sugar, milk, and cinnamon for French toast when Lou got back.

Katie smiled at how familiar it all had become. It wasn't her fault she had fallen so quickly and so hard for Lou when she made everything feel like home. The cabin was too cozy, charming in how rustic and no-nonsense it was and imbued with Lou everywhere she turned. How could she not feel comfortable there?

She peeked out the window again, but there was still no sign of Lou or the dogs walking back up from the barn. She had time to waste, so she wandered back into the living room and found the self-help book on the shelf, flipping to where she'd left off at chapter three.

Staying Busy.

When we have too much time alone with our thoughts, they can become intrusive or appear at unwanted times, especially following the loss of a loved one. Establishing a routine that helps keep your mind distracted and gives you purpose can be a key tool for moving into the next phase of your life.

Katie shut the book again. She didn't know why she was so drawn to it, as if it was the sole thing standing between her and truly understanding Lou, but she needed to stop. Lou wasn't one of her marketing personas created to sell a product, nor was she some code that needed to be cracked. She was a whole person, with pain and trauma that Katie couldn't fix.

Her heart ached for what Lou had suffered. Katie knew she needed to step back and let her share at her own pace. But she couldn't help herself. Maybe she could take a cue from the book and find something else to distract herself with. She pulled out her phone and snapped the first photo she had taken since arriving in Montana of the cozy living room and the view beyond. She texted it to Megan.

"Morning. Still not murdered."

Megan liked the message, but didn't say anything. Katie checked her other texts.

"Flight Update: We were unable to process your request. Please call the airline to complete your rebooking."

Katie's finger hovered over the linked number that would connect her to her ticket out of Montana. She hesitated, then swiped left to delete the message. Mexico could wait another day. She wasn't ready to go, and she wasn't going to pretend that she was anymore. Montana was growing on her, especially when the sun was out. And if she had learned anything from the whole ordeal, it was that life was too short to walk away from good things while they lasted.

The coffee was ready, so she went to pour herself a mug, adding a generous dollop of the thick cream from the fridge. Divine. It was funny how such a simple thing made all the difference. The simple cup of warm comfort almost transported Katie to another time, connecting her to all the other homesteaders who had made their way into Montana for a life of straightforward satisfaction. Seattle may have prided itself for its coffee culture, with national chains and local roasters competing for real estate on every corner, but none of them could hold a candle to Lou's generic arabica with fresh cream.

Struck by inspiration, she poured another glug of cream into a mixing bowl, then looked around for a whisk. The coffee was starting to kick in, giving Katie a burst of energy, so she pulled up her favorite workout playlist and turned her phone up to full volume and danced around the kitchen as she whisked the raw dairy into a glorious, fluffy mass of whipped cream. It had formed nice, stiff peaks by the time the second song ended, reminding her of the mountains surrounding them, and she shimmied over to the table to set the bowl down.

Still dancing, she started heating the cast iron pan over the burner, then turned to set the table. She didn't notice Lou come in until she heard a throat clear behind her. Katie dropped the forks she was holding and whirled around, mortified. Oh, God. She was the worst dancer ever. So bad that she had been asked not to participate in her second grade ballet recital. She probably looked insane. How long had Lou been standing there?

Lou leaned lazily against the doorframe, wearing an appreciative smile as she looked Katie toe to head. "Don't let me interrupt you," she drawled. "You looked like you were having fun."

Katie dropped two pieces of toast into the pan. They sizzled and filled the room with the warm, spicy scent of cinnamon as butter frothed around the edges. "You said you were going to wake me up to help you this morning."

"I was going to," Lou said. "You just looked so peaceful sleeping, I couldn't bear to disturb you."

"I wouldn't have minded." Katie flipped the bread, revealing one side cooked to golden brown perfection. "Breakfast is almost ready, and there's coffee in the pot." Knowing Lou wasn't avoiding her was a big relief.

Lou was already serving herself a mug. "Thanks for cooking again. I wasn't expecting that."

"It's the least I can do for all your hospitality. And I actually really like being in the kitchen, when I have the time. I'd forgotten how much I enjoy this." Cooking was one of creative outlets, but she had put it on the back burner to pour that energy into her career. Later nights meant less inspiration and more takeout, and once Jackie left and she had no one to cook for, she just didn't see the point. It was too pathetic to cook and eat meals alone. But Lou appreciated her, and the effort she put in. That made it fun again, made it worth doing.

"And I'd forgotten how much I enjoy having someone cook for me," Lou said, drowning her French toast with thick, purple huckleberry syrup and an overflowing spoonful of whipped cream. "This is amazing."

Katie flushed, pleased with the praise and with herself. If food was the way to Lou's heart, well, that was something she could do, and do well. "So, what's the plan for today? I saw it finally stopped snowing."

"Haven't seen any sign of the plows yet, so you may still be stuck here for a while. Any word about your flight?"

Katie shook her head quickly, her mouth full of French toast. The syrup was unlike anything she'd ever had, sweet and tart and rich and flavorful. She wondered if she would be able to cajole Lou into letting her leave with a jar or two of it, a token to remember her and Montana by. She had to keep reminding herself that as perfect as everything was, it was all going to come to an end. It was the only thing keeping her from crossing lines she shouldn't. "No, not yet."

"Well, finish up and get changed, and I'll take you around the property," Lou said in her no-nonsense style that Katie found so attractive. "If you still want to see it, of course."

"Do you have any warm clothes I can borrow? I only packed for Mexico." Not just because she wanted to wrap herself up in something that smelled like Lou and cling to the daydream about what their life as a couple might be like a little longer.

"Let me see what I can dig up," she said, going into the bedroom. Katie followed her and sat cross-legged on the bed as Lou rummaged through the chest of drawers before pulling out a thick snowsuit. "Everything I have is going to be too big on you, but these ones have suspenders so at least they're not going to fall off. And you can wear my thick coat, I'll just layer up with others."

"Won't you be too cold, though? I have my rain jacket, I'm sure that's good enough."

"No, I'll be fine, I'm more used to it. Plus, I've got extra padding." Lou patted her stomach fondly and turned back to the chest of drawers to produce a pair of wool socks that looked handmade. "You'll have to make do with those rain boots of yours, but these will help keep you from freezing out there."

"Let me guess, you knitted these from Jason's sheep or something?" Katie asked, wondering if there was anything the woman couldn't do.

Lou threw her head back and laughed. "If only I could knit that well. No, I order those from Vermont. Best socks on the planet. And Jason doesn't even have sheep, just cows and... you know what, nevermind. Not important. What is important is giving you a good tour before we lose the daylight."

Katie thought Lou's rapid change of subject was a little odd, but maybe she was just excited to show off her land. Katie would be, if it was hers. She pulled the snowsuit on and Lou helped adjust the suspenders for her height, clipping them into place then lingering by Katie's side just a second too long. Katie almost yielded to the impulse to kiss her again, but then Lou moved away, so she pulled on the alleged best socks in the world and followed her out.

"Welcome to Paradise," Lou said, throwing open the door as Katie stepped into her boots.

"It really feels like it, doesn't it?" Katie laughed with delight. Snow crunched pleasantly underfoot and the sun shone overhead, making everything glitter with scattered light. If heaven was real, surely it looked like the landscape around her, silent and calm. Katie might have believed she had died and gone there, if it wasn't so cold that it almost hurt to breathe and her eyes didn't feel like they would freeze shut if she blinked.

"It really is. Paradise Valley, the most beautiful place on Earth."

"Are those the Rocky Mountains?" Katie guessed, pointing.

"Technically yes, they're part of the Rockies. But this specific range is the Absarokas."

The wind gusted, and Katie shivered.

"Not too cold?" Lou asked, as if she was reading Katie's mind.

"Not at all." She grinned, and stepped straight into a snow drift, sinking nearly up to her waist before losing her balance and falling over.

Lou offered her a hand up. "Careful, it's deeper there than it looks. But don't worry, we're not walking today. I have something better." She reached down into what Katie thought was just another snowdrift and pulled up the corner of a tarp. Giving it a hard shake that sent the snow flying, she pulled the cover off to reveal a shiny, black snowmobile. "Have you ever ridden one before?"

Katie shook her head.

"Didn't think so. It's easy enough. I'm driving, so all you have to do is hold on." Lou swung her leg over the saddle and plopped down. She stuck the key in the ignition and the machine roared to life. "Hop on," she yelled over the noise.

Katie was happy to oblige. She stepped over the seat behind Lou and sat gingerly, unsure where she was supposed to hold on as instructed. The snowmobile shot forward and she clung to Lou's waist so she wouldn't fall off, and then they were racing across the snow. Katie closed her eyes and rested her head against Lou's back, feeling like she was flying. They hit a bump and she was jolted out of her seat, then landed back in it, still clinging to Lou. It was exhilarating and terrifying at the same time, and she never wanted it to stop.

Lou turned the machine sharply to the right, braking in a wide spray of snow. She was laughing as she shut the snow-mobile off. "God, I love doing that."

Katie opened her eyes and loosened her grip. The cabin was just a speck off in the distance, and they were parked in the far corner of a field. A barbed wire fence poked up through the snow to their left, the posts just barely visible. In front of them was a steep drop off.

"This is the back edge of my land. That's the river, but of course it's just about frozen over now," Lou explained. "In the summer it flows slow and deep and you can cast a line without looking and pull out a trout. The huckleberries grow all along the banks, hundreds of pounds of them. Well, if we get to them before the bears do."

"Bears?" Katie looked around cautiously. She hadn't even thought about bears.

"Bear, elk, moose, blacktail deer, antelope, coyotes, and we even hear wolves sometimes, though I haven't seen them come onto the property yet."

"Wait, go back to the bears. Doesn't that worry you?" Katie hated to imagine Lou out there alone, trying to fight off a rabid bear.

"Not really. It was their land first, and I take precautions when they're active. It's just part of living out here."

"Are they active now?"

"No, it'd be pretty rare to see one until April or so."

"That's reassuring." Katie inched closer to Lou anyways, keeping an eye on the distant treeline in case something moved.

Lou pointed past the fenceline. "That's all Jason's land, been in his family since the original settlers out here. He grazes his cattle back here after the snow melts. The new calves are so funny when they see grass for the first time, they just kick up their heels and run." Lou's eyes crinkled, and Katie knew she was imagining the spring scene. She wished she could share the memory, but it was hard to picture when everything looked so cold and barren.

"Do you want to see the garden next?" Lou asked.

"I want to see it all," Katie answered eagerly. Each part of the farm held a different part of Lou's heart, and her reverence for the land was palpable. There was so much to discover, and besides, when was she ever going to get a private snowmobile tour in Montana again?

They got back on the snowmobile and Lou took her to the large, fenced in garden where she painted a magical picture of large raised beds overflowing with abundance. Lou gestured enthusiastically at the broad plot where potatoes would sprout up through the mud and the trellises where tomatoes and pole beans vined. It was hard to imagine the landscape bursting with lush vegetation in the bleak midwinter gloom, but Lou's passion was so vivid that Katie could almost taste the sweet strawberries that lay sleeping somewhere deep beneath the blanket of snow.

Lou was a different person outside of the cabin, vivacious and energetic. Any reservedness or caution was gone when she spoke about her land, what she had done in the past and where she planned to expand and grow in the future. She was openly and unabashedly in love with what she had built, and Katie basked in the warmth of the pride that radiated from her as they zipped around the land.

Next up on the tour was a greenhouse that had been dug into the ground, where carrots and leeks were just starting to sprout in their sheltered oasis. That anything could grow at all in the frozen north seemed like a miracle, not that Katie believed in those. Especially not Christmas miracles. But there was an undeniable thrum of magic in the little room that nurtured life even through the darkest days.

Lou retrieved a wide broom from behind the greenhouse door, and Katie helped her sweep the accumulation off the large panes of glass to let the precious rays of light reach the seedlings. The thick snow was heavier than it looked, and her shoulders ached by the time the greenhouse was clear. Lou talked about her plans to build a second greenhouse attached to a solar array so passionately that Katie could almost picture it in the spot Lou pointed out.

They flew past dormant beehives on the snowmobile, and Lou described the acre of land she had dedicated to pollinators bursting with blooms in the late summer. A flash of movement caught Katie's eye, and she noticed a small bird flitting between the dried stalks that poked up through the snow. The bird landed on one of the dead flowerheads and belted out a cheerful song before pecking at the seeds left behind.

Unfamiliar Latin names rolled off Lou's tongue, sweet as the honey their pollen made: *Rudbeckia, Centauria, Coreopsis, Eschscholzia.* She mimicked the calls of the migratory birds that would return to perch high in the trees and feast on the insects the flowers drew in, and laughed when Katie tried to join in whistling out their tunes. Everywhere she looked held the promise of summer, a promise she would never see fulfilled. Her heart longed for the moments that would never be. By the time the meadow was in bloom, she would be back in her concrete world hundreds of miles away.

As Katie discovered each corner of the sprawling farm, she started to realize she had been wrong about Lou the whole time. Yes, she had been hurt in the past, but she didn't need Katie to heal her. The farm was already doing that. Lou was thriving on her own, content with what she had accomplished and a clear vision of where she was going.

Katie ached for the same self-assuredness. She'd never been able to fully find her place in life without molding parts of herself to be someone she wasn't. But Lou had made no such demands of her, all while remaining unapologetically herself.

They circled back around to the barn, and Lou showed Katie the chicken coop with its two dozen hens that laid all the eggs they had eaten. Lou held her hand while the huge draft horses nibbled carrots and sugar cubes from Katie's outstretched palm, then kept holding it even after they were done giving the animals their treats. They were leaning against the fence, watching the goats frolic in the snow and laughing as they head butted each other, when Lou beamed up at Katie, glowing with pride.

"So what do you think of it all?"

"It's amazing," Katie whispered, feeling so full she thought her heart might burst.

Lou's eyes glittered with the reflection of the vast, blue sky as she leaned closer to Katie. "Are you...?" She trailed off, leaving the rest of the question unspoken before clearing her throat and trying again. "Are we...?"

"Yes," Katie said. "We are." Her heart raced as she tilted her head to meet Lou halfway.

Their frozen breath drifted together and became one. The air between them sparked and sizzled, crackling with increasing intensity as their lips got closer and time slowed down. Lou's eyes were locked on Katie's as she leaned closer, her lips parting slightly as her grip on Katie's hand tightened.

The sound of an engine cut through the stillness, getting louder with every second. Ugh. The moment was ruined. Again.

"That's probably Jason," Lou said, sighing before she walked around the barn to find out.

A wiry man in a sherpa-lined coat, cowboy hat, and black boots rounded the corner and jumped on Lou, wrapping her in a bear hug and knocking her hat off as he almost wrestled her to the ground. "How was L.A.?"

"Good to see you, too, Jason," she answered with a quick smile. Katie noticed she avoided his question as she plucked her hat from a snow drift. "This is Katie."

"A pleasure to finally meet you, ma'am," he said, sweeping his hat off his head and raising the back of her hand to his lips. Katie would have slapped any man who tried that on her in Seattle, but coming from the cowboy, the quaint gesture was kind of charming.

"You too," she said. "I've heard a lot about you."

"Likewise," he said with a warm grin.

Katie looked at Lou in surprise. When had she talked to Jason about Katie? And what had she said? Lou didn't seem to notice Katie's expression at all, though. She was too busy glaring daggers at Jason. Katie was dying to know what Lou had said about her. She just hoped it was nothing bad.

"Well, I just wanted to come 'round and make sure y'all made it through the storm alright." He glanced up at the sky, which was still clear but starting to darken as the sun sank towards the horizon. Katie had been so focused on soaking in every second with Lou she hadn't realized they'd already been out the whole afternoon.

"The house and barn are both still standing, so I reckon we made it through alright," Lou said with a crooked smile.

"While I'm here, I was hoping to go over a couple things before the Christmas Dance Friday, if you have a few? And the last load of presents is in my truck."

"Of course," she said. "As long as Katie doesn't mind? I know you hate things like that."

"No, it's fine," Katie said quickly. "Don't let me get in the way."

"I won't keep her from you long," Jason said with a casual wink that made Katie wonder again what exactly Lou had told him about her.

They walked into the tack room and crouched over a folding table, deep in conversation. Katie wandered around the barn, petting the animals while she waited. She decided the big brown horse with the white bangs that fell into his eyes was her favorite, and she snuck him an extra sugar cube while she scratched his neck.

Katie was starting to get bored. Lou and Jason were still huddled over a thick binder, talking about some band and potluck dishes and rental chairs. She yawned. It had been an early morning and a busy day, and the warmth of the barn was making her sleepy. She needed some fresh air to wake up, and she was starting to feel antsy.

"Hey, Lou?" she called.

"Sorry, it'll just be a few more minutes," Lou said.

"That's fine. I'm gonna walk back up to the house and get dinner started though, before it gets too much later."

Lou peeked around the corner. "You're sure you're alright walking alone? It's getting pretty dark out there and the house isn't near as close as it looks."

"Yeah, I'll be fine. The walk will do me good. And I have the flashlight on my phone if I need it."

"Okay, be safe. I'm excited to see what you come up with tonight."

Katie walked out of the barn, past Jason's towering truck and the snowmobile that had given her memories she would cherish for the rest of her life. The sky was her favorite shade of blue, the dusky, witchy hue it turned just before going totally dark. The mountains in the distance were black silhouettes painted against the horizon. She squinted. It looked like clouds were forming around the jagged peaks, but it was hard to tell. She hoped they were bringing more snow, so she wouldn't have to find some other excuse to stay a few more days.

You could just ask her to stay longer. But Katie wasn't used to that kind of open communication and the vulnerabilities it exposed. It was better when others made the first move so she didn't have to risk being rejected. She had dealt with enough of that in her life and it had hurt her more than she cared to admit. Plus, it was nice to be pursued.

She was almost certain Lou had been about to kiss her, but it wouldn't be the first time Katie had misread a situation like that. The first girl she ever summoned up the courage to kiss in a smelly basement at a college party had seemed into it, right up until she pushed Katie away and informed her that she was just kissing Katie because she was drunk and not actually into women before wandering off to grind on some frat boy. Katie's cheeks burned with embarrassment at the old memory. She had been so naive then, and so confused.

She was halfway back to the cabin when she realized her wish for more bad weather might actually come true. The wind whipped up across the fields, catching the ends of her scarf and wrapping it across her face. Glancing up, she noticed the clouds had moved in more quickly than she'd thought possible, and the first flakes of snow were already starting to fall. Katie lengthened her stride, keeping her eyes on the ground in front of her so she wouldn't trip into another snowdrift. Lou was right, the cabin was a further walk than she'd thought, and she was starting to feel the stinging bite of the wind on the tip of her nose.

The snow fell in thick clumps and piled up quickly on the long driveway, but Katie ignored it and focused on putting one foot in front of the other, her gaze firmly fixed to her rainboots and the ground before them. Worst case, Lou would be driving past with the snowmobile soon, and she would just hop on for the rest of the way.

It really was starting to feel like she had been walking forever though, and that she should have already gotten there. She felt in her pockets for the gloves Lou had loaned her, then cursed herself when she realized she'd left them sitting on a shelf in the barn next to the box of sugar cubes. Oh well, she would only be out a few more minutes. It wasn't that big of a deal. She flexed her fingers to get the blood flowing in them and pushed on.

Lou's little house had to be just ahead. It had to. Katie glanced up to check. All she could see in any direction was snow, thick flakes that pelted towards the earth and piled up on everything they touched. She squinted into the storm, trying to spot the glow of the house's lights or the smoke from the fire they'd left smoldering that morning, but there was nothing but white.

Fuck.

Deep breaths. The one thing she wasn't going to do was panic.

She looked over her shoulder, trying to gauge how far away she was from the barn and where she might have gotten off track, and saw nothing but her own footprints. Her footprints. Of course. She would just follow them back to the barn and wait for Lou to finish up with Jason. That was the best plan.

Wind howled across the field and she tried to run, realizing her footprints were quickly filling with fresh snow. She couldn't lose them. She barreled through the drifts, panting with exertion as she raced against time. How much snow had fallen? Her tracks were barely visible. How long had it even been since she left the barn? It didn't seem like she had walked far enough to be as lost as she felt, and she couldn't have wandered that far off the driveway. She looked around, trying to tell which divots in the snow were her footsteps, and which were just natural blemishes blown around by the wind. She couldn't tell anymore.

Her lungs burned from sucking in frozen air, and she stopped to catch her breath and figure out what she would do next. Hyperventilating and passing out wouldn't help anyone. She wiped beads of sweat from her forehead with her scarf. At least she wouldn't freeze to death. Lou's heavy coat was doing its job well.

Too well. Even though it was snowing, it wasn't that cold, and Katie was drenched with sweat. She unzipped the jacket to cool down a little. The breeze felt amazing against her hot skin and damp pajamas, so she took the jacket off and tied it around her waist. Feeling refreshed, she set off again in the direction where she thought the house must be.

It wasn't. She walked for at least fifteen minutes in that direction, but still no sturdy log cabin appeared through the blinding snow. Katie shivered and reached for Lou's coat, but it wasn't around her waist anymore. It must have gotten untied somewhere along the way and she hadn't even noticed. She hoped Lou wouldn't be too mad at her for losing it. She would buy her another one.

It was so cold, and Katie was tired of walking. The deep snow drained her energy, and her legs felt like they weighed a thousand pounds as she shuffled forward. She just had to keep going, and she would eventually find her way back somewhere.

Her next step was into a snowdrift. Katie stumbled to her knees and let out a scream of frustration. She shivered again, and then she couldn't stop shivering as the chills took over. *Stand up,* she willed herself. *You have to keep going.* But she couldn't. Her body was all out of strength.

"Lou!" she yelled. Her cry was lost to the wind. In the distance, she could hear the faint roar of a snowmobile engine.

Chapter Seven

"Katie?"

The voice was far away, barely a whisper through the howling wind. In fact, she was pretty sure she was imagining it.

"Katie?"

There it was again, a little louder. Katie groaned. She wasn't ready to get up. The bed of snow she was curled up in was too soft and cozy to move from. She would just sleep a little longer.

"Oh my God, Katie! Katie. Wake up." Lou's voice, right beside her. Katie smiled. Waking up next to Lou was nice. But even though it was definitely Lou's voice, it didn't sound like Lou. Lou was calm, cool, collected, and this voice sounded panicked. "I'm here, Katie. I've got you. Wake up. I've got you now, I'm here. You have to wake up."

Katie tried to reach up to shush her, tried to tell it was okay, she just needed to sleep for a little while and then she would get up when she was ready, but her lips wouldn't move. She could feel Lou picking up her hands and rubbing them. It hurt, and she moaned. She just wanted to be left alone.

"Goddammit, Katie, wake up!" Lou was pulling her arms now, trying to get her to sit up. "Open your fucking eyes right now."

Lou was mad at her, and it was the worst feeling in the world. Katie hadn't meant to upset her. "Sorry," she whispered. She had to force her jaw to unclench to get the word out, and it started chattering as soon as she did.

"Oh thank God, you're alive," Lou said. "I know you're cold and I know you're tired, but I need you to fight, Seattle." She was wrapping something around Katie's shoulders, rubbing them as she did. "We have to get you inside and warmed up, but you have to get on the snowmobile. Can you do that?"

Katie shook her head. She didn't want to go anywhere.

"Too bad, you have to. So suck it up, and get up." Lou pulled at her arms again.

It took every ounce of Katie's strength to stand, and once she was up she immediately collapsed into Lou's arms. Lou half-carried, half-dragged her onto the snowmobile, where she slumped over. Surely none of this was necessary. She just needed a good nap, and then she'd be fine to walk back to the cabin. If she could just get her teeth to stop chattering.

"Just hold on," Lou said, hoisting her back up to sitting again. Katie didn't know if she was talking about the snowmobile or just staying alive. Maybe both. "You have to hold on."

Katie nodded against Lou's back. She could do that.

The ride back to the house felt comically short, as though Katie had fallen just a few feet away from the doorstep. Maybe she had, but the blizzard made it impossible to tell. It was still torturous. The wind was even worse on the snowmobile, and felt like it was driving shards of ice into her veins. Before she knew it, Lou was picking her up and carrying her across the threshold.

"I've got you," she kept repeating. "You're safe now. I've got you." Lou carried Katie to the woodburning stove and laid her on the floor, pulling a throw pillow from the couch and tucking it under Katie's head. "God, you're ice cold and soaking wet. We have to get you out of these clothes. Can you do it?"

Katie shook her head. Her hands burned and she couldn't feel her fingertips. Her whole body ached as it convulsed with shivers.

"I'm going to help you then, okay?"

Katie nodded, and Lou's hands went to the buckles at her shoulders, deftly unclipping the bib of the snow pants. She stripped Katie's pajama top off, and then the bottoms, leaving Katie shivering in her underwear. Shouldn't she be putting clothes on? She didn't see how getting naked was supposed to help her get warmer, but she didn't mind, either, as long as Lou was the one undressing her. Lou held Katie close as she unhooked her bra with one hand and peeled the sweat and snow-soaked garment away. Her breath was warm on Katie's skin, and Katie saw steam curl up from where it met her frozen flesh before she closed her eyes again.

"Stay with me, Seattle. I need you to stay awake." Lou covered Katie in blankets and tucked a pillow under her head. "Don't move. I'll be right back."

Katie couldn't have moved if she wanted to. Everything hurt. She heard Lou go into the bathroom and open the medicine cabinet, then heard the distinctive rattle of a pill bottle. Guilt added a new layer of pain to the waves wracking Katie's body as she remembered the anxiety meds she had seen before. She hadn't meant to worry Lou.

The wood floor creaked with Lou's footsteps as she walked back across the room. She went into the kitchen, and Katie heard her set a pot on the stove. The burner clicked three times and then ignited.

"Any warmer yet?" Lou came back into the living room.

"N-n-n-n-n-o." Katie could barely get the word out. "Co-o-o-ld-e-e-r." She could feel the heat radiating from the fire, but it wasn't doing anything to ease the chill.

"I'm going to lay beside you for body heat," Lou said quietly before slipping under the blankets and wrapping Katie in her arms. Lou flinched when her hands covered Katie's. "Jesus fucking Christ, you're freezing."

Katie snuggled into Lou. She was so warm, so soft. So safe.

"Oh, Katie. I'm so sorry. This is all my fault. I should have checked the weather. I should never have let you go off alone, or spent that long finalizing things with Jason."

"Shh," Katie said, rolling over to face Lou. Her back was finally starting to get warm but her chest was still freezing. At least the chills were subsiding, leaving her muscles with a dull ache in their place. "It's not your fault. I'm sorry I didn't just wait for you. And I lost your coat."

"It doesn't matter. None of it does." Lou whispered, her lips inches from Katie's. "I found you in time. That's all that's important."

Katie closed the distance and pressed her lips to Lou's. She could claim delirium from the cold later, but she couldn't wait another second to know what it was like to kiss the most incredible woman she had ever met. Lou inhaled sharply as their lips met, but she didn't pull back. Katie deepened the kiss, tasting whiskey and sage and mint and hay as Lou's mouth opened to invite her in.

"I've wanted to do that since I got into your truck at the airport," she admitted breathlessly.

"Me too," Lou said, and pulled her back in for another kiss.

It was everything Katie had imagined and more. Her only regret was that she had to almost die to find the courage to do it. She'd always thought when people talked about sparks flying, they meant it in a metaphorical sense. Even though she'd been certain she was in love with various women before, she'd never felt such an intense connection. But when she touched Lou, her entire body lit up, electrified by desire. A current ran between them, joining them so securely Katie felt like she'd never be able to let go. Just two souls locked together until the heat of passion burned them both to a crisp.

Lou caressed her back, pulling her in closer until Katie was sure they were going to fuse into one. The chill that had consumed her very core burst into flame as they embraced, and Katie moaned out her desire as she hitched her leg around Lou's waist. Lou responded by grabbing her ass and holding her in place as her tongue danced with Katie's in the flickering firelight.

The bitter chill was gone, replaced by a pleasant warmth spreading outwards from her center as lust took over. She needed Lou, more than she'd ever needed anything in her life. Kissing her was as easy as breathing, and it suddenly felt stupid that she'd waited so long to do it. Katie reached up to run her fingers over Lou's short hair, so soft and prickly at the same time.

Lou gasped and pulled away. "Your hands are still ice cold."

"Sor–"

"Shh." Lou hushed her. "Don't you dare say it." She kissed Katie on the forehead then sat up, tucking her flannel shirt back into her jeans.

"Wait," Katie pleaded, missing Lou's warmth, her touch, her lips. "I don't understand. I thought you wanted…" She trailed off.

"I do, but we shouldn't do this, not now. It wouldn't be right of me."

Katie couldn't think of anything more right. What had she done to make her pull away? Didn't Lou understand how much Katie needed her? None of it made sense, but Lou was already standing up and walking to the kitchen. Katie shivered and wrapped the blanket around herself. She'd gotten so caught up in the heat of the moment, she'd forgotten how frozen her toes still were. She wriggled them to try to thaw them, and pain shot up her feet.

"Here," Lou said, handing her a mug of something warm. "This will help."

Katie peered inside the mug. Steaming orange liquid sloshed inside, filling her nostrils with a sickly sweet scent that reminded her a bit of cough syrup. "What is it?"

"Hot water and electrolyte powder."

Katie took a sip, and spit it back into the cup. "It's disgusting." She'd never liked sports drinks, and being served one warm was a new layer of hell. "Thank you, though."

"Suck it up and drink it, you need it." It was clear Lou wasn't going to take no for an answer.

Katie dutifully swallowed a mouthful, if only to appease Lou, then set the mug down on the coffee table. "How about something stronger?" She asked, thinking of the whiskey bottle above the fridge.

"No, alcohol is the last thing you need, that'll just make it worse. Right now, you need the sugar and the heat." Lou handed the mug back to Katie, then crossed her arms. "Drink it, and if you feel better, we'll see about getting some food in you."

"I already feel better," Katie said. "But if it makes you happy..." She took a long swallow, and then another. A few seconds later, she realized Lou knew what she was talking about. Like always, it seemed. Even though the drink left an awful, sticky feeling in her mouth, it filled her with warmth and energy she hadn't even noticed she was lacking.

"Thank you," Lou said. The line of anxious worry etched across her forehead was beginning to soften. "Now how are you feeling, really?"

"Better," Katie said. "Tired."

"Just stay here and rest while I make dinner." Lou helped her up to the couch and pulled a remote from the coffee table drawer. "Put on whatever you like."

Lou went to rummage around in the kitchen while Katie scrolled through movies, finally selecting a cheesy rom-com that wouldn't require her to think too much. She heard the whir of the microwave in the background, and a few minutes later, Lou came back to the living room bearing two steaming bowls of chili. Katie's stomach growled as soon as she smelled it, and she dug in.

"This is incredible," she managed to say between spoonfuls. "And you said you weren't much of a cook."

"Mandy made it a few weeks back," Lou said, sitting down beside her. Their knees touched, and Katie felt that jolt again. "I just happen to be pretty handy with the defrost button."

When Lou returned to the couch after clearing their bowls, she put her arm around Katie's shoulders. Katie snuggled into her, finally warm again, and feeling full and happy. Her head was tucked into Lou's shoulder, and she could hear Lou's heart beating, a steady and reassuring thump-thump that made Katie feel like she was home.

Chapter Eight

The first thing Katie noticed when she woke up in the morning was that she was in bed, even though she couldn't remember how she got there. The second thing she noticed was how sweltering hot it was underneath all the blankets piled on top of her. The third thing was that she wasn't in bed alone. Lou was laying next to her on top of the covers with one arm flung over Katie's waist, snoring lightly. Katie would have been perfectly happy to lay there with her a while longer, except for that second thing. She wiggled out from her cocoon, being careful not to wake Lou up.

It didn't work. Lou's eyes flew open the second Katie moved and her arm tightened around Katie's waist. "Are you okay?"

The fourth thing Katie noticed was that she was still naked. "I'm fine," she said. "Better than ever. But what happened? Did we...?"

"Nothing happened," Lou said. She sat up on one elbow. "You fell asleep while we were watching the movie and I carried you in here so you would be more comfortable. But then I didn't want to leave you alone, just in case."

"What time is it?" Katie asked. Lou shrugged, so she reached for her phone. 9:04. She looked back up at Lou in surprise. "It's late. We need to go feed the animals."

"Jason already did it," Lou said. "I texted him last night and asked him to come over this morning. I couldn't leave you." The line of worry was back, carved firmly between Lou's eyebrows. Katie longed to reach up and smooth it away.

"You don't have to worry about me."

"Yes, I do. I'm responsible for your safety out here. You're my guest."

Is that all I am? Katie didn't dare ask the question out loud. Her heart told her it was more.

"But we need to get moving, get your things packed up. Your flight leaves in a few hours." Lou's words shattered the illusion as if she was reading Katie's mind.

"My flight?"

"To Mexico?"

"The airline never rebooked me. I meant to get that sorted out yesterday, but I got distracted with everything," Katie lied. "Plus, won't they all be canceled again because of the blizzard last night?" Was Lou trying to get rid of her? The thought hurt more than it should have.

"That wasn't a blizzard, just a little snow squall. I called Marlow last night after it blew over, he said flights are going out today as scheduled."

"Oh," Katie said, feeling like the wind had been knocked out of her. She wasn't ready for it to end. Impulse took over, and she reached for Lou's hand. Nothing ventured, nothing gained. "I thought, well, I was hoping... maybe I could stay a few days longer?"

Lou squeezed her fingers, then let go as she looked away. "I don't think that's a good idea, Seattle. It's too dangerous out here for someone like you. I almost lost you yesterday, I'm not going to risk that happening a second time."

"It was just an accident, I just got turned around. It won't happen again, I'll be more careful. I won't go anywhere without you. But I'm not ready to leave yet."

"I can't take another accident," Lou snapped. "Don't you get it? You almost died, Seattle. *You. Almost. Died.* If I had been ten minutes later, you wouldn't have made it. I can't always be there." Her face crumpled, and Katie noticed tears welling in her eyes.

Katie took her hand again, speaking as gently as she could. "Look at me, Lou. I'm fine. Yesterday was scary, but I'm fine. And you *were* there when I needed you." She paused, thinking of anything she could say that might make Lou change her mind. "Remember what you said the other day, that I'm exactly where I need to be? You were right. I was meant to come here. The universe sent me this adventure for a reason. And I'm still trying to figure out what I'm supposed to learn."

"Do you really believe in that stuff?" Lou asked. "The universe guiding you or whatever?"

"Maybe." Katie shrugged. "Not really, it kind of started as a joke with my friend, but I'm becoming more open to it. A year ago I would have told you it was bullshit, but now I'm not so sure."

"Why's that?"

"A few months ago one of my friends got laid off and I was so jealous. I just kept saying 'I wish that would happen to me.' And then it did. I didn't really mean it, I was just burned out and tired, but now it makes me wonder. Careful what you wish for and all that. And then my flight got diverted here, and I got to meet you? How often does that happen? So let's just say I'm open to the idea."

Lou looked at her for a long time, then shook her head and chuckled. "Fine, I guess you can stay a little longer. But no wandering around the homestead alone."

"You don't have to worry about that," Katie said. She was trying not to show Lou how shaken up she was from the night before, but it rattled her if she thought about it too long. She definitely had no intention of going off by herself again.

"We can't lay around all day, though," Lou said. "I do have to go into town to run some errands." She stood up and stretched. "Get dressed, you're coming with me."

Bozeman, Montana didn't seem as suffocatingly small the second time Katie rode through it. She studied the buildings with new interest, noting the bank, the small movie theater, the bars, and grocery store. It wasn't Seattle, but it had all anyone needed. There were even a couple of sushi restaurants.

All the shops along the main street were decorated with garlands and shining white lights that glowed warmly in the snow, but suddenly Katie didn't mind it anymore. Unlike the wealth-flaunting consumerism on garish display in the Seattle streets, the Christmas decorations in Bozeman were quaint and wholesome, making the town feel magical. Or it could have been Lou's hand resting casually on her knee that filled her body with warmth and belonging. Either way, the little excursion was putting Katie into a great mood.

Her heart leapt into her throat when she realized they were driving on the road out of town, back towards the airport. For a brief moment she wondered if Lou had changed her mind and was just going to dump her there without any of her belongings except the wallet and passport tucked into her purse, but that was a little ridiculous. More than anything, Lou had shown she was a good person to her core, and Katie trusted her.

Lou hung a left into the parking lot of a large ranch store and parked the truck among a sprawling lot of other pickups. "Careful, it's icy. I'll come around and help you down."

She was so thoughtful, Katie thought she might melt into a puddle right there on the seat. Whatever happened with Lou in the long run, she was raising the bar for women everywhere. It felt good to be taken care of.

Lou opened the door and offered her hand. It was a good thing she did, because Katie's feet slipped out from under her the second they touched the ground. She would have fallen on her face if Lou wasn't there to grab her around the waist and hold her up until her balance came back.

If someone had told Katie the most romantic moment of her life so far would take place in between two oversized pickup trucks in a parking lot in Montana, she would have laughed in their face. But when the sun peeked between the clouds to illuminate Lou's face, it took her breath away. And when Lou pulled her close and kissed her hard, Katie felt weak in the knees.

"I couldn't wait any longer to do that," Lou said, nuzzling her nose against Katie's. "It was all I could think about on the drive up."

"Same." Katie smiled, her lips still tingling.

"Ready to go inside?"

Katie nodded. She would have gone with Lou anywhere.

The ranch supply outlet was a new experience for Katie. It was as large as any big-box store, but dedicated entirely to things like farming and livestock. Endless rows of tools she had never seen before stretched out in all directions, each one demanding to be discovered. She could have spent hours there browsing the aisles and listening to Lou explain what everything was for, but Lou seemed like she was on a mission. Katie followed her to the back of the store, where she began loading bags of feed onto a large, flat cart.

"I can help," Katie said. "Just tell me what to grab."

"We need five of those alfalfa pellets." Lou pointed a little further down the aisle at a black bag with a yellow horse galloping across the front.

Katie couldn't stop the pig-like grunt that slipped out as she tried to lift the bag. Cute. It was way heavier than she'd thought, especially because Lou made it look so easy to grab the giant sacks and hoist them onto the flatbed cart. On top of weighing a ton— or fifty pounds, as the bag claimed— the sacks were unwieldy, but Katie was determined not to let Lou see her struggle. Finally she worked the bag up so it was perched precariously on her hip, and waddled down the aisle to dump it on the cart. Lou watched her, eyes crinkled up with silent laughter, but said nothing.

They passed through a clothing section on their way to check out, and Katie pulled Lou into the racks as she pored over the options. Even the clothing in Montana was different from what she was used to, but if she was going to stay a while longer, she needed something better to wear than what was in her warm weather suitcase. She picked out a sensible pair of flannel-lined jeans, then tossed in a flannel shirt and a mustard-colored, canvas coat with a thick fleece lining. The standard Montana uniform, judging by what everyone else in the store was wearing.

"Think I'll fit in here now?" She joked, spinning to show off the coat.

"I think you'll look great," Lou said, chuckling. Katie loved the sound of it, low and throaty.

They got to the checkout and Katie pulled out her card first, sticking it in the machine before Lou noticed. It was the least she could do after eating all Lou's food and taking over her bedroom, she wasn't spending any of the money she'd budgeted for Mexico anyways. Lou had seemed ready to pay for her clothes, too, insisting they ring them up together. Katie definitely wasn't going to let that happen.

"Why'd you do that, Seattle?" Lou asked as they walked back out to the truck.

"Because I wanted to," Katie said, reaching for Lou's hand. She liked the way her fingers fit between Lou's, even when they were both wearing gloves. Like their hands were made to fit each other. She didn't want to go a second without touching Lou, but she knew she still needed to take it slow for both of their sakes. She was in Montana to figure out what she wanted, what she was doing with her life, not to fall head over heels for a woman she was going to have to leave.

"I don't need charity," Lou said, sounding slightly offended.

"I know," Katie said simply, squeezing her hand.

"I live simply because I want to, and because it's the right thing to do, not because I have to."

"And I just wanted to show how much I appreciate everything you've done for me," Katie said. "Suck it up." Katie winked, turning Lou's words from the night before against her. They loaded the feed in the bed of the truck and Lou drove them back towards town. "So, where to next?"

"Reckoned we might get some lunch in town," Lou said. "I know a great spot none of the tourists or Californians go to." She turned down an alley and parked behind a building, then showed Katie into the dim restaurant through an unmarked door.

The only sign that it was a business at all was the sign displaying their open hours on the door. Inside was a narrow room with two pool tables, a bar at the far end, and red pleather booths lining either side. It smelled like old cigarette smoke, even though there was clearly a No Smoking sign on the door, and seemed like the kind of place that had stayed unchanged for decades.

"Hey, Claire," Lou called, waving at the bartender.

"Hey, Lou!" The woman replied cheerfully. She looked like a bartender Katie would have expected to see in Seattle more than Bozeman, with bright purple hair, an undercut, and fully tattooed sleeves on both arms. "Long time, no see. Want your usual?"

"You know it." Lou turned to Katie. "What are you drinking?"

"Espresso martini?"

Lou laughed. "Not here." She raised her voice a little. "Claire, make that two, please."

"You got it. Have a seat anywhere, I'll bring those right out for you."

Lou gestured for Katie to pick a table. They all looked the same, so she slid into the booth closest to her.

"So you must come here a lot," Katie said.

"Every time I come into town. Winston works the lunch shift back in the kitchen on weekdays and he makes the best chicken fried steak in town."

Kasey the bartender arrived with two frothy pints of beer and they placed their food orders. Katie tried to keep from wrinkling her nose. Beer probably would have been her last choice of drink back in Seattle, where bitter IPAs seemed to be the after-dark lifeblood of the city, but she guessed the options were more limited in Montana.

"Cheers," Lou said, raising her glass.

Katie touched hers to it, then tasted the beer. It wasn't as bad as she'd expected it to be, sort of buttery and spiced and not very hoppy at all. Maybe knowing it was Lou's favorite helped, or maybe Montana was changing her, making her into a beer person. "This is actually pretty good, what is it?"

"It's from a brewery in Missoula, I think this is their Christmas ale." She winced. "Sorry, I forgot you hate the holidays. I always just get whichever one they have on tap, I didn't even think about it. I can get Claire to pour you something else."

"It's okay, I kind of like it. It's different." Katie took another sip. "You all really get into the holiday spirit out here, don't you? Didn't Jason say something about a Christmas Dance, too?"

"I guess we do. Gives us something to look forward to in the middle of a long winter, brings a little light back to things when the days are so short. Plus it's a reason for people to gather and forget our differences and celebrate, give candy to the kids and dance the night away."

"Can I go?"

Lou raised an eyebrow. "I didn't think you'd want to. I didn't even think you'd still be here." She hesitated long enough for Katie to start to regret asking, then shrugged. "But sure, I don't see why you couldn't."

Katie grinned. "I always wanted to go to a dance with a girl, but I was always too shy to ask one so I just went with the boys who asked me and hated every second of them."

"I can't imagine you being shy," Lou said.

"I wasn't out at school then. I didn't come out until college, and that's when I started to get a little more confident."

"Well in that case, Katie, will you go to the Christmas Dance with me?"

"I would love to," Katie said, feeling like her heart was about to burst open with joy. It was all she had ever wanted, she just hadn't known it until right then.

Katie pushed her plate back. She was stuffed with chicken fried steak and it looked like she'd barely made a dent in her plate of food.

"That was awesome," she said. "What's next?" The food was rich and heavy, and she was thinking a nap sounded good. Even better if Lou joined her.

"I have one more errand to run. Why don't you hang out here, have another drink? Tell Claire to put it on my tab. I'll be back in an hour or so."

"I can go with you." Katie loved spending time with Lou, and even a simple day of errands was one of the happiest she could remember.

Lou gave her a crooked smile and shook her head. "No, you can't. I have therapy."

"Oh." Katie felt like an idiot. "Yeah, I'll be fine here."

"No wandering off?"

"No wandering off," she promised.

Lou left, and Katie moved over to the bar, deciding it looked less pathetic if she was sitting there by herself than at a booth alone. Plus, she was dying to ask Claire some discreet questions about Lou if the opportunity arose. She ordered another Christmas ale, giving the bartender a friendly smile as she did. The taste was actually growing on her a little bit, and drinking Lou's usual drink in her regular bar felt like another way to try to understand her.

The door jingled, and two men walked in. They could have been Jason's brothers, with the same lanky build, tight jeans, and cowboy swagger; but then again, they looked like every man she had seen in the ranch store, too. They couldn't possibly all be related, so Katie assumed that was just what men in Montana looked like, sort of like the tech bros in Seattle all had their uniform of quarter-zip fleeces with company logos and bland khaki pants. The two cowboys sauntered up to the bar and took the two seats next to Katie.

"Howdy, Claire," one of the men said, tipping his hat. "Can we get two double shots of whiskey and one of whatever the little lady's having."

"That's very generous of you, but I'm not interested." Katie said, skin crawling. Did he really just call her little lady like some weird womanizer from the forties? Gross. It was better to nip these things in the bud before they got out of hand and she inevitably got called a bitch for not wanting to fuck someone for a cheap pint.

"Oho, look who thinks she's too good for us," the man said to his buddy. "Pour her one anyways," he directed Claire.

Whatever. The man could spend his money however he wanted. She wasn't going to drink it. The second beer was already starting to make her head swim a little too pleasantly, she didn't need a third. She checked her phone, wondering when Lou would be back.

"You from around here?"

Shit. The man was still talking to her. "Nope. Just visiting." She looked back at her phone, hoping he would see she really wasn't interested in small talk or anything else with him.

"Figured. A Montana girl wouldn't turn her nose up at a free drink. Let me guess, Los Angeles?"

"Seattle." Why'd she even say that? She should have just ignored him.

"Same thing. So ya come out to see Yellowstone, or what?"

What? Wasn't that in California? No, that was the other one, Yosemite or whatever. Was Yellowstone in Montana? If so, it was news to Katie. "No."

"In town for the football game?" The man drained his shot and waved for another one.

"No."

"I give up then, what brings a pretty girl like you all the way out here in the middle of winter?"

"A flight mixup." Couldn't they get the hint that she wasn't interested in talking to them?

"Well, whaddya think so far?" Apparently not.

"It's a lot nicer than I expected. I could see myself living here someday." Where had that come from? Why did she say that?

"Too bad, we're full."

"That so?" Katie asked, raising an eyebrow. "Seems like a whole lotta emptiness, from what I've seen."

"What he's trying to say is, we don't take too kindly to people like you moving in and buying up all our land." The man's friend spoke up for the first time.

"People like me? What's that supposed to mean?" Lou had said something similar earlier, and it grated.

"Outsiders. City folk. People who will never try to fit in here, just try to change to be the way they want it. Bitches, like you." There it was.

"You don't even know me," Katie protested. Normally she would just leave, but Lou had told her to stay put. Besides, what if the men decided to follow her? The bar was safer with

Claire looking on. And if she didn't stand up for herself, they would just try it on the next poor woman who wandered into the weird little bar.

"Maybe not, but I've met you a dozen times before." The man sneered at her. "What makes you think you're right for Montana? You know how to ride a horse? Rope a steer or run barrels? If a grizz is charging you down and it's not a bluff, you gonna be able to pull a trigger? You ever even shot a gun before? Been hunting? Gutted a fish?" He slammed the second double shot back.

"Maybe I have," Katie said, raising her chin defiantly. She definitely hadn't. She didn't even know what half those words meant. Run barrels?

The man looked her up and down. "Yeah, that's what I thought. Go back to the tourist bars, and then go back to wherever it was you came from."

"That's enough, Bradley," Claire cut in. Finally. "She's a friend of Lou's, she's more than welcome here."

"Whatever, we're leavin' anyways. Got shit to do back on the ranch before Christmas," Bradley said, dropping a twenty dollar bill on the bar.

"You better not be driving," Claire called as they left. She looked at Katie and rolled her eyes. "Don't you pay them no sort of mind. They talk too much, but they're all bark and no bite."

"Is it true though?" Katie asked. The whole exchange was making her reevaluate everything she'd thought about Montana.

"Is what true?"

"Outsiders aren't welcome here."

Claire shrugged. "Sorta. I swear, the nicest people in the world live here once you earn our trust. But we're protective of our home. We have to be. Everyone who comes here can see how special it is, and then they move here and try to change it. Well, if they all do that, we'll lose the very thing that makes it special in the first place. We're just out here trying to keep our way of life alive." She cleared the empty shot glasses from the bar and wiped it down before taking the cash over to the register. "Hey, you want me to pour that beer he paid for, now that he's gone?"

"Nah, just keep it as a tip." Katie got it, even if she didn't think it was fair. People said the same thing about Seattle all the time: we're full, go home. And she'd worked in social media for long enough to see how people ruined everything, from restaurants to hiking spots, hidden beaches, cheap vacation hacks, or secret menus. She couldn't even blame the two men for judging her. She probably would have done the same, if they'd shown up to one of her favorite bars back in Seattle looking as out of place as she was there.

"So how'd you meet Lou?" Claire asked, wiping the bar down. "Old friends?"

"She saved me from the airport when all the flights were canceled. What about you?" This was her chance.

"She's been coming here as long as I've worked here, coming up on about four years soon. Every other week on Thursdays for lunch, always gets the chicken fried steak and a beer. You're the first person she's ever brought by, though."

"Really?" Katie asked.

Claire nodded. "I'm a little surprised she brought you here. We like to keep our spots to ourselves, as you can see. And no offense, but this doesn't really seem like your type of bar."

"Well, the secret's safe with me." Katie laughed. "I don't even know what the name of this place is."

"Exactly," Claire said with a wink. "Now you're catching on. So how long are you in town for?"

"Another few days."

"Staying out by the fairgrounds?"

"No, out at Lou's place."

Claire crossed her arms and raised an eyebrow, her demeanor shifting. "Well, just so you know, we Montanans aren't just protective of our land, we look after our own as well. Lou's a great woman. None of us want to see her hurt." Her tone was still casual, but the threat was too thinly veiled to be mistaken. And there was something else there, too. Jealousy?

"Hurting Lou is the last thing I want to do."

"Good." Claire spun on her heel and walked into the kitchen, leaving Katie alone at the bar.

Katie pulled out her phone to check her text messages. There was one that she hadn't seen from Megan, sent earlier that morning.

"Murdered yet? Y/N?"

"N." Katie typed back. "I kissed her." Megan didn't need to know she had almost died for it to happen. "And we're going to a Christmas Dance tomorrow."

"Send me a selfie."

"I will." Katie had to remember to take one. She didn't have any pictures with Lou yet. "I don't know what I'm going to wear though."

"No, send me one now."

"?"

"I need to make sure you haven't been kidnapped." The three dots popped up. Megan was still typing. "Because it's kind of hard to believe that the Katie I know, who has spent the last fifteen years shitting on the holidays, is going to a Christmas dance."

Katie rolled her eyes, then snapped a photo and sent it. "Just me."

"Aww, you look happy, though."

"More than you know."

The door jingled, and Lou reentered the bar. "Ready to go?"

"Born ready," Katie said lightly. Even if it was Lou's favorite lunch, the bar and its patrons made Katie more than a little uncomfortable. She tried to brush it off, but their words still lingered in the back of her mind.

Chapter Nine

"There was one more place on the homestead tour we didn't get to yesterday," Lou said as they pulled into the long drive. "Do you mind if we make a quick stop there now?"

"Not at all," Katie said. She wanted to see everything Lou wanted to show her.

Lou had been quiet for most of the ride back to the farm, other than saying her therapist had given her a lot to think about. Katie held her hand, giving Lou the space she needed to process her thoughts. Instead, she occupied herself by staring out the window into the valley called Paradise, her own thoughts spiraling from the conversations she'd had at the bar.

Maybe the cowboys were right, she wasn't cut out for life in Montana. It was just a silly fantasy she was trying to force, but none of it made sense. And going back out to explore the homestead again after her ordeal put her on edge, especially since the sun was already starting to sink behind the mountains in the west. There was nothing Lou could possibly see in her.

She was weak and useless and so far out of her element and the comfort of being in control and—

No. No spiraling. She needed to snap out of it. Why did she care so much what a couple of douchebags had said to her in passing because they were mad she rejected their advances? But something else nagged at Katie, too.

Claire.

Katie was dying to know what the story there was. The bartender was just a little too friendly with Lou in the most subtle ways, and Katie suspected there was more than either Lou or Claire had let on. If they'd slept together, it wouldn't surprise Katie. What did surprise her, though, was how jealous the thought made her.

Lou drove them all the way back to the house, lost in her own contemplations, then let the dogs out and led Katie back to the shed she had seen the day before. She brushed the snow off a padlock, then fished around in her pocket for the key. At that point, Katie almost believed the shed door would open to reveal a portal to another realm. Montana seemed magical enough for it to be possible. So when the double doors swung open to reveal a staircase going down into the earth beneath the house, it didn't seem that absurd. It was creepy as hell, though.

Lou pulled a string overhead, and a single light bulb illuminated the staircase. "After you," she said.

Katie briefly wondered if this was the part where she was going to get murdered. Megan was definitely getting in her head too much, along with everything else. All the fear, the doubts, the what-ifs, those were the things she'd been trying to escape. And so far, she had. So why were they creeping back up to the surface to torment her again?

Was this a mental breakdown?

"Everything okay?" Lou asked, and Katie realized she had frozen at the top of the stairs.

"Fine," Katie said, and stepped down.

She emerged into a room that was something between a basement and a cave tucked beneath the floorboards of the house. The stone walls were lined with shelves stacked high with jars, each meticulously labeled. Crates piled high with potatoes sat beside thick carrots and fat beets and round heads of pale green cabbage.

"My root cellar," Lou said, swelling with pride as she entered the room behind Katie. "This is what makes it all worth it."

"You grew all this?" It was so much more than Katie had imagined.

"And canned it."

"I'm impressed," Katie said, walking closer to see all the things on the shelves. Glass jars of bright tomatoes took up the entire top shelf along one wall, with vibrant green beans occupying the shelf below them. Katie looked around in awe, trying to take in every detail. Tucked into the corner, she noticed something unexpected. A tall wine rack sat ignored, filled with dusty bottles. Lou was full of surprises.

"I didn't know you were into wine," Katie said, pulling a bottle down and dusting off the label. "This was a good year."

"I'm not," Lou said, looking pained. "Rachel was. She loved going to wineries and picking out bottles to save for special occasions. When she..." She cleared her throat. "After the accident, I couldn't bring myself to get rid of them, so I brought them here."

"I'm sorry. I didn't mean to bring it up." Katie put the bottle back on the rack, guilty for having disturbed the unorthodox shrine to a woman she couldn't help but feel was her competition.

"You don't need to be," Lou said. "Keeping them is just a little way I can honor her memory. Come on, let's find something to make for dinner. Spaghetti okay?"

"Spaghetti sounds great," Katie said turning to follow Lou back up the stairs, even though she was still full from lunch. A shelf at the other end of the cellar caught her eye. "Is that all honey?" There must have been hundreds of the jars in all different sizes, each gleaming with amber nectar.

"The bees have been good to me here," Lou said with a sheepish smile. "I'll never get through it all."

"You should sell it."

"I do sell it, at the Bozeman farmer's market in the summer."

"I want to buy a jar."

"You can just have one." Lou grabbed the biggest jar from the shelf and handed it to Katie.

"But how much would you normally sell it for?" Katie asked. "Whatever it is, I'm sure you could get twice as much if you sold it online. Do you know how much this jar would go for in Seattle?"

Lou shrugged. "I thought about it, but I don't really know how to do any of that stuff, and I'm too busy to figure it out."

"I could teach you," Katie said, the wheels beginning to turn in her mind. Finally, a way she could be useful to the woman who could do everything. "This is what I've done for years. First we just need to get a website set up, and then you won't even have to advertise that much, because once people try this they'll never buy any other brand of honey again. And people love to buy organic, from small farms. You'd want to keep it limited, of course, the scarcity will make people pay a premium."

Lou was looking at her like she had suddenly started speaking French. "I don't have time to learn any of what you're talking about. I do just fine at the markets, I don't need to go complicating things."

"But you have so much surplus, and it's really not that complicated once you get the hang of it. I can get it all set up for you."

"Look, Seattle, I appreciate the offer. But I'm not interested."

Whatever, the idea was brilliant. But Katie knew better than to push the topic, as much as she wanted to be useful on the ranch. She could float it again later, when Lou was in a better mood and not exhausted from therapy and Katie bringing up her dead wife.

"So, spaghetti?" Katie said, changing the subject.

"My grandma's old recipe," Lou said, looking relieved as she grabbed an onion and some garlic from one of the shelves.

"Oh, are you Italian?"

Lou shrugged. "Allegedly. But no one in the family can tell you who came from Italy or when, so who knows?"

"You should do one of those tests," Katie said.

"When hell freezes over," Lou laughed. "I'm not giving the government my DNA."

"It's interesting, though. My mom swore we were half Irish, that's why she named me Kathleen." She rolled her eyes. Such a dumb name. "But when she took the test, it was pretty much all German. Barely any Irish at all."

"So Katie is short for Kathleen?"

"Unfortunately. What about Lou? It must be short for something, right?" Katie already knew the answer, but she couldn't let Lou find out she had been snooping.

"Louisa," she said with a grimace. "I don't know what my parents were thinking."

"Lou definitely fits you better," Katie said.

They trudged back up the stairs and out of the root cellar, their arms laden with ingredients. Katie started walking towards the front door, then realized Lou wasn't with her. She turned back to see Lou hunched over the low double doors, locking back up.

"How come you lock up your food but not your house?" Katie asked.

"Because the bears know how to open those doors but not the house. And I lock up the house in summer when tourists come nosing around."

"But not in winter?"

"If someone gets lost or stranded in the snow when I'm not around, I'd rather stumble on them inside than dead on my doorstep."

"I guess that makes sense," Katie said, following Lou towards the kitchen. Montana people were different. Trusting and suspicious at the same time, warm but distant. She was reminded again what an outsider she was there. The words from the men at the bar were still getting to her. "Are you sure it's okay if I come to the dance with you tomorrow?"

What if they were there?

Lou sighed. "It should be. I think it will be, but none of them have seen me with a woman before. I mean, Jason knows and I'm sure the rest of 'em suspect it, but it's not really something that comes up much either."

Oh, God. Katie had just been worried about not fitting in because she was from out of state, she hadn't even thought about how they would react to her and Lou showing up as a couple. Were they even a couple? "Maybe this was a bad idea. I'll just stay here tomorrow."

"It's up to you. But I'd really like it if you came." Lou looked away, but not before Katie saw the hint of a blush on her cheeks. "And if anyone gives us shit, Jason'll take care of it. His barn, his rules. I'm not worried about it."

"So you've never taken anyone to the dance?" Katie asked, fishing for more information about Lou's love life. She was desperately curious to know if Lou had been with anyone since her wife, but she was too shy to ask outright.

Lou shook her head. "Nope."

"Why not?"

"Guess I haven't found anyone worth taking. Haven't really been looking." Lou started dicing the garlic and onions.

"It's probably hard to have a dating life out here," Katie said, fishing for info. "But that bartender seemed pretty into you."

"Claire? Did she say something?"

"Well, she didn't seem very happy to hear that I'm staying with you." Katie moved out of Lou's way and went to fill a pot of water to boil for the pasta.

"Might've kissed her once at the rodeo," Lou said, glancing at Katie out of the corner of her eye as she turned redder than the tomatoes in the jars on the counter. "It was a while ago, but she's been pestering me to go out with her again ever since."

Katie felt a flash of jealousy burn the pit of her stomach. She knew it. And what did a while ago mean? A month? A year? "Why haven't you?" She asked carefully.

"Because I have nothing in common with her. And she's just not my type." Lou scraped the vegetables into a pan to sizzle in a thick pool of melted butter.

"What is your type?" Katie leaned casually against the counter, her heart racing.

Lou looked up from stirring. "You."

Lou's directness surprised Katie. What on earth could a woman as amazing as Lou see in someone like her, an outsider? And what was Katie supposed to say in return? It was too soon to tell Lou how she really felt. Or was it? "Lou, I–"

Lou silenced her by kissing her softly, and Katie melted into her arms. She fit so perfectly pressed against Lou's body, drawn there by a magnetic attraction that Katie couldn't resist. Every nerve ending on her body was alive and begging for Lou's touch. Lou's lips parted hers tentatively, and their tongues met, tasting and teasing each other in the dim light of the kitchen. More. Katie needed more. Her hands slid over Lou's curves, exploring her body with a sudden desperation to know every crease, every mound, every fold of skin.

The pressure of Lou's lips changed from a question into a demand, and she pushed Katie against the wall, boxing Katie in with her arms as the insistence of her tongue melted the last of Katie's resolve. She grabbed Lou's shirt and pulled her closer still. Her entire body was trembling with need, and she moaned her plea into Lou's mouth.

Lou pulled away. "Shit, the onions."

Katie smelled the acrid smoke then and looked over at the pan. The onions and garlic were shriveled and black, smoking in the cast iron. Lou yanked the pan off the burner and set it on a cold one, then opened the window to air the kitchen out.

"So I guess we can't just order delivery?" Katie asked, leaning against the wall because her knees were too shaky to do anything else. A long delivery time would give them just enough time to finish what they'd started.

"Not out here," Lou said. "We'll just have to start again."

Chapter Ten

C hapter 10

The blizzard swirled in every direction, with nothing but heavy white flakes as far as the eye could see. Katie shivered and pressed forward, kicking through the snow in desperation. Where was she?

"Lou!" Katie tried to scream, but the sound caught in her throat. Why couldn't she find her?

She saw a glimpse of tan canvas in the distance. Lou's coat. She tried to run forward but her legs were heavier than they should have been, as though someone had tied weights to them. No matter how far she moved, Lou seemed to get farther away. Katie pushed on. She needed to keep her in sight. She couldn't lose her.

"Lou," she screamed. "I'm coming."

Katie woke up soaked in sweat. She threw the covers back and looked for Lou, who wasn't there. She had refused to share the bed with Katie again, claiming she wanted to stay up late to read and didn't want to bother Katie when she was finally ready to go to bed. Katie tiptoed to the door to check if she was still awake. Images from the nightmare still flashed in her mind, and she just needed to make sure Lou was okay.

The light in the living room was still on, and Lou was snoring lightly on the couch, her book splayed open on her chest and a half-drunk glass of whiskey on the table beside her. Katie stood in the door and watched her for a moment. Lou looked younger when she was asleep and all the lines of worry were smoothed from her face. She looked peaceful and perfectly at home, but Katie couldn't imagine she would be comfortable spending the night like that.

Katie crept over to Lou, not wanting to wake her as she desperately resisted the temptation to curl up next to her. One of the dogs lifted his blocky head to look blearily at Katie, then sighed with a soft *whuff* and laid back down in front of the fire.

Katie took the book off Lou's chest and replaced it with one of the thick wool blankets, tucking it gingerly around her in case the night got colder. She reached for the lamp to turn it off then paused, too curious for her own good, and looked down at the book in her hands.

Reclaim Your Life After Loss.

That damn book again. Katie turned it over, hoping whatever page Lou was reading had some clues to offer about why Lou was so warm one second and so distant the next. Every time Katie felt like they were getting closer, she could feel Lou pull away again, and it was just. So. Fucking. Confusing. Lou had kissed her, and then barely spoken to her the rest of the evening. She said she wanted to go to the dance with Katie, and then she acted like she wanted to be nowhere near her. None of it made sense.

Chapter 10. Allowing Yourself Love Again.

Katie's breath caught in her throat.

There is no timeline for grief, but eventually the day may come when you are ready to open your heart to the joy and potential of love again. You may decide to seek that love out, or you may happen across it by chance. Those first feelings can be difficult to navigate, and in this chapter I am going to lay out some common questions you may be struggling with as you open yourself to new feelings and possibilities.

Katie shut the book and set it on the coffee table, tears welling in her eyes. She could never compete with a dead woman. Of course she couldn't. The thought was horrible, and she would never want to. But deep down, she wished she could have found Lou first. It would have made things a lot less complicated.

It was just another reminder that she needed to slow things down. Crawling under the covers and curling up on Lou's shoulder was tempting, just so she could be close to her. But she needed to let Lou come to her when she was ready. If she was ready. Katie leaned over and turned off the lamp, then tiptoed back to bed.

"I don't have anything to wear," Katie moaned, flopping back on the bed with the phone pressed against her ear. "And Lou won't take me into town to go shopping, she said there's already too much to do and not enough time."

"Okay, well let's go through what you have and we'll figure out some options. Switch it to video," Megan instructed.

Katie flipped her camera on to show Megan the empty suitcase with its contents strewn across the bed. "Literally nothing."

Megan's pixelated face frowned on the screen. "Hmm. Well, what is Lou wearing?"

"I don't even know," Katie whined. "She wouldn't tell me. Just said it's a surprise."

"And you're absolutely certain this isn't some weird Satanic sex cult murder ritual thing?" Megan continued to be ridiculous, but that was why Katie loved her.

"I wish it was a Satanic sex cult. It's just a little barn dance thing. A Christmas hoedown in the country."

"I bet you would like to hoe down." Megan snickered. "What's that red one?"

"This?" Katie held the skimpy scrap of fabric up to the camera. "Bikini."

"No, that other red thing."

"The flannel shirt?"

"Yeah, why not?"

"I mean, I guess I have to. Ugh." Katie's voice cracked.

"Are you crying? Don't cry. What's wrong?" Megan's tone immediately switched from playful to concerned.

"I just want to look good. I never got that prom experience. I want her to be proud to be seen with me. Is that stupid?"

"She would be stupid not to be proud to be with you. You're hot, smart, funny. A total babe. No matter what you end up wearing."

"Aww, thanks, Meg."

"Is she around right now?"

"No, she went down to the barn to finish chores before we leave."

"So are you finally going to sleep with her tonight?"

"I don't think so. I don't think she's actually over her wife dying. Every time we get closer, she pulls back again."

"You know she's probably never going to be over it, right? A spouse dying isn't really something you get over. You just figure out how to live with it."

"But how can I ever live up to that?"

"Do you want to? I thought you said you weren't going to get in too deep."

"I already am and I don't know what to do."

"Come to DC. You can still get here and spend Christmas with us, and then we'll do New Year's Eve together, just like old times. I'll introduce you to that friend I was telling you about. By the time you fly back to Seattle, you'll have forgotten all about Montana."

"I can't." Katie said. She needed more time with Lou.

"Do you want me to come there, then? I will. I'll get on a plane right now. I'm worried about you."

"You can't do that, what about Q? Besides, I'm fine here. Really." She was anything but fine, but if she told Megan that she was worried, Megan really would show up in Bozeman. That was just the type of friend she was. "I gotta get dressed, Lou said we were leaving at 7:00."

"Okay. Text me if you need anything. I mean it."

"You know I will." Katie finished saying goodbye and ended the call.

She picked up the flannel shirt and closed her eyes, half-wishing a fairy godmother would appear and transform her into whatever the Montana equivalent of a princess was. Her real godmother hadn't spoken to her in almost fifteen years, not since Katie had come out to her, and no one else was going to swoop in to save the day either.

She got dressed, then examined herself in the mirror. The outfit wasn't as bad as she'd thought. Her ass looked pretty good in the jeans, and the embroidery on the back pockets drew attention to it. She knotted the tails of the shirt at her waist, showing just a sliver of skin. There was a lot to love about the look- it was comfortable, soft, and fit her perfectly. Katie didn't hate it nearly as much as she'd expected, but she was worried she would be underdressed for a dance.

She picked up her phone and searched for a Christmas song to help put her in a festive mood. Clicking the first one that came up, she tossed her phone on the bed to finish getting ready. The only thing that felt suitable for her hair was a French braid- elegant and casual all at the same time without trying too hard. She pulled out her makeup bag for the first time since arriving in Montana and applied a quick coat of mascara and a swipe of tinted lip gloss. Anything more would have felt like overkill with the understated look.

Bells jingled with the outro of the song, and she reached over to turn it off. It was almost time for them to leave. She tossed her phone in her purse and realized she could still hear the bells jingling. Weird. She was certain she had turned it off, and a quick check confirmed she had. So where was the sound coming from?

Katie went out into the living room to see if the television had been flipped on by accident, maybe by one of the dogs. Except they were down at the barn with Lou, and everything was dim in the living room. She peered out of the front window and saw a light approaching the house from the barn. It looked like Lou was on her way back. Katie slipped into her jacket and stepped outside. The jingle of bells got louder in the evening air, and then she saw it, emerging from the dark.

She rubbed her eyes, disbelieving. It was impossible. Santa wasn't real.

The sleigh was real, though, an ornate sled with a bench in the front and piled high with presents in the back. Lou's powerful team of horses pulled it across the snow on parallel runners, and a proud figure atop the bench in a warm, red suit guided them all.

"Ho, ho, ho," Lou laughed, her eyes twinkling with radiant joy. "Ready to go?"

Katie was speechless. She felt like a little kid again, transported to a time when magic was real and the world made sense. Tears welled up in her eyes and she blinked them back slowly, afraid what she was seeing would disappear when she opened them again. One of the horses shook its head and the bells jingled again. It was real.

"Lou?"

"The one and only," she said.

"I thought we were taking the truck."

"Let the dogs back in the house and hop on up," Lou said. "I'll explain it all on the way to Jason's."

Katie did, feeling like she was stepping into a movie as she grasped Lou's hand and stepped up into the sleigh. The bench next to Lou was piled high with blankets, and Lou moved them away so Katie could sit beside her before covering them both up with the thickest one.

"You look beautiful," Lou said softly.

"I hope jeans aren't too casual; I didn't have many options."

"It's perfect." Lou must have sensed Katie didn't believe her. "You'd stand out more if you weren't wearing jeans. But why do you care so much what other people think of you anyways?"

"I want people to like me. I want them to respect me," Katie said honestly, wondering if she should tell Lou about the men from the bar and how their words were still eating at her. "I don't want them to judge you because of me."

Lou shrugged. "We can't stop them if that's what their minds are set on doing. Doesn't bother me none, so don't worry about me and let's go dance our boots off without givin' a shit if people are looking."

"So what's the deal with all this?" Katie asked. She'd never been in a horse drawn sleigh, and she gasped as it lurched forward when Lou clicked to the horses. Once they were moving, the ride was pretty smooth.

"It's a tradition," Lou said. "His grandfather built this sleigh, so it's a real antique. When he died, Jason's father did it. And then after he passed a few years back, I volunteered to be Santa for a while until Jason feels ready to step into the role." She reached under her seat and pulled out a fake beard and mustache. "Here, hold the reins," she said, passing them off to Katie so she could affix the facial hair to her face.

"Do I have to do anything?" Katie asked, anxious she would send the horses the wrong signal, crash the sleigh, and ruin Christmas.

"Just hold them like that. The horses know what they're doing." Lou reached under the bench again and pulled out a Santa hat. "How do I look?"

"Like Santa," Katie said, "but I prefer you as Lou."

Lou laughed, the sound mingling musically with the bells as they crested a knoll. Her joy was infectious, and Katie found herself giggling too. She wiggled closer to Lou until their thighs were touching under the blanket. Lou lifted her elbow so Katie could snuggle in under her arm.

"Cold?" Lou asked. "I have whiskey and coffee in the travel mug under the seat."

"No," Katie said with a happy sigh. "Everything is perfect." Maybe fairy tales were real, after all.

Her only complaint was the sleigh ride was too short and the light from Jason's barn came into view too soon. The sound of twangy country music and laughter filled their air as people spilled out of the barn to witness the spectacle of Santa's arrival. Katie scooted away from Lou, nervous to face the crowd of strangers that knew nothing about her. Her worry was unfounded, though, all eyes were on Lou.

"Ho, ho, ho!" Lou cried, deepening her voice as she stepped into the role of jolly gift-giver. "I heard there were some good kids in the Valley this year. Is that right?"

"Yes!" the kids screamed.

"Uh-uh," Lou scolded gently, wagging her finger. "I know you all know better than to scream like that around horses."

"Sorry, Santa," the kids whispered, in awe of their hero.

"Very well then," Lou said, "how about we get right to the presents?" She climbed into the back of the sleigh and began calling out names, the kids running up one at a time to claim their gifts.

Katie looked around, wondering if she was just supposed to sit there until Lou was done, or if she should get out of the sleigh. She looked around at the people gathered. Parents of the kids laughed with each other. Men in cowboy hats and tight jeans laughed with ladies in boots and flannels. Katie realized Lou was right, she couldn't have been more appropriately dressed for the occasion.

"Need a hand down, Miss Katie?" A low voice drawled beside her. Jason tipped his hat and offered up his elbow. "Careful, it's a little icy right here, I ran out of salt."

"Thanks," Katie said, balancing on him as she stepped out of the sleigh. "This looks like quite the party."

"We do enjoy our fun out here, even if it might look a little different than what you're used to," he said. "Come on inside, I'll grab you a drink."

"I'll wait for Lou," Katie said, afraid to face the masses alone.

"You sure about that? Looks like she'll be a while." Jason nodded towards the sleigh. Children were climbing all over the vacated bench, ripping into boxes, and peppering Lou with questions while their parents snapped pictures. Jason was right, Lou would be occupied for a while.

"Alright, a drink sounds great then," Katie said and followed Jason into the barn. "It's beautiful," she said, looking around in amazement. Wooden beams spanned the ceiling, each one bedecked in evergreen garlands. Hay bales were stacked from floor to ceiling, making a rustic backdrop for a makeshift stage. The band seemed to be on break, probably because everyone had rushed outside for Santa's arrival, and gathered around a folding table that held no fewer than eight crockpots all plugged haphazardly into a single extension cord.

"I can't take any credit," Jason said humbly. "My grand-daddy built it and my wife decorated it. I just show up." Katie doubted that. "Now, what can sort of drink can I get for you?" He started listing options, but Katie wasn't really listening anymore. She'd just noticed the Christmas tree.

It towered as tall as the hay bales at the other end of the barn, glimmering with soft, white lights. There were none of the ostentatious, shiny balls she was used to seeing covering every inch of the tree. Just simple ornaments that looked like they were made by the children swarming Lou outside. Ribbons of burlap and plaid were woven through the boughs, and small, carved, wooden animals dangled unpretentiously from the tips of the branches. It was perfect.

Jason cleared his throat.

"Any of those sound great," Katie said, hoping he couldn't tell she hadn't been listening to a word he said.

"Well, here, this one's my wife's favorite," he said, handing her a steaming cup of hot apple cider. The strong scent of cinnamon whiskey cut through the sweetness of the fruit, and she took a sip. "Speaking of..." He waved at a woman re-entering the barn, two small boys in tow.

The kids were the spitting image of Jason, little mini cow-boys in matching flannels. Katie had never seen anything cuter in her life. Their mother bent down to tell them something, and both boys nodded before scurrying off to join their friends playing around the base of the Christmas tree. The woman walked over to Katie and Jason and served herself a steaming cup of cider.

"Katie, this is my wife. Mandy." He beamed with pride when he said her name.

"I've heard so much about you," Mandy said, ignoring Katie's outstretched hand and pulling her into a hug. "Welcome to our home. Well, barn. May as well be our home, as much time as Jay and the boys spend out here."

"Lou about wrapped up out there?" Jason asked.

"Gettin' close," Mandy said. "You oughta go help her get the horses in."

Jason tipped his hat to Katie and Mandy. "You need anything, you just ask Mandy. She'll take good care of you. Me and Lou'll be right in once we get the team settled."

The band was making their way back up to the makeshift stage, and the sound of guitars being tuned filled the warm barn. A few moments later, they launched into a rollicking, country Christmas song that Katie couldn't help but tap her foot to. Some of the people milling around made their way onto the dance floor and began moving in unison, clapping and spinning with the twangy beat.

"Come on, let's dance," Mandy said.

"I don't know how," Katie said. Even back in Seattle, she was a total wallflower at clubs until she had more than a few drinks in her.

"I'll show you." Mandy linked her arm through Katie's and steered her towards the open floor. "It's easy. Step right three times and then do a box step. Then we go the other way."

It had been at least twenty years since Katie's last elementary school P.E. line dancing class, a week of a unit about group dances around the world. Her steps were hesitant at first, and she felt like everyone in the barn was staring at her.

"See, you got it!" Mandy grinned. "Now we turn."

Soon, Katie found herself surrendering to the music and letting her body take control of the motions. She still fumbled some of the more complex steps, but no one was getting mad at her for it. Everyone was laughing, cheeks rosy from the cold and the booze, and no one seemed to care that she was a stranger. By her second cider and the third song, she was starting to forget that she had ever felt self-conscious in the first place. She skipped down a tunnel made of people, then spun straight into Lou's arms.

"Hey," Katie said, laughing. "I didn't know you came in."

"I love watching you dance, and you were having too much fun to interrupt," Lou said. Her eyelashes sparkled with melting snowflakes and the tip of her nose was as red as Katie's flannel shirt. "I see you met Mandy."

"She's great. This is all great. Thank you for inviting me."

The band began to play a slower song, and Lou's arm tightened around Katie's waist. "May I have this dance?"

There was nothing Katie wanted more. She slipped her left hand into Lou's, and rested the right one on her shoulder. It didn't matter if she knew the steps or not, or if people stared at them. All that mattered was her and Lou, circling slowly in the center of the dance floor while the lead singer crooned.

"When December comes back around

And all the lights go up in town

The only place I want to be

Is slow-dancin' by the Christmas tree

It's Christmas in Montana

This year I'm beggin' Santa

To have you in my arms

Together we'll be warm

Just you and me

Next to the Christmas tree."

Katie closed her eyes and sighed in contentment, feeling like the song had been written just for her. It was a love ballad and a lament, and goosebumps prickled up on her skin as Lou pulled her closer. If everything in her life– the pain, the rejection, the trauma– had been put there to lead her to Lou, then it was all worth it for that one perfect dance.

Jason cleared his throat, and Katie's eyes flew open. He was beside them, dancing with his wife while he stared pointedly at Lou, and then straight up at the rafters, one eyebrow raised. Katie glanced up at the same time Lou did, and saw the spring of mistletoe hanging directly above them. Her lips parted slightly as her eyes met Lou's asking the question silently. *Is it okay?*

Lou nodded, and reached up to pull Katie's face to hers. Their lips locked, and once again Katie was consumed by the ravenous hunger that gnawed at her since she'd first set eyes on Lou. Her cheeks burned as she felt the stares coming from all directions, and pulled away before the kiss could deepen into something less chaste.

It wasn't that Katie cared what they thought of her. She could stand up for herself if anyone had anything hateful to say about their winter fling, she had no reputation to maintain. But Lou's whole life was there in Montana, and Katie couldn't help but wonder if the public display of sapphic affection would impact her livelihood when Katie left. Or her life. But as she looked around the room, she realized no one was paying them much attention at all, except for Jason, who flashed her a quick wink and a thumbs up.

To Katie's relief, no one said anything less than welcoming to her the entire night, which was over far too soon. She could have spent forever dancing on the creaky wood floor to the lilting Christmas tunes and it wouldn't have been long enough, but before she knew it, Lou and Jason were stepping out to re-hitch the horses and the guests began to meander out towards their waiting trucks, before idling even longer to chat as their kids dozed off in the warm back seats.

Katie finally understood why people were so into the holiday thing. It wasn't a competition to see who could give the best, most expensive gifts or pile the most blinding lights onto their houses, like all the holidays she'd known before. It wasn't guilt trips about being far away, or her mother crying for the tenth time that she would never have a grandbaby to infect with her narcissism. No, it was the feeling of contentment, the small glow of warmth in the middle of a long, dark winter. It was the people who opened their homes and hearts to her and welcomed her in. It was Lou.

Chapter Eleven

The sleigh jingled around the corner of the barn as the horses stepped carefully around the deeper snow drifts. Lou offered Katie a hand up, then held it in her lap long after Katie was settled on the bench beside her. Katie sighed contentedly and leaned into Lou.

"Did you have a good time?" Lou asked, loosening the long reins and urging the horses into motion with a sharp click of her tongue.

"The best time," Katie said. "I'm sad it's over."

"Are you tired?"

It had to have been close to midnight, and Katie stifled a yawn triggered by the mere suggestion. "Not at all."

"Cold?"

She shook her head. "Not with the ten blankets you brought."

"Let's take the long way home, then," Lou said, turning the horses to the left and towards the back pasture.

The sleigh crunched across the snow, leaving twin tracks in their wake. Besides that and the horses' occasional snorts and the jangle of the bells, the night was silent and still.

"It's so peaceful out here," Katie whispered, scared to speak too loudly in case she broke the spell. She wasn't even sure if Lou heard her.

"Mmm," Lou hummed in agreement, her chest rumbling against Katie's arm. She pulled the horses to a halt. "Look up."

Katie gasped in amazement at the sight before her. Stars rose from the peaks of the mountains to stretch across the vast eternity of sky, an endless sea of glowing specks as far into the universe as the eye could see. She had never seen anything like it. It didn't even look real.

"This," Lou said, smiling in satisfaction, "is Big Sky country."

"I see why they call it that, now," Katie said.

She had never felt so small. The realization that should have terrified her or made her feel insignificant was somehow comforting. There were billions of people on the little blue planet that was just one tiny dot among many, but somehow, miraculously, the universe had led her to Lou. And they were all alone, with not another soul for miles, on the most romantic date she'd ever been on. She couldn't wait another second.

She planted her lips on Lou's as though she were drowning and Lou was her only chance at fresh air, trying to convey the depth of the emotions she was feeling through the passion of her kiss. Lou responded with a soft moan, and let go of the reins to wrap her fingers through Katie's hair. Katie rolled on her hip and swung her leg across Lou's lap, straddling her on the bench as they kissed. She felt wild and free, uninhibited and sexy. Her pussy clenched and moistened as she ground against Lou, and her nipples hardened as they brushed against Lou. Lou groaned again, deeper this time, and her fingers dug into Katie's hips as she pulled her closer. Katie shivered.

"You're cold," Lou said, pulling back so their lips were just barely touching. "I need to get you home."

"No," Katie said. "I just want you. More than anything. And I don't know how much longer I can stand it."

Lou's eyes widened slightly, and she nodded slowly. "Get in the back."

Katie scrambled over the bench into the back of the sleigh, heart pounding with excitement. Vacant of the presents from earlier, there was just enough room for them both to lie down. Lou tossed back the warm, handmade blankets, then swung her legs over the bench and crawled over to join Katie underneath them.

Katie pulled off her gloves, and Lou pulled the blanket over their heads. They fumbled for each other in the dark, Katie working at the buttons of Lou's jacket while Lou slid her hand up Katie's thigh and rubbed the seam of her jeans right where it fell between her legs. Katie traced her fingers slowly beneath Lou's shirt, across her stomach, and up to caress her nipple as their mouths found each other again.

Her pussy throbbed as Lou pressed against it, teasing and torturing through the layer of denim that separated her from the pleasure she was craving. She whimpered and spread her legs wider as Lou's lips departed to kiss down her neck.

"Please," she begged.

Lou's tongue lapped at the space between Katie's breasts as she massaged them against her face. She was in no hurry, teasing one nipple into a stiff point before switching hands and paying attention to the other.

"Please," she whimpered again, pushing Lou's head down further.

Lou chuckled against Katie's skin, her breath hot and feral. She climbed between Katie's thighs, accepting the invitation, the kisses getting lower and lower until Lou stopped, her lips lingering on the sliver of skin between Katie's belly button and the waistband of her jeans. Katie held her breath in anticipation.

"Should I keep going?" Lou asked.

"Yes," Katie moaned, feeling like she would die if Lou didn't.

Lou's hands replaced her lips, and she undid the button of Katie's jeans. Katie lifted her ass off the floor of the sleigh and Lou slid the jeans over her hips, then pulled them all the way off.

"Mmm," she hummed again, tracing her fingers over Katie's bare thigh before burying her nose in Katie's soft pubic curls.

Katie squirmed away from the sudden pressure against her clit, but Lou draped her forearm across Katie's hips and held her easily in place. Two fingers parted Katie's slit, and she gasped as Lou licked her opening, tasting her dripping juices. She took a deep breath in, then released it slowly in a shuddering sigh.

Lou paused, her breath warm against Katie's folds. "Everything okay?"

"Yes," Katie said. "Just trying not to cum all over your face before I get to enjoy this." She felt Lou's face crack into a grin against her.

"I wouldn't mind." Lou plunged her tongue into Katie, and Katie dissolved into bliss.

She arched her back and her thighs tightened on either side of Lou's face as Lou worked her magic on Katie's pussy, thrusting her tongue as deep as it would go and lapping up everything that trickled out. Katie's knees were starting to tremble when Lou turned her attention to her clit, tracing lazy circles around it with her tongue, then sucking directly on the sensitive nub as Katie bucked and moaned beneath her.

"Oh, God. Oh, Lou. Right there," she gasped, as the pressure built deep in her core, swelling and burning until she couldn't contain it anymore. Lou flicked her tongue, soft but steady on Katie's sensitive clit, and Katie exploded with a feral scream as the waves of pleasure broke over her again and again until she was a trembling, throbbing mess on the floor of the sleigh.

Lou lapped at the wetness flowing from Katie's pussy, chucking with satisfaction at what she had accomplished. Katie tried to catch her breath, but let out another moan as Lou's tongue returned to tracing its languid circles around her sensitive clit. The sensations were overwhelming, just on the edge of being too intense but still pleasurable enough that Katie's hands went to the back of Lou's head, holding her in place.

The second orgasm came even faster than the first, and Katie moaned Lou's name, feeling more complete than she ever had before. Lou emerged from between Katie's legs, her face shining with Katie's wetness in the moonlit night. Katie sat up and kissed her, tasting herself on Lou's lips. Her pussy clenched with an aftershock, and she almost asked Lou to make her cum a third time. But there was something she wanted more.

"Your turn," she said, her voice rasping with desire as she pushed Lou onto her back.

"The tip of your nose is frozen," Lou said, kissing it lightly. "We should probably be heading back."

"Just a few more minutes," Katie pleaded. It didn't matter how long they stayed wrapped up in the blankets and each other beneath the starry night, if they stayed until the snow melted and spring came and the farm burst into glorious color around them before fading back into fall. It would never be long enough. A lone star shot across the sky, blazing a trail brighter than the rest before disappearing as quickly as it had come.

"Make a wish," Lou whispered, staring off into the space between the stars of Orion's belt.

I wish I could be the person you need me to be, Katie thought, clinging to Lou as though she would blink out of existence at any moment, as ephemeral as the shooting star. She wondered what Lou had asked the universe for, wondered if it had anything to do with her. Probably not. Lou didn't seem like the type to believe in fairy tales and happily ever afters. She'd probably wished for something practical, like favorable weather and a good harvest.

One of the horses shook its head and snorted, causing the bells on its harness to jingle and break the spell. Lou pulled her arm out from under Katie and buttoned her shirt, then wriggled back into her jeans and sat up. Katie sighed and began to do the same. It actually was pretty cold, and the blankets weren't doing much without Lou's soft warmth beside her. She glanced up at the sky again, hoping for another wish, or maybe some sort of sign, but nothing jumped out at her from the vast canvas of the universe.

Katie climbed back up on the bench beside Lou and pulled a blanket around both of them, then rested her head on Lou's shoulder. Lou wrapped her arm around Katie's waist in a move that felt almost protective, or maybe it was just because Katie felt so safe in her arms.

"Listen," Lou said. "Do you hear them?"

At first, all Katie heard was the wind, the bells, and the sound of the horses snorting. Then the gust died down and she heard a mournful tune that made the hair on the back of her neck stand up on end. The haunting choir seemed to surround them, coming from everywhere at once. "Are those...?"

"Wolves," Lou confirmed. "That's what got the horses all riled up. Isn't it beautiful?"

"Kind of creepy," Katie said, peering through the cloud of her frozen breath towards the treeline in search of glowing pairs of eyes emerging from the woods. The wolves were eerie, but she trusted Lou would know what to do if they tried to approach.

"They're pretty far off. They're hunting something, but it's not us," Lou said confidently, but she urged the horses to go a little faster and held onto Katie a little tighter. The howling chorus accompanied them all the way back to the house, but none of the wolves showed themselves along the way. "Why don't you head on in and warm up? I'll get the horses settled and be up in a bit."

"I can help you," Katie said. It wasn't fair for Lou to do all the work alone, and she was enjoying the time spent together.

"It'd take me longer to show you how to do everything than just do it myself, and it's already late. I'll be back before you know it." Lou kissed Katie tenderly on the forehead before shooing her towards the door.

The dogs greeted her as she stepped inside, and she gave them both a treat from the jar in the kitchen before starting to run the water for a hot shower and stripping free of her clothes. It had been a magical evening with Lou, beyond anything she had ever dreamed possible. The water streamed over her head and down her back, but it couldn't wash away the warm glow that lingered everywhere Lou had touched her. She felt like a new person, vulnerable and tender but satisfyingly whole. She'd thought she'd had good sex before, but making love with Lou was making her question everything she'd known about passion and intimacy. It had been so good. Life changing, as stupid as that sounded.

And did Lou feel the same way? Of course she wouldn't, what a dumb thought. Lou had already met her soulmate two decades before Katie came into the picture. What could Katie have to offer her when it came to intimacy? From Lou's perspective it was probably average at best. Katie sighed, wishing again that she could have been the one to meet Lou first.

She heard the front door open and shut as Lou returned from the barn, and she switched off the water. Stepping out of the shower, she wrapped herself in an oversized green towel, then padded out into the hallway to see what Lou was doing. She found her in the kitchen feeding the dogs, a pot of water boiling on the stove for tea.

Lou looked Katie head to toe, biting her lip appreciatively before breaking into her crooked grin. "You make that towel look as pretty as any ballgown. I'm surprised you're still up, though."

"How could I go to bed after..." Katie trailed off, blushing. Maybe Lou didn't want to talk about it. Or maybe Katie was the one who wasn't ready to figure out what it all meant.

"Tea?" Lou asked, holding up the bottle of whiskey.

"Tea sounds great," Katie said, leaning against the counter.

Lou poured a generous shot for each of them into mugs, then added boiling water and dried herbs from her pantry. "What are we doing here, Seattle?"

Katie swallowed hard. "I don't know. What do you want us to be doing?"

"Not playing games," Lou said, sighing as she sat down at the little table by the window. "I'm too old for all that."

"None of this is a game to me. Tonight was the best night of my life. For multiple reasons." Katie's heart raced as she spoke. Everything she said was true, but admitting it felt dangerous.

"I'm getting to be quite fond of you."

Katie sat at the table across from her, and took her by the hand. "I like you a lot, too, Lou." It was still too soon to confess how deeply in love she had fallen. The last thing she wanted was to scare Lou away. She wanted to walk beside her, every day, as long as their path let them.

Chapter Twelve

K atie whipped butter and sugar together, adding vanilla and then eggs before pausing to squint at the recipe on her phone screen. Lou was down at the barn finishing up the morning chores, and Katie wanted the whole house to smell like cookies when she got back.

The trio of plastic cookie cutters that had inspired the surprise sat on the counter, the star, tree, and bell each waiting to be pressed into service. She had found them at the back of one of the kitchen drawers while she rummaged around making breakfast, and the sight of them had struck a nerve of nostalgia for all the happy holiday seasons before...

Nope. She wasn't going to think about that.

Besides, it was never too late to change. She whistled the Christmas song the band had been singing during her slow dance with Lou the night before, swaying as she sifted the dry ingredients into the cookie dough. The mix came together quickly, and she tossed it in the fridge to chill while she looked around for something to decorate with.

An ancient box of food dyes was hiding behind a bag of powdered sugar in the pantry, the cardboard nearly falling apart and stained with drops of the various dyes. Katie flipped it over to check the date, then decided she'd rather not know. Oh well. It was a bunch of fake chemicals anyways, so how expired could it really be? She only needed a little bit to make some icing.

She thought about calling Megan to spill all the dirty details on what had happened the night before. There were six unopened text notifications she hadn't replied to yet asking how it had gone. But Katie wanted to keep it to herself for just a little longer, until she had had time to figure out what it all truly meant.

Waking up beside Lou was wonderful, getting to kiss her and hold her and bask in her comfort was the best way she had ever started a day. It was kind of terrifying how much Katie wanted to leave her old life behind for good and take a chance on something better in Montana. But it was way too early to be thinking about that. And as much as she loved it there, could she really give up everything she had built back in the city? Her entire career? The shattered fragments of a social scene she was starting to put back together after Jackie tore it all apart? The thoughts were heart-wrenching, and dwelling on it made her feel like she was being pulled in two.

It was much easier to think about Christmas and how she was going to make it special for Lou. Though Katie was sure the outside world was progressing as normal, only Katie and

Lou existed in their little cabin cocoon. The moments together felt separate from time, intimate and infinite, yet somehow it was already Christmas Eve, and she didn't even have a present for Lou, or time to get one or order something if anywhere even delivered out to the farm, and even if they did she didn't know what she would get Lou, who already had everything she needed right there on the farm, and—

Katie took a deep breath and poured herself a glass of water before she could spiral any further. She'd only known Lou for like a week, they definitely weren't at the gift-giving level yet. She was stressing about nothing. She took the dough out of the fridge and rolled it out, then cut out shapes and placed them on a cookie sheet to bake.

Lou walked in just as she was pulling the first pan from the oven.

"I missed you," Katie said, kissing her quickly then looking away shyly, wondering if she was being too bold.

Lou pulled her back in for a second peck, a smile lighting her face. "I was only gone a couple hours. I see you've been busy. Are those Christmas cookies?"

"I guess I'm just in a festive mood today," Katie said, swatting Lou's hand away as she reached around her to grab one. "They're hot, and I still have to decorate."

A flicker of sadness crossed Lou's face before it was replaced with her familiar, crooked grin. "Well, I can't wait to try one. They smell amazing."

"And then I thought we could put the decorations back up? Do you have a tree somewhere?"

Lou chuckled and nodded at the window towards her truck. "We can go get one. Where'd this holiday spirit come from?"

"I guess I just needed the right person to show me a little Christmas magic," Katie said, grabbing Lou by the hand and twirling her around the kitchen. She didn't care if it looked silly, she was too excited to spend another day with Lou, getting to know her and making her laugh. Kissing her. Caressing her. And so much more.

Lou pulled Katie close, reading her mind. She tucked her hands into Katie's back pockets and kissed her again and again until Katie was breathless and her body humming with desire. She could finally understand why the women in old Western movies were always swooning, now that she had her own strong, brave cowgirl to sweep her off her feet.

"I'm glad your plane got diverted here," Lou said softly when she pulled away. "I'm glad I got to meet you, Seattle."

"Me too," Katie said, fighting the urge to pull Lou into the bedroom and spend the whole day with her there. Christmas was less than twelve hours away, and they had so much to do to make it perfect. And it had to be perfect. Lou deserved nothing less. "Now, where did you stash those decorations?"

"Up in the crawlspace," Lou nodded up at a square door cut into the ceiling that Katie hadn't even noticed before, before climbing up on one of the kitchen chairs and pulling down a folding ladder. "Stay here, it's full of cobwebs and maybe even some critters. I'll hand stuff down to you."

One by one, she passed down cardboard boxes labeled *Christmas Decor* and Katie piled them on the table. There were way more decorations than Katie had anticipated from the modest display she had seen when she first arrived at the cabin, and suddenly the task seemed daunting. She was happy to undertake it if it meant more time spent with Lou, though, and it was clear Katie's newfound holiday spirit was bringing Lou joy. Katie would have walked to the North Pole to find Santa himself if it would make Lou's eyes sparkle and her nose wrinkle up like it did when she was trying to suppress her throaty laughter.

"Last one," Lou said, passing Katie the final box.

"I had no idea you loved Christmas *this* much," Katie laughed and motioned to the boxes that seemed to cover every surface of the counter.

"I always did," Lou said, trailing her hand over the worn cardboard. "But Rachel loved it even more than me. She picked out most of this stuff."

"I'm sorry," Katie said, heart shattering a little bit at the raw pain in Lou's eyes. Why did she always have to say the wrong thing and ruin a nice moment?

"No, I'm sorry." Lou smiled, but it looked a little forced. "I shouldn't have brought her up and made everything sad and weird. This year is about showing you a real Montana Christmas. Without extra baggage."

"I don't want you to think you can't talk about her," Katie said, resting her hand on Lou's forearm. "You can. It doesn't bother me."

"She would have liked you."

"Really?"

Lou let out a sad chuckle. "Actually, probably not. Not if she met you back then. Rachel had a jealous streak, and like I said, you're exactly my type. But now, if she's out there somewhere looking down on all this, I think she'd be pretty glad you came into my life." Lou sighed and her voice cracked when she spoke again. "I don't think you realize– probably because I haven't told you– but I really needed you to show up when you did. I was barely hanging on here by myself."

"Lou..." Katie didn't know what else to say as Lou blinked back tears, so she wrapped her in a hug.

"It's okay, I'm okay." Lou pulled away and rubbed her eyes, then brushed some invisible dirt from the hem of her shirt. "What I'm trying to say is this is a good thing. You're showing me I don't have to keep my brick wall stacked quite so high anymore. It's okay to take new chances."

I love you.

The words came so close to slipping out, but fortunately the timer dinged and saved Katie from the embarrassment just in time. She pulled the second batch of cookies out of the oven, vanilla-scented steam curling into the air.

Lou sidled up to hug Katie from behind, watching over Katie's shoulder as she moved the cookies to the cooling rack. "You sure I can't have one now?"

"They're too hot right–" Katie broke off in a gasp as Lou kissed her neck, sending shivers down her spine. Her body melted into Lou's as Lou's hands began roaming away from Katie's waist to grope at her chest.

"You're too hot right now," Lou murmured into her neck, nipping playfully at the skin. "If I can't have a cookie, then how about a different treat?" Her hand slid down to cup Katie's crotch.

Katie closed her eyes, savoring the sensation for just a second. The impulse to drag Lou into the bedroom and spend the afternoon tangled up in each other's limbs was strong. Later. She only had two more days to make the most of her Montana Christmas, but they would never get anything done if they couldn't keep their hands off each other.

"Shouldn't we go get a tree before it gets dark?" Katie asked, wriggling away before she dissolved completely under Lou's magic spell. She hated having to be the voice of reason, but getting the full Montana Christmas experience was important to her. "We have all night for everything else."

Lou checked her watch. "Reckon we should. Go get bundled up, and meet me out by the truck."

Katie glanced over her shoulder as she left the kitchen, just in time to see Lou swipe a cookie from the cooling tray. Lou grinned sheepishly, then scarfed it down as Katie laughed and went to get ready. She found Lou outside loading a chainsaw into the bed of the already-running truck and hopped up into the toasty cab.

"I already texted Jason," Lou said, climbing up beside her. "He's going to unlock the gate for us."

"We're going to Jason's?" Katie asked, surprised.

"His trees are better." Lou smiled mysteriously but didn't elaborate. "You'll see when we get there."

"So you lock your gates out here but not your doors?" Montana was still mystifying in a lot of ways.

Lou shrugged. "Guess so. So tell me, why do you really hate Christmas? Can't just be because you think it's tacky."

"That's a big part of it. I don't talk about the rest very often. Or think about it." Katie swallowed hard. Lou had been vulnerable enough to open up to her, and she deserved the same in return. "I came out to my parents around Christmas, sort of by accident. It didn't go very well."

Lou grimaced, and put her hand on Katie's thigh, giving it a gentle squeeze. "I'm sorry. Are things better with them now?"

"Kind of? We're not close, but I think they've accepted that no amount of praying is going to change who I am. And, I mean, it could have been a lot worse. They didn't kick me out or anything, just made life miserable for me until I moved out. And they eventually apologized. Sort of."

"How did they find out?"

"My mom caught me watching lesbian porn. It was winter break, sophomore year, and they were both supposed to be at work. My mom came home early and flipped out, called my dad and made me tell him." Katie sighed. It still made her mad, still hurt more than she ever wanted to admit. "I never got another Christmas present from then again, or birthday present." Not to mention the two and a half years of emotional and religious abuse she endured after. It didn't matter anymore. She had made it through and saw no point in reopening the wounds more than that. "What about your parents?"

Lou turned up Jason's driveway. "They always knew." She chuckled. "I mean, look at me. There was no keeping that a secret. And I've been lucky, they've always supported me. Maybe too much at times, but we had to be close, movin' around as much as we did. And I don't know what I would've done without my mom after Rachel died."

Katie stared out the window as they drove past the barn and through a gate that was open, as promised. Cows huddled around each other in a snow-covered field, but Lou continued past them, up a long drive that wound beyond a sprawling ranch house and towards a clump of trees in the distance. Lou hummed along to a countrified Christmas tune playing softly over the radio as she put the truck in park.

"We'll have to walk from here, the snow's drifted up too high to drive through. But it's just up there." Lou pointed at the trees.

"What is this, some kind of Christmas tree farm?" Katie asked, stepping down into knee-deep snow. Evergreen trees of all shapes and sizes grew in tidy rows around them, snow decorating the branches and blowing up in the breeze.

"Used to be, back when Jason's dad ran the place. He always said the tree farm had been there as long as Christmas had been in Montana."

"So why did Jason close it down?"

"People stopped buying them. You don't have to walk through snow with a chainsaw to get a plastic one, just have to drive to town and brave a salted parking lot. So he stopped trying to sell them and started focusing on other things to feed his family."

"I would have guessed everyone had a real tree with as much as people say they value tradition around here."

"Things change, even tradition." Lou said. "Not that it's any of my business to be putting out there, but he almost lost the whole place. If Jason hadn't switched to dairy, he probably wouldn't have the farm today. So that's the tradition his boys will know, but maybe by the time the farm goes to them, things will have changed again. Or maybe they'll sell it all to rich fucks from California to build vacation homes on. But hopefully I'll be dead before that happens." She grabbed the chainsaw from the bed of the truck, laughing wryly.

"Do you want help with that?" Katie asked, feeling guilty that, as usual, Lou was doing all the heavy work. Katie never touched a chainsaw in her life, though she'd watched enough horror films with Megan to have developed a healthy fear of them, but she didn't want Lou to shoulder the burden alone. Especially since it was at her request.

"I've got it," Lou said with a playful wink, and reached for Katie's hand instead.

They walked slowly between the rows of trees. Each one looked perfect to Katie, but none stood up to Lou's scrutiny. After a while, Katie stopped looking at the trees, and just soaked in the scene of beauty around her. Montana was overwhelmingly gorgeous, and each day held something new to discover. Katie took a deep breath, feeling the cold bite of the air as it burned her nostrils and froze her nose hairs, then burst out laughing from a sudden rush of gratitude and joy.

"What?" Lou asked, looking at Katie like she had suddenly gone crazy. Maybe she had.

"I finally get it," Katie said, tears escaping the corners of her eyes. She wiped them away before they could freeze to her face.

"I don't think I do," Lou said, chuckling softly. "But I'm happy if you're happy."

"That old saying, 'Don't miss the forest for the trees.' It never made any sense to me, because, like, the trees are the forest, you know? But now I see, I've been spending my whole life missing the big picture." She was babbling and didn't know if she was making any sense, but it didn't matter. "And yes, I'm happy. Happier than I think I've ever been."

Lou squeezed her hand. "Good. You deserve to be."

No one had ever told Katie that before, and it was hard to believe it was true. She'd always felt like happiness was something she needed to earn, that each milestone was a step closer to a day when she would feel worthy of being content. But with Lou, all that doubt and self-consciousness was stripped away, leaving only the naked potential of the present. Katie crumbled, and her tears of laughter turned into deep sobs of cathartic release. Somehow, in navigating all the twists and curves of life, the universe had brought her to that moment. It was too miraculous to believe but too vivid to deny.

"I know, I know." Lou murmured comfortingly. "Whatever it is you've been hanging onto, I can tell it's been causing you more harm than good. It's better to get it out. Let it all go." Lou held her until her shoulders stopped heaving, rubbing Katie's back gently as she cried into her shoulder.

"I needed that," Katie said when she could speak again, her voice muffled by Lou's thick coat. She looked up over Lou's shoulder, her vision still blurry with tears, and saw it.

It felt like a sign. It was perfect. The one. Short and squat, it grew stunted between two much larger trees. The trunk was slightly crooked as it leaned out into the row, fighting for the space to be itself but trapped between giants in a place it didn't belong. Scraggly branches clawed towards Katie, as if they were pleading with her to free it from its prison.

"What about that one?" Katie asked, pulling away from Lou.

Lou turned to look. "It's a little on the short side, and it'll be hard to prop up. We can do better for your first Christmas in Montana. I want it to be perfect."

Did she say first Christmas? As in, there might be others?

Katie's heart beat a little faster. "It already is perfect. And so is that tree."

"Then I love it," Lou said. She walked over to the tree and pulled the cord of the chainsaw. It roared to life. Katie jumped. It was louder than she had expected, and a flock of birds fluttered out of the branches of one of the tall trees.

"Wait!" Katie cried, suddenly realizing that she wasn't saving the tree, she was dooming it. It didn't belong inside, it belonged there in the field to grow freely. Who was she to decide to cut its life short?

Lou turned off the chainsaw.

"I don't want it to die," Katie knew how ridiculous she sounded. They were there to cut down a tree, of course one was going to have to die.

"It would die there either way," Lou reassured her. "Too much competition."

"It just feels like a waste."

"We won't waste it. After it's given us a little yuletide joy, we'll toss it in the creek. It'll slow the water just enough to make a little pool and the fish will find a safe place to lay eggs in its branches. Or we'll turn it into wood chips to use as mulch in the garden to grow more food. It has so much more potential than to wither here in the shadows, leeching up the nutrients the other trees need to grow even stronger."

Katie nodded, and Lou fired up the chainsaw again. It was over quickly, and the tree fell into the snow with a soft whump.

The space between the larger trees opened up, revealing a new view of a mountain peak in the distance, framed like a scene painted onto a Christmas card. Katie felt for her phone, then realized she had left it back at the cabin. She stared intently, hoping her memory was good enough to preserve the moment forever.

"Now I might need a little help getting this back to the truck," Lou said.

Katie picked up the tree by its trunk near the top, and Lou took the thicker stump at the bottom. Between the two of them, it wasn't heavy, just unwieldy and difficult to maneuver through the snow. They were both huffing and puffing by the time they made it back to the truck and hoisted the little tree into the bed.

The sun was beginning to set as they drove back across Jason's ranch, painting the clouds above a brilliant red. Jason was waiting for them at the gate.

"Find a good one?"

"Found a great one," Lou said. "Thanks again, Jay."

"Any time," he drawled, tipping his hat to them. "Merry Christmas to you both."

"You, too," Katie and Lou said at the same time.

They looked at each other and smiled. Jason shut the gate behind them, snapping the padlock shut in the rearview mirror.

Chapter Thirteen

Lou stopped the truck by the barn, and Katie helped her refill the animals' water buckets while Lou tossed thick flakes of fragrant hay to the horses. The evening chores went quickly with both of them working together, and it was relaxing just being around Lou and watching her in her element.

Katie was glad Lou was finally letting her in and letting her help. Doing manual labor gave Katie a new sense of pride and accomplishment, even if the buckets were heavy and the water frigid as it sloshed onto her pants. At least it meant something in a tangible way. She was contributing to something that mattered, and was almost sad when it was time to go back to the cabin.

"Red or white?" Lou asked randomly as she parked the truck in front of the door.

"Huh?"

"Wine. Which do you like better?"

"In winter, red." Lou was already heading towards the root cellar before Katie caught on and guilt crept in. "Lou, you can't..."

"Why not?"

"You're supposed to save it for a special occasion."

"This is special, it's Christmas Eve. And there's no one I'd rather share it with." Lou's tone left no room for argument.

"Then I'm honored," Katie said, her knees going a little weak. Under the tough, no-nonsense exterior, Lou was the most romantic, loving, giving person she'd ever met. She knew what the wine collection meant to Lou, and honored didn't even begin to cover how much it meant that Lou found her worthy of drinking it.

She went inside the house and turned the old-school radio on, spinning the dial until it landed on the same station that was playing in the truck. There was no denying the twangy country Christmas songs were cheesy, but it was sort of endearing, and Katie found herself singing along to the ones she knew.

Lou came back from the root cellar, dusting off the old bottle as she walked into the kitchen. She looked at it lovingly, eyes full of unspoken memories, then handed it to Katie and began searching the drawers for a corkscrew. Katie ran her thumb over the embossed label that proudly proclaimed it's Napa heritage in a font that had been out of vogue for at least a decade. No wonder, because the wine itself was fourteen years old. She passed the bottle back to Lou to uncork, trying to believe she really was worth it. Lou poured them each a glass.

"To your first Montana Christmas," Lou said, handing Katie one and raising her own.

Katie clinked her glass against Lou's. *To Rachel,* she thought, feeling the dead woman's presence everywhere. But Lou didn't seem sad about it, she was smiling her easy, crooked grin as she watched Katie take her first sip.

"How is it?"

"Good," Katie said. "Really good." She was no wine connoisseur, but the red Lou had selected was just the right blend of dry tartness with a light, fruity sweetness lingering after she swallowed.

Lou drank hesitantly, then wrinkled her nose. "It all tastes like mildew to me. But I'm glad you like it." She finished her glass in two gulps, rinsed it, and replaced the wine with a generous shot of whiskey. "Now, we've got some decorating to do."

The wine was going right to Katie's head, making everything comfortably warm. She turned up the radio and followed Lou into the living room. Lou unpacked the little electric candles first, passing them off to Katie to set in the window sills. The room was bathed in a cozy glow as Katie plugged them in one by one. Lou followed behind her, wrapping colored lights around each window.

When the room was decorated and half the bottle of wine was gone, they carried the tree inside. Katie held it steady while Lou screwed it into the base and– just as Lou had predicted– it was so lopsided it barely stood upright.

"I just can't get it straight," Lou grunted in frustration.

"So why waste your time trying?" Katie laughed. "It's perfect as-is."

The scent of fresh pine filled the cabin, clean and bright as the snowy field where they had cut it down. More boxes yielded more lights, a few small nutcrackers, and an assortment of delicately carved wooden ornaments of Montana wildlife. Katie hung them carefully while Lou tied red velvet bows to the boughs.

"These are stunning," Katie said.

"My dad made them," Lou said proudly, cradling one before placing it on the tree.

"He's really talented." The little animals were carved with incredible detail, seeming almost lifelike as they frolicked between the branches of the illuminated tree.

"Here," Lou said, handing Katie a star and stepping back to admire the tree fully decked out in baubles and lights. "You do the honors."

Katie climbed up a wobbly stepladder, wondering if she was too tipsy for her balance to be trusted. Lou reached up to steady her, her firm hand stabilizing Katie as she stretched up to fit the star over the crown of the tree. She was always there when Katie needed her to be, always saw what Katie needed before Katie even realized it herself.

"Now come down here and kiss me," Lou said. When Katie turned around, Lou was holding a dusty, plastic sprig of mistletoe over her head.

Katie jumped into her arms, wrapping her legs around Lou's waist without even stopping to think if Lou would catch her. Of course she would. It was Lou. She would never let Katie down. And just as Katie thought, Lou's arms wrapped around her legs, gripping her tightly as Katie's mouth descended onto hers.

Lou carried her into the bedroom, their lips locked together in a sloppy, drunken, passionate kiss. She tossed Katie on the bed and climbed on top of her. "I've been waiting for this all day."

"Me too," Katie said.

Lou kissed the divot between Katie's collarbones, making her whimper in anticipation. They undressed each other slowly, reveling in each other's bodies by the warm glow of battery-operated candlelight. Each brush of bare skin against bare skin set Katie's nerve endings on fire.

Lou's breath was heavy and warm against Katie's neck and she squirmed under Katie's touch. Katie grinned, then tucked her head and took one of Lou's ample breasts into her mouth, feeling her own pussy throb with desire as Lou moaned.

"Get on my face," Lou said, rolling to the side. "I want to taste you."

Katie straddled Lou's head, facing away from her so she could still play with her tits. Lou's nipples hardened under her fingertips, her breath hot and fast between Katie's thighs. Katie arched her back and sank down slowly until her pussy hovered just above Lou's face.

Lou grabbed her hips and pulled her down all the way, moaning as she thrust her tongue into Katie. "Mmm," Lou hummed, the sound muffled.

The vibrations sent a wave of pleasure through Katie's body. It was just as good as Katie had imagined the first moment she set eyes on Lou. She stretched forward, relaxing more of her weight onto Lou until she was resting her head on Lou's thigh. She lay there for a moment, fingers playing lazily in Lou's soft pubic curls, basking in the magic Lou was working on her.

Lou's body tensed as Katie slipped her middle finger between Lou's folds, and she moaned again, sending more of those toe-curling vibrations against Katie's clit. Katie had to have her. She parted Lou's slit with two fingers, then dove in. Lou tasted so good, sweet and clean and salty-tangy, and Katie couldn't get enough. They feasted on each other, giggling and moaning as they each tried to make the other cum first. When they did, it was together, in a wash of pure ecstasy that left their faces and the sheets soaked.

Katie rolled off Lou and turned around to lay beside her, previously unaware that such bliss existed. Lou was smiling, her eyes closed and face glistening with a light sheen of sweat and Katie's release. She almost looked like she was glowing.

Everything was perfect. Katie yawned and curled into Lou, then drifted off to sleep in her arms.

The first time Katie woke up, Lou was gone. She checked the time, rubbing sleep from her eyes. It was early. Super early. But she had to pee. She stumbled to the bathroom and relieved herself. Lou was nowhere to be seen, and a quick glance out the window showed the truck was gone, too. Probably down at the barn feeding the animals. Katie crawled back into bed.

The second time Katie woke up, Lou was walking into the bedroom carrying a tray full of food.

"Merry Christmas," Lou said, setting the tray down on the bed beside Katie before sitting down herself.

"No one's ever made me breakfast in bed before." Katie sat up, amazed at the spread and the effort that had gone into it. Two plates overflowing with thick slices of bacon, scrambled eggs, and toast with strawberry jam sat beside steaming mugs of coffee. A third plate was piled high with pancakes and maple syrup. Katie didn't know where to begin. "I wish I had something to give you."

"Just being able to spend this time with you is the greatest gift I can imagine," Lou said, cutting into the pancakes.

Katie took a bite of eggs. "So what's the plan today?"

"No plan." Lou stroked Katie's thigh. "We can spend all day in bed if you want. Or we can go out for a walk, or take the snowmobile out, or watch movies all day, or go into town. Whatever you want to do."

"The first sounds best," Katie said. Just one touch from Lou had her ready to abandon the breakfast and spread her legs. A whole day of making love to Lou sounded like an ideal way to spend Christmas.

Lou cleared the plates then rejoined Katie under the covers.

Chapter Fourteen

Katie's legs were all tangled up in Lou's and her hair was damp with sweat as they made out beneath the sheets when she thought she heard the slam of a car door right outside the cabin.

She pulled away. "Did you hear that?"

"Hear what?" Lou asked, rubbing Katie's nipple with her thumb and forefinger in slow circles. She brushed over the hard peak and smiled when Katie squirmed. "Mm, you love it when I do that, don't you?"

Katie placed her hand over Lou's so she would stop moving for a second. "I do, but I swear I heard a car outside. I don't hear anything now though, must have been my imagination."

"Don't tell me you're imagining things besides what I'm about to do to you." Lou pinched her nipple.

Katie squealed, then pulled Lou's face close to kiss her again. Lou kept rolling and squeezing her nipple as the ache inside Katie grew. No matter how many times she came, Lou could still turn her on instantly, working Katie's body until she begged for release. Like they'd already done three times that morning.

A loud knock came from the front of the house. Lou pulled away and looked at her in horror, and Katie knew she wasn't imagining it that time. The front door creaked, and they heard footsteps thump across the wooden floor. Someone was in the house.

"Stay here," Lou hissed. She wrapped herself in a blanket and crept towards the door while Katie watched in terror.

"Louisa?" Katie heard a woman call, just as Lou yanked the bedroom door open and stepped out into the hall.

"Mom?" Katie heard the confusion in Lou's voice. "What the fuck are you doing here?"

"Oh, Louisa, how could I not come? It's Christmas after all, and we're worried about you."

"Is Dad here, too?"

"Of course!" The woman– Lou's mom– sounded cheerful. "We couldn't let you spend the holiday alone, now could we? We've barely heard a peep from you since you got back from Los Angeles, and you haven't been up to Butte to see us at all. So we decided to come down and surprise you."

"Well, it worked. I'm surprised. But you didn't need to come. I'm doing fine here."

"Are you wearing a blanket? Have you even gotten out of bed today? Your hair is a mess." The woman tsk-tsked. "See? Your mother knows when her little girl needs her. Now, go get dressed before your father comes in."

Lou slipped back into the bedroom, her face as red as one of the jars of beets down in the root cellar. Katie felt as mortified as Lou looked, and she couldn't help but think of her own mother catching her in the act all those years ago.

"Sorry," Lou whispered. "I had no idea they were going to show up like this."

"Your mom sounds nice," Katie whispered back, still in shock.

"She's a lot."

"What do you want me to do? Hang out in here until they leave?"

"What?" Lou looked confused. "Why would I want that? Just get dressed and come out and meet them."

The thought was so terrifying Katie almost wished the noises had been a random intruder there to murder them instead. She didn't meet parents, especially not after only knowing someone for a few days. With Jackie, it had taken years to get to that point, and it hadn't exactly gone well.

Lou tossed Katie a pair of jeans from her open suitcase on the floor. "It's fine. They're going to love you."

"If you say so." Katie wasn't so sure about that, but what other option did she have? She begrudgingly got dressed and followed Lou out into the living room.

"At least you decorated," Lou's mom said without looking up from the books she was reorganizing by color on the shelves. "It looks nice in here."

"Mom."

"You could have picked a nicer tree, though, don't you think? This one's all crooked."

"Well, it fits. Nothing straight in this house. But, Mom–" Lou cleared her throat.

"And I saw you baked cookies! I didn't know you picked up baking. You know, I've just been so worried about you all alone out here..."

"Mom! Stop. I'm not alone."

The woman finally looked up, eyes widening as she finally noticed Katie.

"I guess not," she said softly, looking at Lou with hope in her eyes. "And who might this be?"

"This is my... this is Katie."

My what? Friend, or girlfriend? Lover? Katie wondered what Lou had been about to say, but it was not the time to ask. Besides, Katie wasn't even ready herself to put labels on what they had. It was too special to force into a labeled box.

"Katie," Lou's mother said slowly, looking Katie head to toe, before pushing Lou aside to wrap her in a tight hug. "I'm Diane. It is *so* wonderful to meet you. Louisa didn't tell us she had company."

"Maybe I didn't want you to know yet," Lou said, crossing her arms. "Where's Dad?"

"Oh, I dropped him off down at the barn. He wanted to check on your animals."

"The animals are fine. I'm fine. Everything's fine." Lou was more flustered than Katie had ever seen her.

"I see that," Lou's mom said, pulling Katie over to the couch. "Now tell me everything. How did you meet Louisa? Are you from Bozeman?"

"It's a long story," Lou said before Katie could answer. "Don't badger her."

"It's okay." Katie smiled. "I don't mind." Lou's mom radiated the same safe energy her daughter did, and Katie could tell her eagerness to know more was just because of how much she cared for Lou. Katie thought it was sweet. "I'm not from here, just visiting from Seattle."

"What brings you all the way out here?"

"A flight mishap," Katie said slowly, unsure how much Lou wanted to share with her parents. Lou gave me a hand when I needed one and..."

"And Katie wound up staying out here a few nights," Lou finished for her. "Mom, I told you not to come by without at least calling first. What if you'd driven all this way and I wasn't even here?"

"I did call. I've been calling for days. You never answered or called me back, besides telling me your flight landed. What's a mother supposed to think?"

"I didn't mean to worry you. I was just busy."

"I see that now." Diane smirked. "Why don't you go make us all some coffee and let me get to know Katie?"

"Sorry," Lou mouthed to Katie before disappearing into the kitchen.

"Now," Diane said, "Tell me about yourself. Have you spent much time on a farm before?"

"No, this is my first time. But I love it. Everything is so peaceful out here."

"You might want to hold your judgment on that until you see it in full tourist season. No offense. So how long are you planning on staying?"

"Until Lou gets sick of me," Katie said. The thought of leaving at all felt like a knife wrenching through her heart. But she and Lou hadn't even begun to discuss that.

Diane lowered her voice. "How is she, really?"

Katie shifted on the couch. The conversation was friendly enough, and it was clear Diane loved her daughter immensely, but Katie didn't feel it was her place to comment on Lou. What she shared with her parents was up to her. "She's been an awesome host," Katie finally said, keeping it light and vague. "Everything she's managed to do here is really impressive."

"That's my Louisa," Diane smiled crookedly, looking exactly like an older version of her daughter.

The door swung open and a grizzled man in a black cowboy hat entered, stomping the snow from his boots. Lou's dad, there was no question about that. They had the same gait, unhurried and confident.

"Louisa's in the kitchen," Diane called without glancing over at him. "Why don't you go say hi?"

"And who is this?" He asked, crossing his arms as he stared Katie down.

"Louisa has a guest and it appears you left your manners outside," Diane chided, though the look she gave her husband was one of adoration. "Katie, this oaf is George."

"Hmph," he grumbled, and went into the kitchen to see Lou.

"Don't mind him," Diane said. "He's a little protective of her, especially after... I'm assuming Louisa's spoken to you about..."

"I know about Rachel," Katie said. "If that's what you're asking."

"She's just been so distant with us. We thought when she moved back here, things would go back to the way they were before. She used to tell me everything, you know."

What was she even supposed to say to that? Katie was sure Lou had her reasons, but she wasn't going to get involved in family drama. She glanced towards the kitchen, hoping the coffee was almost ready and Lou would be back in soon. Maybe she should have just stayed in the bedroom. It was great Lou's parents loved her as much as they did, but she had only spent five minutes around them and could already see how exhausting it probably was for Lou.

Fortunately Lou came back right then, carrying two mugs of hot coffee and followed by her father, who carried two more. Lou handed a mug to Katie with a sly smile. The steam rising up carried the faint scent of whiskey. Katie's suspicions were confirmed when she took a long sip and tasted the sharp alcoholic bite as Lou squeezed in between Katie and Diane and draped an arm around Katie's shoulders, possessive and protective all at the same time.

George wasn't nearly as relaxed as his daughter. He hadn't even sat down, and paced around in front of the sofa as he began. "What are you really doing here with Louisa?"

"Nothing," Katie said, taken aback by the accusatory tone and wondering what she had done wrong, what he expected her to admit to.

"Dad..."

George continued his questioning, undeterred by Lou's stern tone. "How long have you been here?"

"A week or so."

"Don't you have someplace else to be?"

"Not really."

"Why's that?"

Katie shrugged. She didn't want to admit that she was unemployed, lost and adrift and unsure of what to do next. What kind of first impression would that be?

"You better not be taking advantage of my daughter," George threatened.

"I'm not. I would never. I care about Lou a lot."

"Do you? Or do you just see opportunity here? You after her money? Her land?"

"Dad! That's enough!" Lou yelled, standing up to stare him down. "Stop it or I'm going to tell you to leave."

"What? I'm just looking out for you, Louisa; someone has to. There are people out there that prey on kind-hearted people like you, you know. I saw a post about it. They specifically go after widows. They can look all that up online."

"Katie's not like that. She hasn't asked for anything at all." Lou insisted. "For fuck's sake, Dad, you spend too much time online. If you even tried to get to know her, you'd see she's brilliant. She's smart, and funny, and an amazing cook." Lou sat back down next to Katie and took her hand. "And I like her a lot."

"George, sit down and drink your coffee and leave the poor girls alone," Diane said. "If Louisa's found someone that makes her happy, that should make us happy. And Louisa, don't swear at your father."

"Mom, it's not that serious. Come on, can't we just have a nice Christmas?"

"That's what we were trying to do, but now it seems like you'd rather we just leave."

Lou closed her eyes and took a deep breath. "I didn't say that," she said through clenched teeth. "I'm glad you came. I'm happy to see you. I appreciate that you drove all this way to check on me." She sounded like she was trying to convince herself.

"Excuse me for just a sec," Katie said, seizing on a chance to escape to the bathroom and regain her composure. She'd always thought she was pretty good at charming people, but Lou's parents' opposing attitudes towards her had thrown her off her game.

Lou would be fine without her, but she didn't think she could field another harsh question from George without breaking down. The bathroom was a welcome refuge, and Katie pulled out her phone and sat on the edge of the tub.

"Merry Christmas," she texted Megan. "The craziest shit just happened. Lou's parents showed up."

There was no response, but Katie didn't expect one. Of course Megan was busy with her own family on Christmas day. She checked her other messages, and saw one from her mother—a perfunctory holiday greeting accompanied by a long Bible verse. Not even a phone call. Katie deleted the message without reading it. All her old hatred of Christmas came flooding back. Everyone had people except for her. And she was in the bathroom alone. Ugh, she didn't want to cry. Feeling sorry for herself had never gotten her anywhere.

Katie splashed some water on her face and took a deep breath. If she stayed in the bathroom any longer, she'd just keep spiraling. She'd rather be sitting out there with Lou's arm wrapped around her, crazy parents be damned.

By the time Katie emerged, the mood seemed to have lightened in the living room, with Lou and her father deep in conversation about sustainable agriculture and regenerative farming practices. Diane smiled gently at Katie when she sat down beside Lou again, but otherwise no one made a fuss about her reappearance.

"So are you originally from Seattle?" Diane asked.

"No, I grew up in the Washington, D.C. area."

"Oh, an east coast girl. So that's why you seem so put together. Me too." Diane smiled conspiratorially. "Upstate New York."

"Do you like it out here?"

"Do I have a choice?" Diane laughed. "George grew up out here, and even though the Army might've taken him all over, he never stopped talking about coming back home. Lou's always been the same way. But I'll admit, it's grown on me."

"They seem a lot alike," Katie said, pausing to stare at the father and daughter so engaged in discussion they were completely oblivious that Katie and Diane were watching them.

"They are. She was his little shadow growing up. Damn near broke his heart when she left for L.A. to chase someone else's dream." Even though her tone was perfectly pleasant, Diane gave Katie a very pointed look– almost as if she was daring Katie to try to do the same.

"I can't picture her anywhere but here."

"I don't think she'll move away again."

Was that another veiled warning? Diane may have been from upstate New York but her passive aggression was on par with any Seattleite.

"I wouldn't ask her to," Katie said, choosing directness instead.

"She seems happier than I've seen her in a very long time. I can tell having you here has been good for her. "

"Must be the holiday spirit." Katie noticed Diane's mug was empty. "Would you like more coffee? I was just about to refill mine."

Diane handed her the mug. "How about some of that whiskey in mine this time?"

The rest of the afternoon was pleasant enough. Diane regaled Katie with tales of Lou's childhood, while Lou groaned in embarrassment. Still, Katie was relieved when– after the second cup of coffee– Diane stood and announced she and George were leaving.

"I thought we were staying down here for supper?" George asked.

"We've intruded on Louisa and Katie long enough," Diane said. "We came down to make sure she's alright, and she clearly is."

George didn't exactly look happy about his wife's declaration, but he nodded amicably and stood. Diane hugged Katie and George shook her hand, and then Lou walked them over to the door.

"Thanks for coming to check on me," Lou said as they hugged her goodbye. "Means a lot."

"Merry Christmas, Louisa. We love you." George's voice was gruff but his eyes sparkled.

"Love you, Dad." Lou shut the door behind them, then leaned against it and waited for the roar of the truck engine outside before turning to Katie. "I am so sorry. I had no idea they were coming."

"Don't be," Katie said, walking over to her. "I'm glad I got to meet them." Mostly. It had still been awkward, but Lou's parents were far from the worst.

"They're a lot." Lou glanced down at her watch and frowned. "And I haven't even started cooking yet. You're going to be starving by the time dinner is ready! I was going to roast a duck but I forgot to put it in and it needhours."

"There's only one thing I want to eat anyways." Katie took Lou's hand to pull her back to the bedroom when her stomach growled.

"I'm sorry," Lou apologized again. "I had this whole thing planned. I just wanted today to be perfect."

"I got to spend it with you, so it was." Katie kissed Lou softly. She never wanted Lou to feel bad, especially not over something so out of her control like her parents' surprise visit. "We can just cook tomorrow and make something easy tonight. Then it will be like two days of Christmas."

"Frozen pizza then?"

"Sounds perfect, I'll find us a movie to watch." Katie sprawled out on the couch, pulling the throw blanket up to her chin. The dogs settled in on either side of her while she flipped through endless Christmas rom-coms. Straight couple after straight couple filled the screen, some in red sweaters and some in green, but otherwise indistinguishable from the next. Ugh. Why couldn't lesbians have their holiday happily-ever-afters, too?

Finally she found a single movie with two happy looking women in the preview image, but only after diving deep into search. Lou came in and nudged one of the dogs aside so she could settle down next to Katie. She set the pizza down in between them, and Katie hit play.

Steam curled up from the plate and the scent of oregano hit Katie first as the opening sequence unfolded on the screen. Her stomach growled, and she reached for a slice at the same time Lou did, feeling the now-familiar jolt of attraction as their hands brushed together.

The pizza wasn't very good, but it was absolutely perfect. Mass-produced, over-sweetened marinara mingled with salty cheese, sad vegetables, and sausage of mysterious origin. Katie couldn't stop eating it, practically inhaling the first slice without caring that it was burning the roof of her mouth.

"Delicious," she mumbled between bites.

"I wish it was a more traditional Christmas feast."

"It doesn't matter," Katie insisted. "All I care about is spending it with you."

When they were finished eating, Lou set the plate on the coffee table and kicked her feet up on it. She lifted her arm so Katie could snuggle closer. Katie lay in her lap, basking in the coziness of the evening. The movie leaned into all the right tropes and was delightfully cheesy, if objectively awful.

Lou's fingers worked their languid magic, tracing down her stomach to the hem of her shirt and pulling it up just enough to rest her hand on Katie's bare skin. Katie loved being held by her. *You're mine,* Lou's firm grip seemed to say. Katie wished she would slide that hand a little lower, below the waistband of her jeans to apply that possessive pressure somewhere better. Her clit throbbed in anticipation. It was getting hard to focus on the movie.

She glanced up at Lou, who seemed completely oblivious to the turmoil she was causing Katie. Her thumb drifted lazily over Katie's belly button, leaving goosebumps in its wake. Katie inhaled sharply and noticed the corner of Lou's mouth twitch up in the faintest hint of a smile, but her eyes stayed locked on the screen.

She definitely knew what she was doing.

When the two women on the screen finally kissed after the slowest burn imaginable, Lou cradled Katie's chin in her hand and turned Katie's face to hers. They kissed for a lot longer than the characters did, getting drunk on the taste of each other and unable to stop.

"Now this is what I planned to spend the whole day doing." Lou's voice was viscous and her eyes dark with lust. "Not that disaster of a visit from my parents."

"Shh," Katie said, sitting up so Lou could pull her shirt over her head. She didn't want to think about the day or their surprise visitors any longer, not when she was practically dripping with desire. Thanks to Lou, there was only one thing on her mind. "Just kiss me."

Their lips met again, Lou's hands lighting every nerve in Katie's body on fire as she pulled Katie onto her lap to face her. Lou's tongue pressed into Katie's mouth, demanding more as her fingers burned a blazing path up Katie's back and unhooked her bra.

Katie's heart raced as Lou pulled the straps over her shoulders, then threatened to beat out of her chest when Lou traced her thumbs across Katie's nipples. Katie groaned, the sound dampened by the ongoing kiss. Just one touch was enough to drive her wild, and Lou was blanketing her body with tender caresses.

The background noise from the TV switched to a peppy Christmas tune, briefly breaking through the overwhelming rush of sensations. The credits, probably. Katie wasn't going to turn around to check.

Her hands were resting on Lou's shoulders, and she slid them down to begin fumbling with the buttons of her flannel shirt. She undid the first few, but it took too much concentration and she was finding it impossible to focus when her nipples were sending electric shocks through her core and into her pussy. She gave up and reached for the hem of Lou's shirt.

Lou pulled away, leaving Katie's lips tingling and lonely. "I got it," she said, pinching Katie's nipples lightly before her hands flitted off to undo the buttons at her wrists.

"You should wear things that are easier to get off," Katie said.

"Maybe you just need more practice taking them off me."

"I'll take all the practice I can get."

Lou's shirt fell away, and Katie reveled in the sight of the shadows flickering across her pale skin. She was so beautiful it made Katie ache. Katie leaned down to kiss her neck, feeling Lou's soft curves beneath her hands. Her clit pulsed as she ground into Lou, riding her on the couch as Lou gripped her ass and pulled her closer.

"Do you want me to get my strap-on?" Lou whispered into Katie's ear, sending a shiver down her spine.

Katie nodded, her heart racing. There was nothing she wanted more, and she was relieved Lou had brought it up first. She had always had trouble asking for what she wanted, but Lou seemed to read her mind and respond in all the right ways.

"Stay here." Lou tossed Katie to the side as if she weighed nothing and strode off into the bedroom.

Katie leaned back into the couch cushion, her breaths coming quick. Her chest flushed red as she imagined what Lou might have in store for her. Fortunately, she didn't have to wait long.

Lou reappeared from the bedroom, still buckling the harness around her hips as she sauntered back to the couch. "Why are you still in those?" She asked, nodding at Katie's jeans.

Katie scrambled up, hands flying to the button at her waistband as she raced to obey the subtle command in Lou's question. She tugged the jeans down over her hips, followed quickly by her underwear.

"So beautiful," Lou said, her eyes darkening with lust as they devoured Katie slowly. "Now where were we?" She sat back down on the couch and motioned for Katie to straddle her again.

Katie climbed into Lou's lap again, her pelvis hovering just above the tip of the toy. Lou reached forward and slid one finger along Katie's slick entrance, making her knees buckle. She whimpered as the toy brushed against her clit. She was already on the verge of coming before they'd even really begun.

"Are you sure about this?" Lou asked, misinterpreting Katie's hesitation as apprehension.

"Very sure." Even more so because it was clear how much Lou cared about her comfort.

"Just go slow." Lou's fingers parted Katie's folds and she shifted her hips slightly, bringing the tip right to Katie's entrance.

Katie gripped Lou's shoulders and sank a little lower, feeling the soft silicone slide inside her. Lou traced a path down Katie's spine, making her shiver and arch her back. The strap shifted inside her, rubbing against her pussy walls until it pressed against her G-spot. Katie froze as her muscles clenched and relaxed, knowing if she moved at all she would explode.

"Good?"

"Uh-huh," Katie moaned, eyes shut. Words were beyond her.

Her body contracted around the toy as she rose up again. Lou's strong hands closed around her waist, guiding Katie as she rode the silicone cock with more intensity. Noises Katie couldn't control left her parted lips and she sank all the way down into Lou's lap, deliciously full and on the verge of complete eruption.

Lou's hips rose beneath her, thrusting softly as Katie's mind began to black out. All she could sense were the waves of pleasure building inside her, desperate to break free. Two new sensations overwhelmed her at the same time– Lou's thumb rubbing firmly around her clit and Lou's mouth teasing her sensitive nipple.

Katie shattered. Her toes curled beneath her and her thighs trembled as pleasure spread through her core to wash over every inch of her body. She moaned Lou's name and slumped forward into Lou's open arms. Warmth trickled from her as her body continued to convulse rhythmically around the toy. Lou held her close and kissed her neck softly. Every muscle in Katie's body was beginning to relax into a state of total bliss. She sighed.

"Everything okay?" Lou murmured into her collarbone.

"Better than ever," Katie answered, though she was suddenly struck with a deep feeling of terror. Everything was too good, and she didn't deserve it. But most of all, she was afraid she was going to lose it.

Chapter Fifteen

For the first time since arriving at the homestead, Katie woke up when Lou did. It was still completely dark outside, and she yawned as she rolled over to face Lou.

"What time is it?"

"Five," Lou said. "Go back to sleep. I'll wake you up when I come back from the barn."

"Actually, I'm not tired at all." Katie was surprised by how refreshed she felt. "I sleep better here." The homestead was dark and quiet, unlike the constant background of noises and lights she'd thought she was used to in Seattle. Maybe it was how totally safe she felt sleeping next to Lou, or it could have just been the warm glow of consistent, fantastic sex, but Katie felt more alive than she had in years. "I want to help with the chores this morning."

Lou shrugged. "If you say so."

They brushed their teeth together and got dressed quickly, then drove down to the barn. Everything was quiet in the predawn hour, and the blanket of stars still twinkled brightly across the endless sky. It was easier for Katie to remember the last time she had gone to bed at five a.m. than the last time she'd woken up so early, but she suddenly understood morning people. There was something alluring about the tranquility that made her eager to break through it and start her day.

Lou parked and Katie followed her into the barn, struggling to pull the heavy sliding door shut behind her. Lou reached over and gave her a hand, making the door feel weightless. Lou made everything look easy, though Katie supposed if she spent long enough working on the farm, she would develop the same subtle strength and maybe even the unassuming confidence that accompanied it.

"What's first?"

"You can water while I feed." Lou was already striding across the barn to collect the empty food buckets from the night before.

Katie hurried to keep pace with her, but it was futile. The work became much more enjoyable once she settled into her own rhythm, and she found herself slowing just to prolong the experience. The barn was warm and full of life as the animals woke up from their own slumbers, then erupted into noise as they each began demanding their breakfasts from Lou.

"I hear ya," Lou called as one of the horses whinnied and stamped in its stall a few feet away from Katie.

Katie watched as Lou scooped food from different bins into different buckets, and grinned sheepishly when Lou caught her staring. She couldn't help it. Lou was too sexy to tear her eyes away from, and she felt herself heating up at the thought of what they might do when they got back to the house.

When the animals had all been fed and watered, Lou showed Katie how to chase the chickens out of their boxes and collect the warm eggs from their nests of straw. Katie would have expected more resistance from the chickens, but they seemed entirely lacking in maternal instinct and indifferent to having their nests robbed. Or maybe they just knew their eggs weren't fertile, and that there was no use fighting back when Lou came by to spirit them away to become omelets and scrambles.

"Ready?" Katie asked, assuming they were finished for the morning and about to go cook the eggs they had gathered.

"Not quite," Lou said, fishing her keys out of her pocket. "I still have to clean the horses' stalls. But I don't expect you to help with that, I know it's pretty gross if you're not used to it. You can go warm up in the truck if you want, or just hang out while I do it. It won't take long."

"I don't mind helping. I like spending time with you."

Lou's cheeks flushed red as she dropped her keys back in her coat. "You're not too difficult to be around yourself."

Lou waited for the horses to finish their grain before she let them out into their snowy pasture. Katie laughed from inside the barn as she watched the horses prance off into the field, waiting for the rest of the herd before they all took off running. The sight of them thundering across the field took her breath away. They were so powerful, with snow spraying up behind them as they lunged forward, racing each other and tossing their heads with joy. They seemed free in a way Katie had never felt before she'd come to Montana, and even though she was standing still in the barn, she could feel her soul thundering off towards the mountains with them as the first light of dawn filled the sky.

Lou handed her a pitchfork and brought over a wheelbarrow. "Ever done this before?"

"You know I haven't," Katie laughed.

"Just pick up anything that looks like shit and any sawdust that's wet." Lou shoved her fork into a pile in the corner of the stall and dumped it into the wheelbarrow.

Katie tried to emulate her, but the waste was heavier than she anticipated and hard to balance. The slick wooden handle spun in her grip and the pile of horse shit dropped back to the ground.

"It's not as easy as it looks. I've done that a million times. You just have to get under it more," Lou said, propping her pitchfork against the wall and coming over to show Katie. Her arms reached around Katie and covered her hands, correcting her grip on the handle. She thrust forward, demonstrating how to get leverage, and guided Katie as she deposited it in the wheelbarrow. "That's it."

They shoveled in silence for a few minutes as Katie got used to the task. When the wheelbarrow was full, Lou took it away to dump on a huge pile of manure outside, and Katie took a moment to catch her breath. Her shoulder muscles ached, and they had only finished one stall. There were still four more to go.

"So tell me something, Seattle," Lou said as she came back into the barn. "Why are you still single?"

The question took Katie by surprise. "What do you mean?"

"I just find it hard to believe someone as great as you hasn't settled down yet."

Katie blushed at the compliment, even though she was sure she wasn't quite as great as she had let Lou believe. "I guess I just haven't found the right person yet."

"Why did it end with...?"

"Jackie? I guess we just weren't right for each other. I was too busy."

"Did you love her?"

"I thought I did." Before she'd met Lou, and been shown the real meaning of life, and love, and everything else that mattered in the world.

"Thought you did?"

"Jackie was needy and I liked being needed, until I had too many other things going on and it wasn't enough for her. Then it all just sort of fell apart." It was hard to believe it had only been a few months since she'd come home from a late night at work to an empty apartment and the note. "I thought this year I was going to get a promotion, and I was trying to put in the hours to show them how much I wanted it. They kept dangling it in front of me, and it felt so close. She thought I was staying out late to cheat on her, and using work as a cover. Once she decided I was, there was no changing her mind again."

"Were you?" Lou's tone was inquisitive, not judgmental.

"No! I would never. I've been cheated on, and I could never do that to someone I cared about."

"By Jackie?"

"No, my girlfriend before her." Katie dumped another pile of shit into the wheelbarrow.

Lou winced. "I'm sorry."

"That was probably my fault, too."

"I kind of doubt that."

"I was too stubborn and trying to force compatibility where there was none."

"Which isn't your fault. She could have ended it, too." Lou grabbed the handles of the wheelbarrow and pushed it into the next stall. "You didn't deserve to have that happen to you."

"It happens." Katie shrugged. "We were young." She hadn't really thought about it in a long time. She wasn't mad anymore, but it had fucked her up for a while.

"Rachel cheated on me, too." Lou looked horrified as the words slipped from her mouth. She stopped shoveling and leaned on the pitchfork. "I've only told my therapist that before."

Katie was shocked. The photos Lou had shown her had painted such a perfect picture of their life together, and it was hard to imagine it was anything less than the daydream it seemed. "After you got married?"

Lou shook her head. "Before. Right after we moved to L.A."

"And you stayed with her anyways?"

"She swore it was a mistake and it would never happen again. And I think she kept that promise. Besides, I didn't have many other options. Spent all our money getting down there and finding a place to live and working extra hours so she could take time off to go to auditions. I was sort of stuck there."

"And you loved her."

"With my whole heart. But sometimes that isn't enough."

"What do you mean?"

"It was just starting to look like she was going to get her big break and I was already sick of L.A. Even if she hadn't died, I was thinking about divorcing her and coming back here." Lou winced. "I feel like a terrible person when I say that part out loud. But our paths to happiness were different, no matter how deep our love was. One of us would have always been sacrificing too much."

Katie reached out and laid her hand on top of Lou's. "You shouldn't feel terrible. I don't think it's terrible. You tried."

"And what about you? What's your path to happiness?" Lou looked deep into Katie's eyes, and Katie knew it was finally time to be honest with Lou.

She swallowed hard. "I want it to be you."

"What are we, Seattle?" Lou's stare was intense.

"Two people who were in the right place at the right time to find each other," Katie said. She hadn't imagined confessing her love in a barn, but somehow it felt right. "Two people who were meant to find each other."

"Be honest with me, what are you looking for here?"

Katie wanted to hear it from Lou first. She was too much of a coward to say the three little words, because if Lou didn't say them back, Katie didn't know if she'd ever be able to pick up the pieces of her heart again. There was no one on Earth more perfect than Lou, and no place more perfect than Paradise Valley. But if Katie said *I love you* before Lou did, it would feel like she was imposing on Lou to say it back. Like she was pushing herself too forcefully into a place where she still wasn't fully sure she could ever belong. So she shrugged.

Lou sighed and turned away with the wheelbarrow full of horse shit.

Katie cursed herself. She could have come up with a better answer than that. Anything would have been better than shrugging, but her panic had taken over. Now Lou probably didn't think Katie cared at all, or worse, she'd start to believe Katie was just there for the wrong reasons.

"Lou, wait," Katie said.

Lou paused in the stall door.

"I want to call you my girlfriend. I want to text selfies of us to my friends and brag about how stunning you are and how much I..."

Lou looked at Katie over her shoulder, one eyebrow raised. "How much you what?"

Katie swallowed her fear and went for it. "How much I love you."

The wheelbarrow thudded to the dirt floor as Lou dropped the handles. "Do you mean that?"

"I do." Katie's whole head was heating up, from the tips of her ears to the back of her neck. Lou didn't say anything, and even the animals seemed to have quieted and were listening to the conversation. Katie's heart pounded, deafening in her ears as everything else seemed to stop.

Why wasn't Lou saying anything?

"You don't have to say it back," Katie whispered.

"After Rachel died, I didn't think it was possible for me to love again. And then I met you. But I'm scared, Seattle. This is too fast."

"I know," Katie said. It was too fast, and it didn't make any sense, but she had never felt a love more real. She needed Lou in her life as much as she needed oxygen or food or water. If Lou felt a fraction of what Katie did, it was easy to understand why she was scared, because Katie was terrified of what lay ahead. The longing to be with her forever was overwhelming, and Katie could no longer stand the thought of a future without Lou. It just wasn't possible.

They returned to the house to eat, and Katie was just starting to daydream about another afternoon much like the one before, lounging on the couch with Lou and making out and enjoying each other's company while soft flurries of snow drifted past the frosty windows. Lou seemed to have other plans though, and as soon as the kitchen table was cleared of their dishes, she began piling it high again with notebooks and binders.

"Do you want to see what I'm working on in the garden next year?" Lou asked, flipping open one of the notebooks to a sheet of graph paper.

Katie pulled her chair around to sit next to Lou, and leaned in to look at the papers.

"This one is the whole homestead," Lou said, flipping back a few pages. "Every block of nine squares is an acre."

The map of the homestead was meticulously drawn in pencil. The cabin and barn looked tiny next to the sprawling horse pastures, and the vast area marked 'wildflower meadow' in Lou's tidy, all-caps print seemed bigger on paper than the area Lou had indicated to her on the snowmobile tour the week before.

"You're putting in twice as many hives as you have now?" Katie asked, noticing the carefully labeled boxes near the far end of the property. "I thought you had more than enough honey already."

"It's not about the honey, I just like the bees. And the world needs them. Makes me feel like I'm helping, in my own small way." Lou was becoming more animated as she spoke, her passion rubbing off on Katie. She flipped to the next page, revealing a beautifully sketched drawing of a boxy hive. "I'll get started building the hives in the next few weeks so they're ready when our new queens arrive."

"Do they ever sting you?"

"They used to when I first started, but it was my fault. I didn't know how to handle them without riling them up. But now that we're more used to each other, they're a lot more docile than you'd think."

Katie tried to imagine herself as a beekeeper. As long as she had a suit so none of them could sting her, she thought she could probably muster up the courage to help with it. And as long as she had Lou at her side, showing her how to do it and keeping her out of harm's way.

Lou turned the page again, to a sheet with four long garden rows drawn on it. It was less neat than the other pages she had seen so far, with obvious eraser marks and question marks accompanying the labels. "This is what I have to figure out," she said, opening another notebook. "What goes where."

Katie scanned the long list of vegetables and herbs. "Do you replan it every year? Why not just keep it the same?" It seemed like a lot of extra work, and if something wasn't broken she saw no need to fix it.

"For one, it makes the soil healthier to rotate the crops around. Diseases can stay in the dirt and attack the plants if I put them there, and every plant needs different nutrients and takes different things out of the soil. Moving them around helps."

"Makes sense," Katie said. "So how do you even know where to begin?"

"Trial and error and lots of erasing," Lou laughed. "These are the front four rows, and I'll probably fill them with beans and peas." She penciled the words in carefully on each row. "I had cabbage and greens there last year, and they use a lot of nitrogen. The beans and peas will replace it." Lou flipped the page, and four more neatly blocked rows appeared. "I can move the brassicas here and they should still get plenty of sun." She frowned for a moment, then scribbled on the page. *Broccoli, cabbage, nasturtium...*

"What's that one?" Katie asked. Of course she knew what broccoli and cabbage were, but she had never heard of the third thing Lou was writing in between the other vegetables.

"Nasturtium?" Lou said, the Latin— at least, Katie thought it was Latin— rolling smoothly off her tongue. "It's a flower."

"Do you eat it or is it just for decoration?"

"The leaves and flowers are edible, taste sort of like arugula. And it's beautiful, but mostly I grow it because it keeps insects away from the vegetables. They especially seem to love anything in the broccoli family here, but the nasturtiums attract them instead and I get a better harvest."

"So it really does matter where all the plants go?"

"It matters a lot. That's why I spend the time every year figuring it out. Once you've had a tomato fresh from the vine, you'll see why it's worth it. There's no love in a grocery store tomato."

"I can't wait to try one." Katie didn't even particularly like tomatoes unless they were cooked into marinara sauce or ketchup, but she would try one of Lou's. With the entirety of Lou's love for the land nurturing it, she was sure it would be the best tomato she had ever eaten.

"You planning on sticking around until July or August, then?" Lou asked. Her tone was light, joking, but Katie knew she was asking seriously.

"I don't know." It was better to be honest, right? "Are you asking me to stay?"

"I'm asking if you want to stay." Lou looked up from the notebook to meet Katie's eyes and rested her hand on Katie's thigh.

"I want to, but..."

"But?"

"I don't know."

"What are your dreams?"

"You mean when I wake up from this one?"

"Like what do you want to do with your life?"

"I thought I was living my dream. Rising in the ranks, getting promotions. Eventually I would have made VP some-where, or started my own agency. Someday I do want to work for myself, once I save enough money to take the leap. I guess that's the dream. Plus all the find the right person, settle down, die happy kind of stuff."

"Were you happy in Seattle?"

"Sometimes. I was mostly stressed."

"Are you happy here?"

"More than I've ever been."

"Then why go back?"

"My life is there. I don't know if I was made for Montana." Katie pointed at the notebook. "I don't know any of this stuff, or how to ride a horse, or rope a steer." The insecurities the men in Bozeman had planted in her slipped out.

"You're never too old to learn. And besides," Lou's hand covered Katie's on the notebook and squeezed gently. "You don't have to know how to do everything. Just like the plants here, each one has its role in the ecosystem to help the other thrive. Our differences are how we can help each other grow. You're the nasturtium to my cabbage."

"Oh please," Katie said, blushing at how romantic Lou was without even trying. "I would definitely be the cabbage."

"Not a chance. You're way too beautiful. I'm round and plain, and you turn heads in every room you walk into."

"I happen to love cabbage. It's not plain at all." Kate leaned forward, letting the playful tone creep back into her voice. "It's robust, and comforting, and cute, and charming, and romantic..."

"Are you sure you're still talking about cabbage?" Lou set down her pencil and tilted her chin as she turned to Katie.

"Did you know the French call people they love cabbage? Well, *chou*."

"You didn't tell me you speak French. I happen to find that incredibly attractive."

"It's about the only thing I remember from French class." Katie laughed. "That and '*Où est la toilette?*' which is probably the least sexy thing I could say." Though one of the most useful on Katie's drunken college summer abroad.

"Everything you say is sexy. Even just sitting here working, I can barely keep my hands off you."

"So don't."

"That's for later," Lou grinned and looked Katie head to toe. "And I'm looking forward to it, but I do really need to get this done before I get seeds in soil blocks next week."

Katie glanced out at the snow-covered world that glowed pinkish orange in the fading winter light. "Next week? I would have figured it would be months away."

"I plant the seeds indoors to give them the longest head start possible. They need it with as short as the growing season is up here."

Even though farming was a world Katie was completely unfamiliar with, she was drawn to the planning part of it, at least. "You know, this almost reminds me of my old job."

"I find that a little hard to believe."

"It does," Katie insisted. "I had to figure out the timing of a lot of moving pieces months in advance too, doing everything in my power to make sure it all paid off when the time came. This scratches that same itch for me." She picked up the pencil. "May I?"

Lou gestured for her to go ahead.

Katie erased a row marked "CORN" and penciled in radishes/cherry tomatoes instead. "Assuming everything on this chart is correct, then the radishes will be ready to pull out just when the tomatoes are ready to go in. And if those only need sixty-five days, it should be ready before the frost?"

Lou leaned back in her chair and crossed her arms. "I'm impressed, Seattle. You catch on quick."

"It's just like setting up overlapping ad campaigns," Katie said, even though it was really nothing like that. Lou's approval made her heart flutter.

"If you say so." Lou chuckled, the rich sound filling Katie with warmth.

Katie's phone vibrated on the table, making both of them jump. Megan's picture filled the screen and Lou's expression changed to a slight frown. Katie clicked the phone off and the screen went dark.

"My best friend," Katie explained. "I should probably call her back, she'll be worried if I don't."

"Don't let me stop you," Lou said. The creases of worry on her forehead softened, but she still looked troubled.

"You don't think... I mean, you trust me, right?"

"I trust you. But I see you texting all the time, I'm assuming that's with her. So if I'm being honest, I don't know what to think."

"Well, she's just a friend, and very straight." Except that time Megan had kissed her to make a boy jealous and then crushed six months of Katie's daydreams about her, but Lou didn't need to know about that. Not yet, at least. It would only confuse things, and for no reason. Katie was more than a decade past imagining Megan as anything but a friend. A sister. "You're the only one I want, Lou. You're the most incredible person I've ever met."

"Do you mean that?"

"With my whole heart. No one has ever made me feel as special or as worthy as you. Even if I don't deserve you."

"Why would you even say that?"

"You've been so nice to me and I feel like I haven't done enough to earn that."

"That's fucked up, Seattle." Lou took both of Katie's hands and pulled them into her lap. "You don't have to earn shit. You deserve all the love and affection in the world, just for being the beautiful person you are. Inside and out."

"There's still a lot I have to work on."

"Can I ask you a harsh question?"

Katie nodded.

"Has everyone in your life demanded you change something about yourself as a condition of their love?"

"I never really thought about it like that before." Katie's parents had withheld their love in the hopes it would make her go back to pretending to be straight again. Jackie had only wanted to do things she was interested in, telling Katie if she actually loved her she would learn to love her hobbies, too. "I guess so. Except Megan."

"That's fucked up," Lou repeated. She sighed. "So, how much of what I've seen is the real Katie and how much was just who you think I want Katie to be?"

"All of it was the real me. Well, except the horse stalls this morning. I probably wouldn't choose to do that again, but I still enjoyed spending the time with you and doing it for the horses. And everything else has been incredible." Katie smiled ruefully. "I guess that's why I'm so comfortable here. You don't push me to be someone I'm not."

"And I never would. Real love doesn't do that."

Katie blinked back tears stirred by the words she hadn't known she'd needed to hear. It was hard for her to believe everything Lou was saying, even if logically it sounded true. She'd spent so many years trying to please people, always feeling like their love was being dangled just out of reach. And Lou was just offering it up.

"Why would someone as amazing and put-together as you want me, though? I'm a mess."

"A very cute mess," Lou corrected. "Who happens to be one of the smartest people I've ever met. You pick things up so quickly, and you're so open-minded to everything. Even when I can tell you're nervous, you dive right on in, so that means you're also brave. You're kind to my animals. You're independent enough to book a solo trip to a foreign country. Every time you walk into a room, my soul feels lighter, like a piece that was missing has finally been put back where it belongs."

Katie's heart raced. She had no idea Lou saw her that way, and even though Lou hadn't directly said the words yet, she felt every ounce of the outpouring of love Lou had just given her.

"Like I said, this scares the ever-loving shit out of me." There she was, doing her mind reading thing again. How did she always seem to know what Katie was thinking? "And it doesn't make a whole lotta sense. But it feels right." Lou laughed. "You know, I almost didn't offer you a ride. I thought you were another stuck up city girl and a night in the airport might humble you a little."

"What made you change your mind?"

"I guess I was delaying coming back here and spending the night drinking alone. And I didn't want someone else to come along and take advantage of you."

"I'm lucky you were at the airport when I needed you," Katie said. "You were coming back from L.A., right?"

"First time in years."

"I thought you hated it there."

"I needed to be there. Legal stuff." Lou closed her notebooks and started stacking them up. "But enough about that, we should get our belated Christmas feast going."

What legal stuff? It was clear Lou didn't want to talk about it, but Katie couldn't let it go. "Hold on. You can't just say that and not give me some kind of explanation."

"The man who killed Rachel had a parole hearing. It was granted." Lou stood. "Any other questions?"

"Are you okay?"

"I'm fine. It pisses me off, but what can you do?" Lou shrugged. "Is what it is."

"Do you want to talk about it?"

"Nope. That's what I pay my therapist for."

Jeez. Okay. Katie could take a hint. "So, I should just–"

"–chop this onion for the stuffing? Yeah."

"Did I do something wrong?"

"No. I'd just rather not think about it if you don't mind." Lou must have seen Katie's face fall. Her eyes softened. "I didn't mean to snap at you. I'm sorry."

"Apology accepted," Katie said, turning to the onion.

"I'm glad you're here. I'm glad I offered you that ride."

"So am I. Though I will say, Montana is seriously lacking in hot tubs and margaritas," Katie joked, lightening the mood.

"And beaches and warm weather."

"You make up for all of it." Mexico was the furthest thing from Katie's mind.

Chapter Sixteen

"It's about time you called me back." Megan sounded exasperated, and Katie could hear her rolling her eyes through the phone. "It's only been three days."

"I'm sorry, Megs. Time got away from me. Everything is just so perfect here. Seriously, I feel like I'm living in a dream. We went for a walk yesterday and it was the most romantic thing. She brought hot cocoa and we danced in the snow under the stars." Katie sighed happily. Every day with Lou was better and better.

"Where is she now?"

"Lou? She went into town."

"Without you?" Megan sounded offended on her behalf.

"I didn't want to go." Katie quickly filled Megan in on Lou's weekly tradition and the weird bar with its unwelcoming patrons. "So yeah, I'm happier just hanging out here."

"For how long?"

"A few hours. She just left."

"No, I meant how long are you planning to stay there?"

"Maybe forever."

"I knew this was going to happen."

"She's just so amazing. I've never met anyone like her before. And literally the best sex I've ever had in my life. Did I tell you she made me breakfast in bed?" Katie flopped down in the living room chair and tossed her legs over the armrest.

"You've told me tons about how great she is. I want to know her red flags."

"There literally are none."

"No red flags? Red flag." Megan sighed. "You're just love-blind. There has to be something."

"I'm serious, I can't think of any." Katie smiled. Lou was just perfect, and Megan was going to have to accept that. "She's so observant, she picks up on everything and knows what I need before I even do. And she treats me so well."

"Everyone has something. I get mad at Rob for stuff he does in my dreams. You pretend to be busy to hide that you're emotionally unavailable. So what's her deal?" Megan was not convinced. "A secret lover? Maybe she's broke. Hidden drug problem?"

Lou's words from a few nights before rang in Katie's ears. She had almost forgotten, but Megan's prying jarred her memory. "Well... she did say one thing. About spending time drinking alone. But, like, that's pretty normal. She's been through a lot of shit."

"Is she an alcoholic?"

"I don't think so."

"Does she drink every day?"

"Pretty much, but so do tons of people, and it's not drinking alone if she's doing it with me. I think you're just looking for something to be wrong with her. First it was 'she's a murderer,' now it's 'she's an addict.' Seriously?"

"I'm looking out for you," Megan insisted. "How much have you really thought this through?"

"A lot! Why can't you just be happy for me?"

"I am happy that you're getting a break you really needed, but I have to be honest, Katie. I don't think she's right for you and I don't think Montana is right for you. I'm just saying that because I care."

"You've never even been here."

"I know who they voted for in the last election. I can see what laws they're trying to pass. It's just not a place I can see you living long term."

Katie had avoided thinking about that as much as she could. She couldn't deny the reality of what Megan was saying. "Lou seems to think it's fine, and she's spent most of her life here. I trust her judgment."

"And what are you going to do about a job? Ask me how easy it is for women our age to get back in the workforce after taking time off. I've only been out ten months and I can't even get a call back for an interview."

"Can we just go back to talking about how happy I am here?" Finding another job was something else she didn't want to think about.

"And I want you to be happy, you know that. But none of this makes sense. Just slow down a little. Maybe try long distance for a while to see if you still feel this way when you have some separation. Get your job and apartment sorted out. You've been through a lot recently, no need to make any other huge changes."

"I'll think about it."

"That's all I'm asking."

Awkward silences were rare when Katie talked to Megan, but the pause felt a little too long as Katie scrambled to change to subject. "So how was Q's first Christmas? You didn't send me any pics."

"I honestly didn't think you cared. You've been so preoccupied."

"Of course I care!" Katie swallowed back the lump of guilt that rose in her throat. Maybe she had been a little distracted with everything she had going on, but she never meant to make Megan feel unimportant in her life. "Did he love it?"

"He had no idea what was going on. He enjoyed ripping up the paper though." Megan laughed, and Katie knew she was forgiven.

"As long as he had fun."

"Speaking of, he just woke up from his nap."

"Okay, well, text me later."

"I will."

The line went dead. Katie couldn't remember the last time Megan had ended a call without saying 'I love you.' It hurt more than the other harsh truths Megan had laid out for her. Megan was the only person in Katie's life who actually felt like family, and even though she was probably just in a rush because of the baby, the omission of those three little words reopened an old, aching wound.

Lou would still be gone a while, so Katie grabbed another book from the shelf and curled up to read. She was almost through the selection of romances, and if she was planning to stay longer she was going to have to figure out a way to replenish the stock.

If she was going to stay. When Lou had kissed her goodbye before walking out the door to go to her therapy session, Katie had been so certain in their forever. And then twenty minutes on the phone with Megan had cast doubt on everything.

Katie set the book down and ran her fingers through her hair, trying to sort out her thoughts. She loved Lou with her whole being, that wasn't in question. But on the flip side, there was no one she trusted more to have her best interest in mind than Megan. And, painful as it was to admit, she had raised some valid points.

Digital marketing was a competitive field, and if Katie wanted a future in it, she needed to get back to work. Even a few months off would put her behind the latest social and tech trends. The longer she was out, the harder it would be to get back in. Being a woman in her thirties didn't help, either. Everyone assumed she already had kids or they were in her near future, and even the most progressive employers saw people like her as too much of a risk, as if a measly twelve weeks of leave would propel their companies straight into financial ruin. And Katie didn't even want kids.

Remote jobs were even more competitive, and Katie wasn't even sure Lou's spotty internet and cell service on the homestead would even make that a possibility. And where would she even work in the small house? The kitchen table? That's not how she had imagined her life.

Her time on the farm had been relaxing so far, but Katie knew at some point boredom would set in. There was no coffee shop to walk to nearby for a latte and the pastry of the day. There was nothing to walk to nearby, except Jason's cows. Without a car, she would be stuck on the homestead 24/7. Was she really ready to commit to that life?

She wished she had more time, but the clock was ticking. She hadn't signed a lease renewal, so she had to move. But with no income, who would rent to her? Katie had to make a decision, and she had to make one quickly. Ugh. There was too much to think about. She felt like she still hadn't even had time to process losing her last job. She never got the closure she needed.

Either way, she needed to go back to Seattle at some point. Her stuff was there, and she was getting tired of wearing the same thing over and over. She genuinely didn't understand people who lived out of their suitcases while traveling for months on end. All she wanted was her favorite cardigan, her fuzzy slippers, and a steaming mug of Earl Grey. Or anything cozy and familiar, that felt like hers.

Katie tried to imagine her thrifted art hanging on the cabin's walls, or where she might tuck the funky lamp she'd adopted from the curb one Saturday after too many mimosas at brunch. It was hard to picture her things in a space that was so clearly designed to be Lou's alone.

She was so deep in thought she didn't even hear the truck pull up or the door swing open. Katie finally looked up when Lou kicked off her boots and padded across the room to greet Katie with a deep kiss. Wonderful, perfect Lou. The trappings of the cabin didn't matter when she was around, because being held by Lou felt like being home.

"How was therapy?" Katie asked when they broke apart.

"It was good. Exhausting, but really good." Lou walked towards the kitchen. "Can I get you anything while I'm in here? A drink?"

"Do you have any tea? I looked around but I couldn't find any."

"No, but we can get some next time we run to the store."

"I'll just have a glass of water."

Lou carried two cups back into the living room, one tall and filled to the brim with clear liquid, the other with just a splash of amber. Whiskey again. Lou set them both down on the coffee table and sat down next to Katie. "So, what did you get up to while I was gone?"

"Not much," Katie said casually. "Chatted with Megan and then read for a while." The white lie slipped out easily, but she wasn't ready to talk to Lou about the doubts flooding her until she had sorted out what to do on her own.

"Do you have plans tomorrow?"

"You're funny; you know I don't. What's up?"

"I have a surprise for you." Lou smiled slyly. "A belated Christmas present."

"I hate surprises," Katie laughed. In her experience, they were overhyped. She never managed to react with enough enthusiasm, or worse, they were just flat out bad.

"You hate Christmas, you hate surprises, anything else to put on that list?"

"I don't hate Christmas anymore, as long as it's here."

"But seriously, if surprises make you uncomfortable I'm happy to tell you now and if you hate the idea we'll forget I ever suggested it."

"No, I trust you." Katie reached for Lou's hand. Lou hadn't let her down yet, and she was more excited than nervous for whatever was in store. It could only be good.

"And what about today?"

"What about it?"

"Got plans?" Lou's crooked smile was so endearing that Katie tried to hide her wince when she lifted the glass of whiskey and drained it in one swig.

Not that she thought Lou had a problem with drinking. It was just something to keep an eye on. Plus, Megan wasn't there. She couldn't see things how they really were. "Just spending time with you."

"That's what I was hoping you'd say." Lou wrapped her arm around Katie's waist and pulled her closer. "We talked about you today."

"Oh really?" Katie relaxed into Lou.

"Don't worry, it was all good."

"So I'm therapist-approved?"

"Something like that." Lou played with Katie's hair, running her fingers through the strands and twirling the ends. "I haven't had feelings this intense in a long time. The whole time I was away from you, I couldn't stop worrying about you. I feel like half a person without you next to me, and I'm so fucking scared that if I let you out of my sight for one second, something terrible will happen. But I'm working on it."

"Are we moving too fast?"

"Might be, but I don't think we could stop it if we tried. Sometimes you just know. The way you fit into my arms is like you were meant to be there. When I come in from the cold, your smile warms me up faster than any fire. And when I look into your eyes, I see my future. I love you, Seattle."

Tears welled in Katie's eyes. It was all she'd wanted to hear, and she felt so stupid for having let Megan plant doubt in her brain. "I love you, too," she responded, her voice cracking as the tears broke free. Was love really enough?

Lou kissed her tears away. "I didn't mean to make you cry. Are they happy tears, at least?"

Katie nodded and blinked quickly before new tears could spill over in their place. Happy, and confused. Lou's mouth pressed against hers, the kiss as intense as the feelings Lou had talked about.

"I love you," Lou repeated when she pulled away to breathe. "Come on." She tugged Katie's hand and stood.

They went into the bedroom, leaving a trail of discarded clothing in their wake. Katie's mind was racing, but she tried to set all the pessimistic thoughts aside so the tender moment with Lou wouldn't be wasted. Who knew how many more of them she would get?

Lou kissed her again, her hands going to Katie's chest as they fell onto the bed together. Her expert thumbs teased soft circles around Katie's nipples, but the familiar jolt of sudden uninhibited need was missing. Katie covered Lou's hands with her own, stopping her.

"There's no need to rush," she whispered. "Just kiss me."

Lou moved her hands to Katie's back, pulling her close as they lay on their sides and kissed deeply. Katie tried to chase all the doubts away. Talking to Megan had been a bad idea, and she was getting in her own head. She just needed to relax.

Katie hitched her leg over Lou's hip as Lou's tongue pleaded with hers for more. She still tasted like bitter whiskey tinged with regret. Katie arched her back as she ground her pelvis into Lou, trying to generate some friction that would warm her up and ignite the desire she knew was hiding somewhere inside her. Lou's hand massaged her ass before sliding slower to tease her slit. Katie groaned in frustration. Why wasn't her body responding like it was supposed to?

"Should I grab the strap-on?" Lou asked, misreading her signals.

Katie sighed and shook her head. "I don't think it's going to happen for me right now."

"Is everything okay?" Lou pulled her hands away.

Katie unhitched her leg and rolled onto her back. "I'm sorry. Just a lot on my mind."

"Anything you want to talk about?"

"Not really." How was she supposed to tell Lou she was having doubts after Lou finally said 'I love you?' She couldn't, not until she figured out where her head was at. Not until she had more answers than questions.

Lou rested her head in her hand, propped up by her elbow. Her eyes were full of questions that she was too polite to ask, but Katie could see the hurt there, too.

"I'm excited about tomorrow," she said. She just wanted to see Lou smile at her again.

"Me too," Lou said, obliging with a brief smile that didn't reach her eyes. She sighed. "Did I do something wrong?"

"No," Katie said quickly. "Not at all. I swear."

"Would you tell me if I did?"

"I would." Probably. If it really bothered her enough. Katie didn't like confrontation and usually just tried to avoid things until she forgot about them.

"Promise?"

Katie nodded.

Lou was quiet for a long time as she studied Katie. A slight frown creased her forehead, and she reached forward to trace one finger across Katie's bare thigh. "I never noticed this before."

Most of the time, Katie forgot the scar was even there, it had happened so long ago. "Yeah, the doctor did a good job with the stitches. You can hardly tell, unless you really look at it."

"What happened?"

"I fell out of a tree when I was eight and nearly impaled myself on a broken branch on the way down. Thirteen stitches, and I broke my wrist when I landed." Katie flexed the joint absentmindedly. Fortunately, she'd been young enough that it healed perfectly and hadn't bothered her since.

"What were you doing in a tree?" Lou laughed.

"I was climbing it!" Katie said with fake indignation. "What, you didn't think I was the type?"

"Not really."

"Well, I used to be a lot more adventurous."

"What made you stop?"

Katie stared up at the ceiling, trying to remember. It hadn't been a conscious decision, just something that had faded out of her life over time. "I wanted to be like all the other girls so badly, so I did all the things that I thought would help me fit in. Hair, makeup, following all the latest trends, joining the pinkest sorority I could find."

"And did it work?"

"Not really, but it did help me figure out how much I love expressing my creative side with clothes and makeup, so I guess it worked out in the end. And eventually I realized I didn't actually want to be those other girls I thought were so perfect, I just had crushes on them and didn't know how to handle that." Katie hesitated.

"But?"

"Sometimes I miss that little kid who was brave enough to fall out of trees for a chance to see the top." Katie laughed again, but it was tinged with sadness. "I grew up and got scared of the world."

"Scared of what?"

"Falling. Failing. You only get one shot at life, I don't want to mess it up. Is it better to take big risks for big rewards, or play it safe and hope for satisfaction in the end? I don't know."

"I won't claim I know either, but I do know my biggest regrets are the things I didn't do, the opportunities I let pass me by. Not the ones I took a chance on, even when they didn't work out."

Katie reached for Lou, wanting to be held. "Sorry I'm such a downer today."

Lou pulled her close, her arms comforting and warm as they closed around Katie. "You're allowed to have feelings and down days, Seattle. It's not going to scare me off."

Katie knew that sooner or later she needed to come clean with Lou and admit her fears about the crossroads she faced, but cuddling with Lou felt so right that she didn't want to let the tender moment go. There would be time for harder conversations later.

Her face was buried in Lou's shoulder and she pressed her lips to the soft skin there, wanting to cover every inch of Lou's body in kisses until she was so familiar with every crease and curve that there would be no chance of forgetting them, or how it felt to be wrapped up in her arms. Lou sighed, but Katie couldn't tell if it was from contentment or if something heavier weighed on her mind, too.

Chapter Seventeen

"Are you going to be ready to go soon?" Lou asked, stacking their plates from lunch in the sink. She had been buzzing with excited energy all morning, and it was contagious.

"I might be if I knew what I needed to be ready," Katie replied, wiping the crumbs from the table. "You still haven't given me any clues."

"It's not really fancy– regular clothes are fine– but, you'll need a swimsuit." Lou smiled mischievously.

"A swimsuit?" *Please not a polar plunge.* It wouldn't surprise Katie in the least if that was Lou's idea of fun, but jumping into icy water was where she would have to draw the line.

"Just trust me." Lou gave her a peck on the cheek and shooed her out of the kitchen to pack.

Katie smiled as the familiar butterflies fluttered in her stomach. Lou was too adorable, and Katie was determined to have a perfect day out with her, wherever they were going.

She pawed through her suitcase before settling on two swimsuit options: a sturdy one-piece that would hold up to any more physical activities Lou might have in mind, and a skimpier bikini that fit her so perfectly it made her feel like the sexiest woman in the world. She tossed those in her travel tote, along with pajamas and toiletries, then checked her hair in the mirror as she slung the tote over her shoulder and rejoined Lou in the living room.

"Be good," Lou cooed to the dogs. "Jason'll be by later, and we'll see you tomorrow."

Both dogs hopped up onto the couch and settled down with matching sighs as if they understood every word Lou said. Lou offered Katie her arm, an exaggeratedly chivalrous gesture Katie was happy to accept as they walked out to the truck.

Even if all they did was drive around, Katie would have been happy to take in all the hidden sights of the frozen Paradise Valley with Lou's hand clamped firmly on her thigh. Uncertainty about the future still lingered at the fringe of Katie's mind, but Lou's grip slowly inching up her leg was enough to distract her momentarily.

She squealed softly when Lou found what she was searching for, wishing she had worn a skirt instead of the jeans that were turning out to be quite the hindrance. Then she remembered where they were.

"Shouldn't you be focused on driving?" She squeaked out, her voice rising as Lou applied the most exquisite pressure.

"I am focused on driving."

Katie peeked over at Lou, whose eyes glittered with laughter but were, indeed, firmly fixed on the road. She closed hers again, leaning back against the headrest and sinking deeper into Lou's touch.

"Besides, we're almost there." Lou said a few seconds later, pulling her hand away.

Katie sighed her disappointment before sitting up to look out the window. A weather-battered sign bearing the name Pray marked their turn. The road looked like it led nowhere, but before long a cluster of low buildings came into view. Lou turned into a parking space as Katie read the sign hanging from the largest of the buildings.

Welcome to Chico Hot Springs & Resort.

"Surprise," Lou said, studying Katie's face with a shy smile. "It's not a hot tub next to the beach in Mexico, but it's the closest thing we've got. And I'm sure the bar could whip up a margarita."

"Lou," Katie said. It was the only word she could choke out, so she reached for her face and kissed her in gratitude, hoping her lips alone could convey what her brain couldn't.

"Don't get too excited," Lou laughed, but Katie could tell she was pleased with herself. "It's nothing like the resorts I'm sure you're used to. But the pools are hot and the view's not terrible, either."

"Shh," Katie quieted her. "It's perfect."

They checked in and went upstairs. It felt like stepping back in time to an old western movie, the kind of place where stagecoach robbers would stopover while fleeing their crimes and sheriffs would confront them over their misdeeds. Lou unlocked the room, which was decorated in the same rustic theme as the hallway leading to it, and held the door open for Katie to enter first.

Katie dropped her bag by the entry and grabbed the sherpaed lapels of Lou's denim jacket, pulling her towards the massive, four poster bed in the center of the room.

"Now?" Lou asked. "I figured you might want to hit the pools first, get all relaxed."

"After the ride over here?"

"I don't know what you're talking about." Lou's grin was as devilish as the look in her eyes. "Maybe you'd better show me."

Katie tilted her chin down to kiss Lou deeply. Reaching for Lou's hand, she pulled it back in place against her crotch and held it there. "Remember now?"

"Hmm," Lou murmured into Katie's neck before nipping it softly. "I'm not sure that I do."

"Just take my clothes off," Katie demanded.

Lou squeezed Katie's breast through her shirt, sending a shiver down her spine. "But I like seeing you like this, all worked up."

Katie tried to pull Lou down onto the bed, but Lou was as solid as a brick wall and didn't budge, only increased the pressure of both her hands massaging Katie's body. "Please,"

Katie whimpered as warm desire built inside her with no outlet in sight.

"It's sexy when you beg," Lou said, moving her hands to the button on Katie's jeans. "Is this what you want?"

Katie nodded. "Please." It was all she could say.

Lou's fingers undid the button, torturously slow. She grasped the zipper between her thumb and forefinger, pausing before she finally slid it down. Katie's clit throbbed, aching for Lou's touch. She wiggled her hips as Lou pulled the pants down over them, then gasped as Lou grabbed her waist to steady her as she stepped free from her denim cage.

"Sit down," Lou commanded as she sank onto her knees between Katie's legs.

Katie perched herself on the edge of the bed and leaned back onto her elbows, gasping as Lou buried her face into Katie's mound of curls. She lay all the way down on the bed, fully aware that there were probably other guests on the other side of the thin wall but unable to stop her moan as Lou's tongue parted her slit and flitted across her clit. She reached for one of the pillows at the head of the bed and clamped it over her face as Lou's tongue dipped inside her to force another moan out.

Lou settled into a rhythm, plunging her tongue into Katie and then licking her length, flicking the tip against Katie's clit and swirling before diving back down to repeat the process. Katie's thighs, which were draped over Lou's shoulders, were twitching, and Lou reached up to hold them firmly in place against her. *Mine,* her touch seemed to say.

Katie was melting into the bed, becoming one big, damp puddle of overpowering sensation. She didn't recognize the pillow-muffled noises coming from her own mouth as Lou sucked her clit. The pressure from Lou's mouth grew as Katie edged closer to orgasm. When her teeth grazed ever so softly over her clit, Katie exploded.

Bursts of light clouded Katie's vision as her body spasmed. Lou held her in place until every drop of cum had been wrung from her, then slid out from beneath Katie's thighs. She pulled the pillow away from Katie's face and kissed her hard. Katie tasted herself on Lou's lips, salty, sweet, and tangy all at once, and felt another aftershock of delight rush over her.

"Now you," she said when her vision cleared.

Lou had already shimmied out of her pants– when did that happen?– and was rubbing herself with one hand. Katie pulled it away and replaced it with her own, feeling Lou's wetness flood over her. She pushed into Lou, feeling her soft inner walls convulse around her fingers as Lou inhaled sharply. Katie curled her fingers forward and rubbed broad circles with her thumb around Lou's clit.

"Katie," Lou was moaning within seconds. "Oh God, Katie."

"I love you," she said as Lou's thighs clenched her arm, locking Katie's hand in place as her pussy spasmed around her fingers.

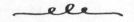

"Holy fucking shit," Lou said appreciatively as Katie came out of the bathroom. "You look like a goddess."

Katie's legs still felt like jelly, but she had managed to shower and change into her bikini to go down to the hot springs. "You like it?"

Lou handed Katie her jacket. "You better put this on or we aren't going to make it down to the pools."

"The sooner we go, the sooner we can come back up here." Katie laughed and threw the jacket over her shoulders. Her body had changed going into her thirties in ways she was still coming to terms with, but Lou made her feel like she had never looked sexier.

"Don't have to tell me twice," Lou said and grabbed her own jacket and two towels.

They went downstairs and through the lobby before entering an interior courtyard surrounding a large pool. Steam curled up from the surface of the water, teasing a tantalizing escape from the frigid air. Katie and Lou hurried across the brick patio and set their jackets and towels on a lounge chair, giggling like little kids as they rushed over to the water and stepped into the hot pool. The pool was less than waist deep, so Katie sunk down to submerge herself . Lou lowered herself into the water and pulled Katie into her arms, kissing her neck from behind.

"Warm enough?" Lou whispered into Katie's hair.

"It's perfect." Katie had never known she wanted to be soaking in a natural hot spring pool surrounded by snowy mountains before, but she suddenly couldn't imagine a more ideal date with the woman she loved. "And we have it almost all to ourselves."

"It's more popular in summer. More tourists," Lou explained. "But I think it's better in winter."

There were a few other people milling around the other end of the pool. Katie wondered which group they fell into, tourists or locals? She didn't recognize them from Jason's party, but that didn't mean they didn't live in the valley. And was it her imagination, or were they giving her and Lou strange looks?

She groped around under the water, pulling Lou's arm from around her waist as she remembered what Megan had said. What the men in the unnamed bar had said. She didn't belong there. If they had been in Seattle or D.C., she would never have given the public displays of affection a second thought. But Montana was different.

Lou gave her a confused look.

Katie dropped her voice to a whisper. "They're staring at us."

Lou looked even more confused. "No, they aren't."

Katie glanced over again. The group of people were laughing. "I feel like they are."

"Who cares? We aren't doing anything wrong." Lou reached out under the water and Katie took her hand hesitantly. "See? They aren't even paying attention to us."

Katie nodded and tried to relax. Lou had put together an amazing date for her, and she wanted to get out of her head and enjoy it. The water was just the right temperature to soak her stress away, was everything she'd wanted from her vacation. But it was really hard to tell if that guy was glaring at her or just squinting at the clock behind her.

"Can we go back upstairs?"

"If you want," Lou said, sounding mildly surprised. "We can come back down later, might be less people when it gets dark."

Katie nodded and stood up quickly, forgetting how cold the air was. Warm water streamed off her, leaving goosebumps in their wake. Multiple men in the group at the other end of the pool turned to stare at her, and she felt her cheeks flush hot as she rushed out of the pool and wrapped herself in a towel.

"They were definitely looking at me," she said when Lou joined her.

"Yeah, that time. Because you're sexy as hell and your nipples are hard as rocks under that bikini top. Anyone with a pulse would look."

"You think so?"

"Absolutely," Lou linked her arm through Katie's and led her to a door proclaiming itself to lead to the saloon. "Let's grab that margarita on the way up to calm your nerves."

"All we do is drink," Katie said, more sharply than she intended. Why did Megan have to be right about everything? "Can we maybe not for one night?"

"Of course," Lou said, hurt and confusion flickering across her face as she let go of Katie. "Are you okay?"

"Fine," Katie snapped. "Let's just go back to the room."

Lou let her lead the way up the stairs and unlocked the door for them in silence. Katie walked over to the bed and flopped down on it, burying her face in the pillow to hide the hot tears spilling from her eyes. She sobbed quietly as Lou settled onto the bed beside her, rubbing her back.

"Katie," Lou's voice overflowed with concern. "Please talk to me."

That was the problem, she couldn't. It was too hard, when she knew it meant risking everything. "I'm sorry," she blubbered. "I know you tried to make everything perfect and I ruined it."

"What are you talking about? You didn't ruin anything. I thought we were having a good time."

"We were and then I fucked it up," Katie bawled. The tears streamed harder, soaking the pillow against her face.

"You didn't," Lou insisted, sounding on the verge of tears herself. "Please, just tell me what's wrong and I'll fix it. You want me to stop drinking? Consider it done. I had no idea it bothered you."

"It's not that," Katie said, even though it was, partly. She took a deep breath and exhaled a great, shuddering sigh before rolling over to face Lou. There was no more kicking the can, and it was time to have an honest conversation with the woman who had her whole heart.

"Just tell me," Lou begged, wiping the remaining tears from Katie's face.

"I love you," Katie began. It was important to start with that part first. "More than I ever knew was possible. You've reintroduced me to the parts of myself that I thought were lost forever, and made me happier these past weeks than I ever thought I could be."

"Are you breaking up with me?" Lou's voice quivered slightly with the question.

"No!" Katie cut her off quickly. "But I have to go back to Seattle."

"Eventually. But what's the rush?"

"My lease will be up soon, and I have to move all my stuff. I can't really afford that place on my own."

"Okay, but then you'll come back here, right?"

Katie swallowed hard, trying to get rid of the lump in her throat, and shook her head. "I'm not ready. I need time, I can't just throw away everything I worked for. I don't know if I could ever get it back." She couldn't bear to look at Lou.

"I'm not moving to Seattle."

"I know, and I wasn't going to ask you too." Katie sniffled. "I thought we could do long distance for a while, see where we are in a year. That gives me time to figure out where my career is going and us time to figure out if this will actually work. I'll come visit every time there's a long weekend–"

"Where is this coming from?" Lou interrupted. "A few days ago we were planning summer here and now you're changing your mind?"

"I just need time. And we both have things to work on, like your drinking."

"Which we can do together. But do you really think I have a problem?"

Katie shrugged. "Maybe not a problem, yet. But it seems like you drink a lot to cope, and I don't know if I can be around that long-term. Which is why I think long distance would be good for us, for a little while."

Lou stood up and walked across the room to look out from the broad window overlooking the mountains. She crossed her arms and sighed. "I can't do long distance."

"All we can do is try," Katie said.

"No, we can't try." Lou spun around, anger creeping into her voice for the first time since Katie met her. "Don't you get it? I can barely make it three hours without a panic attack when you're out of my sight, and that was only because I had my therapist there to talk me through it. Long distance would break me. Every second of every day would be torture, wondering when the call will come that something terrible happened and I wasn't there to help." Tears were streaming down Lou's face, too.

"But I love you," Katie protested weakly. Wasn't true love supposed to conquer everything?

"Then stay."

"I'm scared I'll regret it if I do. I have to go back and find out."

"So all of this was a joke to you? Just a vacation fling?"

"No! You're the most incredible woman I've ever met, but I can't just move across the country for someone I've known less than two weeks. It doesn't make sense."

Lou crossed the room to hand Katie her phone from the nightstand. "Book your flight then."

"Lou..." Katie wanted to take it all back but it was too late. It was killing her to see Lou hurt, even as her own heart was shattering into a million pieces.

"Don't." The smile was completely gone from Lou's eyes, leaving only a cold, vacant stare. "Don't make it harder."

Chapter Eighteen

Katie's heart refused to let her believe it was over, carrying false hope even as her brain screamed at her to just accept it. Lou had packed up their damp swimsuits while she'd booked her flight between bouts of crying. They'd driven back to the homestead early so Katie could pack her bags. Lou had slept in the living room and made her coffee in the morning and then shuffled Katie out the door so fast she barely had time to process what was happening. Her face hurt from crying, but otherwise she was completely numb.

She glanced out the side mirror for one last glimpse of the cabin behind her. It was still hard to believe she was leaving some of the happiest moments of her life behind, but she had to hold onto hope that there were still plenty more ahead. Just with someone else. The tears she'd thought were all cried out rose up again to spill down her cheeks.

"Can we stop?" Katie choked out as they neared the barn at the front of the property. "I need to say goodbye to the animals."

Lou rolled her eyes as she pulled over next to the gate. "Five minutes. I want to leave plenty of time in case there's traffic on the highway."

Katie had probably seen a total of fifteen cars since she arrived in Montana, so she doubted Lou was worried about traffic on the way to the airport. It was obvious she just wanted to be rid of Katie.

Lou nodded towards the barn, indicating Katie should go in without her. Okay, then. Katie stepped down from the truck and walked up to the heavy barn door. She felt Lou's eyes on her, silently judging as she struggled to pull it open wide enough to slip in.

The barn was warm and its animal scent comforting as Katie entered. The horses whinnied softly to her, and she went to them first. She hugged one around his massive neck, and sobbed as he lowered his heavy head to rest on her shoulder, hugging her back.

"I'll miss you. I love you," she told him, scratching his neck before moving to the next horse.

She said her goodbyes to all the animals, then lingered for a moment, taking it all in one last time. Her hand rested on a leather saddle she would never get to use to learn how to ride. The men from the bar were right. She wasn't cut out for any of it. And she was running away from the greatest thing she'd ever had, because she was a coward.

Lou wouldn't meet her eyes as she made her walk of shame back to the truck, which was probably for the better. Katie was scared she would see hatred there. She climbed up onto the wide bench seat and stared out the window. They passed Jason's property, and Katie felt another pang of regret. She didn't dare ask Lou to stop again so she could say goodbye, and he probably didn't want to hear it if Lou had already told him what happened.

"Lou?" She didn't know what she wanted to ask, but it felt like there were things that still needed to be said. Or maybe she just wanted to hear Lou's voice without the harsh edge again. "I don't want you to hate me."

"I don't." Lou was clenching the wheel of the truck so tightly her knuckles were white and the back of her hands were red.

"We only have, like, forty minutes. I don't want them to be like this."

"What do you want me to say, Seattle? I'm hurt. I feel like you lied to me about what you were here for. And I still love you and have to put you on a plane, knowing I'm probably never going to see you again but I'll have to spend every day of the rest of my life thinking of you and hoping you're okay. Did you want me to be cheerful?"

Katie ached to reach out to her, to hold her hand and feel Lou's protective grip one last time. She couldn't help but feel like she was making the biggest mistake of her life, one that wasn't too late to undo. "Hurting you was the last thing I wanted to do."

"Yeah, well..."

"Just promise me you'll be alright when I leave?"

"Managed thirty-five years without you, so I reckon I will be." Lou stared stony-faced at the road ahead.

"Look how pretty the sky is today," Katie said desperately. Anything that might pull a hint of a smile from Lou to let her know she was forgiven.

"Really?" Lou sighed.

Okay, fine. Katie would shut up. It *was* a glorious sky though, a deep blue that looked too oversaturated to be real and morning sunlight bouncing golden rays off wispy clouds that stretched forever into the distance. And soon she would be on a plane, taking off into it, leaving her happiest moments behind for Seattle's gray gloom.

Weathered wooden barns stood eternal between vast pastures dotted with horses and cows, and the mountains circled the valley in their endless embrace. Paradise Valley could make someone think it was untouched by time. Yet, signs of modernity still poked through: a billboard for a dispensary in Bozeman here, new-build construction there. It seemed the deep, firm roots of tradition could do nothing to stop the branches from reaching towards change.

The buildings of the small town where the highway met the interstate were coming into view when Lou finally spoke again. "You know, I really thought you were different."

"In what way?" Katie asked cautiously, not sure if she really wanted to know. Her heart hurt enough already.

"I could actually see a future with you. And you let me believe you saw the same with me."

"I did," Katie said, but her mind flashed to the cramped kitchen table. "With you, but not relying on you for everything, which is what it would be if I stayed. If that makes any sense."

"I see."

It was clear Lou didn't want a response, which was good because Katie was in no position to give one. Her throat was raw with sorrow and her whole chest ached but she had to hold it together for a few more hours.

Lou sped past the car dealership, skipping the exit that would take them into downtown Bozeman. Katie had hoped she would drive through the charming little town all decked out for the holidays so she could take it in one last time, but Lou seemed hellbent on getting her to the airport even though there was still plenty of time before her flight.

"Alright, then," Lou said, pulling to a stop in front of the airport and turning her hazard lights on.

"Alright, then," Katie echoed, staring at Lou's lips and wishing she could kiss them one more time.

"Let me know when you get home safe." Lou hit the unlock button.

So that was it? She wasn't even going to get out of the truck to say goodbye?

Katie fumbled with the door handle. She was used to Lou opening it for her, and the numbness of grief was starting to make her lose all her senses. It was over. Sweet, chivalrous, considerate Lou was gone, replaced by a stone wall. Finally, the door swung open and Katie scrambled down. She was desperate to get away and seek out sanctuary in the airport bathrooms where she could break down in peace.

An hour and a half later, Bozeman was just a rapidly shrinking speck beneath the wings of the plane. Katie craned her neck as the plane circled around after its ascent, hoping to catch one final view of the little homestead, but all the valleys looked the same from the air. She wondered if Lou was somewhere down below, stretching for one last glimpse of Katie, too.

Chapter Nineteen

"**I**'m miserable," Katie moaned, staring up at the ceiling. "I hate it here."

"You've only been back, what, two weeks? It'll get better once you find a job you love and start being social again." Megan coughed. "What are you doing?"

"Laying on the floor second-guessing every decision I've made in my life. You?"

"Smoking a bowl on the back patio. Rob's at the office and he dropped Q off to spend the day with his parents, so I finally get some me-time. But anyways, I'm sorry you're going through all this. Again."

"I thought I'd at least still have her as a friend. I didn't think she'd ghost me completely."

"That just goes to show you're better off without her."

"Why did I have to fall in love with her?"

"Because you're vulnerable and were hurting and she let you imagine a world without all that. Which is good. Now you know what it feels like to have someone treat you right.

Maybe that's why all this happened, so when you find your real soulmate you'll know."

"What if she was my real soulmate and I just let it all go?"

"If she was, her lifestyle would have been compatible with yours. Her goals would have been more aligned. But look, you need to stop dwelling on this for today, at least. Go do something fun. You remember how to do that, right?"

"And what if I can't find a job?" Katie continued, ignoring everything Megan said. "I've been spamming resumés and haven't gotten a single call."

"It's going to happen, just stay positive."

"But what if it doesn't happen in time? I don't have anywhere to go."

"You can always come back to D.C. Stay with us until you find a job and a place here. But seriously, you need to stop thinking about all this for a few hours and do something for yourself. Go buy some books."

"Ugh, I can't go outside, I haven't showered in, like, three days."

"Then go take one, grab your favorite novel and a glass of wine, and distract yourself for a while."

"Okay, fine. For you." Megan would never know the difference, anyways.

"I love you and I'm proud of you. You got this, and you'll come out of it better than ever."

"Thanks, Megan. Love you, too."

As soon as she ended the call, her phone buzzed again with a text message.

"I better see a selfie of you with wet hair in thirty minutes."

Katie smiled ruefully. Megan knew her too well. She groaned and went into the bathroom, avoiding looking at herself in the mirror. She didn't want to see the greasy strands of hair she'd pulled back into a sloppy bun or the dark circles that she could almost feel weighing down her face. Yeah, it was definitely time for a shower.

Actually going into the bathroom to get undressed and turn the water on was the hardest part, but as soon as she'd accomplished that, she began to relax. She wasn't going to follow the rest of Megan's advice, though. Reading romance would only make her think of Lou and everything she'd lost. She would find some other way to spend her afternoon, probably by expanding her job search radius and applying to anything new that popped up.

The warm water felt good washing the stench of wallowing from her skin, and she scrubbed harder with a loofah that probably should have been replaced six months earlier. The pale glint of the faint scar running from her thigh to her hip caught her eye and, even though the water was hot, Katie shivered remembering Lou's calloused fingers tracing it ever so gently.

Maybe she should go climb a tree. Free her inner child and all that. One thing Seattle did have was plenty of trees.

Katie snorted. She doubted her upper body strength was up to the task anymore. But maybe the whole inner child thing wasn't the worst idea. Lou was right; she'd suppressed too many parts of herself to please other people for too long. It was distressingly hard for Katie to remember what used to make her happy back when all of her time was her own.

She wrapped a towel around herself and another around her hair, then sent a picture off to Megan. Going out somewhere still didn't sound appealing, so she boiled a kettle of water for tea and got dressed in clean pajamas while it steeped. She pulled an oversized t-shirt on, soft with age and paint-splattered from her and Megan's failed college furniture flipping attempt. She smiled at the memory, then had an idea.

The dusty box was sitting on the shelf in the closet, still unpacked from the last time she'd moved. They had to be in there, unless she'd gotten rid of them. But she wouldn't have done that. She finally found the old leather case she was looking for buried underneath a stack of her old college papers and pulled it out.

The zipper still stuck in the corner, just like it always had, and then her old tubes of paint spilled out onto her desk. She slid the postcard-sized pad free from its elastic strap and flipped past watercolor landscapes of her old college campus and the cherry blossoms in East Potomac Park before finding a blank page near the back of the book.

She wasn't even sure if she could remember how to paint, and the colors were probably too old and desiccated to use anymore, but she went to the sink and filled an empty soup can with water. At least the lighting at her desk was good.

It was one of those rare January days in Seattle that promised spring would eventually return, and even though clouds still hovered low in the sky, soft rays of sunlight pushed through them to illuminate her desk. She picked up the paintbrush, running her thumb across the stiff bristles. It was hard to believe she hadn't even touched them since she moved to Seattle. Ancient flecks of paint lofted through the air and settled on the desk. She had loved painting once, but somewhere along the way, she'd been convinced it wasn't a practical use of her time.

She squeezed a dab of paint onto a brittle, plastic palette and dripped some water onto it until the pigment started to run. The view from the window was rather uninspiring– mostly just a brick wall from the building facing hers with a small sliver of Puget Sound if she craned her neck– but at least it would be easy to paint. The brush felt unfamiliar in her hand as she dipped it in the muted gray pigment to block in the base of the clouds. She held it over the paper.

"Fuck." Where should she even start?

The oversaturated brush made the decision for her, dripping heavily onto the page and spreading in an uneven flood of gray across the page.

"Fuck," she repeated. It was a rookie mistake.

Katie squinted at the page. The blob almost looked like the towering mountain behind Lou's cabin. She put the brush to paper again, manipulating the paint with clear intention as the outline of the peak began to take shape.

Okay. That was something she could work with.

She exhaled a long breath she'd been holding and began to paint faster, her old artist's instincts taking over. A dab of blue and the big Montana sky began to fill in the upper half of the page. She saved the cabin for last, each stroke a memory with Lou she needed to honor before she could let them go.

Her phone vibrated, breaking her from the trance.

Unknown number.

She thought about letting it go to voicemail, but her flow was already interrupted and it was probably important. She set the brush in the can of water and swiped to answer.

"Kathleen Miller?"

"This is she."

"Hi, this is Jennifer calling from PNW Bancorp. I got your application materials for our Director of B2B Marketing and was wondering if you had any time this week to come in for an interview?"

"Oh, yes, let me check," Katie said, pretending to fumble with her planner. "It looks like I have time on Wednesday morning between nine and eleven or Thursday after two." Hopefully that struck the right balance between flexibility and boundaries.

"Ten-thirty on Wednesday?"

"Sounds great!" She forced herself to sound chipper.

"Perfect, we'll see you then. Come right on up to the seventh floor and let Lucy know you're here for an interview."

"Awesome, see you Wednesday."

She set her phone down and reached for the brush again, but her will to paint had vanished, stifled by the demands of the real world. The damp spots on the page lightened as they dried, hardening her mistakes into permanence. There was nothing more she could add to the little homestead that was so far away. Her heart ached for Lou to offer a crooked smile and tell her things were going to be alright, but she would never hear her gravelly drawl again.

Katie slammed the watercolor pad shut.

It hurt too much to look at, each detail scraping her throat raw and burning across her chest until she felt like she couldn't breathe. She knew Megan was right and everything would get better with time, but that didn't ease the pain of the present. There was no way around it, and she would just have to find a way to get through.

The apartment buzzer sounded out of nowhere, making her jump. They probably just keyed in the wrong apartment number. She definitely wasn't expecting anyone, so she ignored it. It buzzed again. She forced herself to stand and trudged over to the intercom.

"Hello?"

"Yeah, this is your delivery driver, I have your food."

"I didn't order anything, you must have the wrong apartment."

"Katie Miller? Apartment 405?"

"That's me, but I didn't–"

"Well, someone did. I'm just going to leave it here if you don't buzz me in."

"Okay, come on up, I guess."

Hope flared in Katie's chest and her heart started pounding. It was exactly the kind of sweet gesture Lou would do. She started to wonder if maybe she was forgiven. But she couldn't remember giving Lou her address, though it probably wouldn't be that hard to track down. Her friend at the airport could have looked up Katie's reservation or something.

The driver knocked at her door and her heart sank as soon as she saw the bag he was holding. She took it and thanked him sadly, knowing it wasn't Lou who had sent it. Her stomach growled as she sat down at the breakfast bar, and she unpacked the contents. Her favorite order from her favorite dim sum place. The same place she had taken Megan the last time she visited Katie in Seattle.

What would she do without Megan? Katie smiled and grabbed her phone to text a thank you. She dug into the feast while she researched the company that had called for an interview. It was some fintech startup she barely remembered applying to, and she would probably be overworked and underpaid. But it was the only bite she'd gotten, and it wasn't like she was in a position to be picky.

She knew she shouldn't, but she opened her last text to Lou. There was still no indication it had been seen. Maybe she just hadn't noticed. Lou was busy and didn't have her phone with her all the time. She might have missed the messages. Or maybe service was down again and they hadn't gone through at all.

Her fingertips hovered over the keyboard as she thought about everything she wanted to say. How she wondered if a new blanket of snow had fallen over the homestead or whether the tiny seeds in rows of trays had sprouted under their lights yet? If the horses were getting enough sugar cubes and the dogs enough treats? And most importantly, if Lou was thinking about her and missing her so desperately, too?

Katie turned her phone off. She wouldn't find closure if she kept trying to reopen the door. As much as it hurt, she needed to leave things be, for both of their sakes.

Chapter Twenty

Katie sat in a hard plastic chair, going over her professional achievements in her head as she practiced what she
would say in the interview. Her first impression of the place
wasn't great, and she had to keep reminding herself of all the
positives. It was within walking distance of lots of good apartments, and the salary range listed for the position was enough
to afford one of those apartments. But it was already giving her
a headache. The lights were unnaturally bright and the whole
place smelled like someone had gotten too overzealous with
citrus-scented cleaner.

I'm not meant to live like this.

"Kathleen? Brad is ready for you now."

His name was Brad? Katie hated him already.

Suck it up, you need this job.

She followed the receptionist through a maze of cubicles and
into an empty conference room. Chic bottles of trendy water
were clustered in the center of the long glass table, flanked by
baskets of protein bars and plastic-looking fruit. Fluorescent

lights hummed overhead, nearly drowned out by a burst of heavy rain beating against the tall windows.

Apparently Brad wasn't ready. Katie sat in one of the tall chairs facing the windows, idly wondering how much they paid to rent the downtown office space. Whatever it was, it probably wasn't worth it. No view could possibly compare to the one from Lou's bedroom window, even one that included the Space Needle.

Making her wait was exactly the dickish kind of power move Katie expected from a boss named Brad, and when the man finally deigned to show up for his own appointment, he was everything she expected him to be. Exactly like her last boss.

"So, Kathleen," he said, crushing her hand in his grip, "I thought I'd tell you a little about the company and then we can get the interview started. Sound good?"

"Great." She smiled placidly and sat up a little straighter in her chair, trying to judge how formal the interview would be and when she could tell him she'd rather go by Katie.

"I've been at PNW Bancorp for just over three months now and it's a really dynamic start up experiencing fast growth in the finance sector. We have a few proprietary apps that we're just getting ready to launch, so I need to bring on a rockstar team player that is really ready to get out there and disrupt things."

Katie was already starting to zone out. Guys like that just loved to hear themselves talk without ever saying anything of substance.

"But enough about PNWB, let's talk about you. Tell me a bit about yourself, why you want to work here?"

"Well..." Katie trailed off. She hated the stupid song and dance of interviews. It was all so fake. "I'm really passionate about marketing and have a lot of experience in the direct to consumer space, including skills that transfer to business to business. I've always been competitive and I love channeling that into marketing to hit new goals and..." She was getting flustered. Brad didn't even seem like he was listening to her as he checked his smart watch. "I'm sorry, what was the second part of the question again?" She was bombing it.

"Why do you want to work for PNW Bancorp?"

"I..." Katie froze. Every over-practiced sentence about looking for a fast-paced environment where she could leverage her skillset vanished from her mind. When she looked at her resume sitting on the conference table in front of her, all she could see was Lou's binders full of future plans and the promise of an August tomato fresh from the vine. Those were the things that felt important to work towards, not promoting some app that solved problems people never had to begin with. "I don't."

"Excuse me?" Brad finally looked at her.

"I don't want to work here. I'm sorry for wasting your time."

He looked taken aback by her honesty. "Then I guess we're done here."

"I guess we are."

He led her back through the office and waited until the elevator came to scoop her up and spit her back out of the building she was suddenly certain she would never belong in. Good riddance.

Two seconds later, the realization of what she had done hit her like a Montana blizzard. How could she have been so stupid? Over a hundred applications and one call back for an interview, and she had wasted it because her mind had wandered into a daydream for two seconds. Squandered her only shot at the title she'd been working for because some guy gave her douchey vibes.

But she would have hated it there.

A group of tourists was laughing about the rain and taking pictures of themselves with their new umbrellas at the bus stop. Katie pulled her hood up and walked past them towards the second stop half a block away, with the bus that would take her north.

If she had already made one massively idiotic decision that morning, another couldn't hurt.

Three hours later, the salesman slid the keys and the paperwork across his desk. "Well, she's all yours."

"But I still need, like, insurance and stuff, right?" Katie asked. Megan was going to flip out when she found out, which was why Katie was waiting to tell her until it was too late to undo.

"Legally, yes. But you can just give any of the companies a call and they'll get you all set up before you drive off the lot."

"Like right now?"

"Yeah, they do this all the time for people."

"And you're sure I got a good one for driving in the mountains and snow?"

"In your price range, you won't find anything more reliable with all-wheel drive. She'll treat you right."

The gravity of what she had done set in when she walked outside and saw most of her savings account sitting in the parking lot in front of her.

She clicked the key fob. The lights of the dark green SUV flashed, and she hopped into the driver's seat. For being almost twenty years old, it was in gorgeous condition. There were no extra frills, but it stopped and started and did all the things it was supposed to during the test drive. Single owner, 180,000 miles. But what finally sold Katie was when the salesman revealed it had been traded in by an older lesbian couple who had just bought the brand new version of the same car. It felt like it was meant to be.

"Oh my God, I've been waiting for you to call all afternoon! How was the interview?" Megan squealed into the phone.

"I don't think I got the job."

"Aww, I'm sure it went better than you think."

"I actually told them I didn't want the job." Katie winced, waiting for Megan's disappointment.

Silence.

"You there?"

"Yeah, I'm sorry, I'm just stunned. You did what?"

"It was awful. I couldn't see myself lasting a year there. Not even a month. The guy had his head so far up his own ass, and everything was so sterile and–"

"Yeah, sounds like an office. So, what are you going to do now? Don't you have to be out of your place in like a week?"

"You can't get mad."

"You are not!" Megan had already figured out what she was going to say.

"I am. I bought a car today, and once they do the final walkthrough next week, I'm going back to Montana."

"Have you talked to her about this?"

"No." Even if she tried to call, Lou probably wouldn't pick up.

"Don't you think you should?"

"She won't believe I'm serious unless I do it in person."

"Are you one hundred percent sure about this?"

"I'm like eighty-five percent sure. But I'd rather regret going than wonder about what-ifs forever. I have to try."

"Okay." Megan didn't sound as disappointed as Katie thought she would.

"Okay?"

"Is anything I say going to stop you?"

"No."

"Then, okay." Megan's flat tone hid whatever she was really feeling.

"Well, I guess I better go pack."

"Yeah, I guess you should."

They said their goodbyes, and Katie ended the call. She almost wished Megan had gotten mad, at least that would have made sense. She didn't expect gushing support, but the nothing she got was worse than any response she could have anticipated. It felt like Megan had stopped caring.

It didn't matter in the long run. Katie was used to disappointing people, and she was fairly certain Megan would come around when she saw how happy Katie would be after the move. She always did. All that mattered was getting back to Lou.

Chapter Twenty-One

The last box sat lonely by the apartment door. All Katie needed to do was carry it down and squeeze it somewhere in the back of her car. The property manager would be by any minute to inspect the unit and collect her keys. She hoped he hurried. She really wanted to be out of town before afternoon rush hour hit.

It was weird to be leaving the apartment she'd called home for so long. She would be lying to herself if she said she wouldn't miss it. There was a lot to love about the old building, like the high ceilings and broad bay windows, and there was a lot she was glad to be leaving behind. For every good memory with Jackie, there was a bad one of growing apart and breaking up. Katie was more than ready for a fresh start.

The buzzer wailed and she hit the button to let the property manager in before she realized that he should probably have a key. Whatever, maybe he lost it or locked himself out on a break. A few minutes later, she heard him knock at the door. She took a deep breath, preparing herself to walk through one last time, then opened the door.

Holy shit.

"Megan? What are you doing here?" She squealed, jumping into her best friend's arms.

"Obviously I had to come. You've lost your fucking mind."

"Well, you wasted the plane ticket. I'm leaving in an hour if this guy ever shows up."

"I didn't waste anything. My return flight leaves from Bozeman."

"What are you talking about?"

"You're in *crisis*, Katie. You think I was going to let you drive seven hundred miles alone? Besides, if you're really going to do this, I have to at least meet her."

"You're an absolute lunatic, you know that, right?"

"But you love me."

"Of course I do." Katie hugged Megan again. "I can't believe you're here. Wait, who's watching Quentin?"

"Rob and his parents. I have three and half days to sort your life out before I have to be back." Megan pushed past Katie into the empty apartment. "So what did you do with all your shit?"

"Sold most of it, set some out on the curb for people to take, and shoved the rest in my car." Her car. It was still strange to think about. "I hope you didn't pack much. We might need to rearrange some things for you to fit."

"We'll make it work." Megan sashayed around the apartment, looking in cabinets and behind doors.

"I already got everything," Katie laughed. Megan really was meant to be a mom, but Katie didn't mind when some of that maternal instinct seeped over to her.

The property manager showed up just as Megan was wrapping up her final sweep, and fifteen minutes later Katie handed over the keys.

"Coffee before we hit the road?"

"Please. I had to get up at four to make my flight."

Seattle was alive with workers streaming in and out of restaurants on their lunch breaks and tourists taking up space in the middle of the sidewalk to argue about whether Pike Place was within walking distance. They ambled comfortably to Katie's regular coffee shop just up the block by the bus stop. Even though Katie was impatient to get on the road, it was still hard to say goodbye to the first place she could really call home on her own.

"Aren't you going to miss all this?" Megan asked.

"Yes and no. I feel like I got what I came here for, and I'm satisfied with it. I'm ready to move on."

Two large lavender lattes later, the city was thirty miles behind them. They had managed to miss most of the afternoon rush hour, and Katie was more relaxed behind the wheel once the traffic dissipated.

"What's the weather supposed to be like?" Megan asked between mouthfuls of gummy bears, her feet up on the dash.

"I didn't really check." It was raining steadily, but as long as she paid attention she was pretty sure she could handle it.

"You didn't check?"

Katie shrugged. "It wouldn't change anything, I had to be out of the apartment today either way. Why add something to worry about?"

"Oh, I don't know, maybe because we're about to drive into some huge fucking mountains in the middle of winter?"

"Look, I didn't tell you to come."

"This is exactly *why* I came."

"Everything is going to be fine." It had to be. It was what the universe wanted. Right?

"Okay, but this is why I worry you haven't really thought this through. What if we get there and she tells you to get lost again?"

"Then I'll keep driving until I get to DC and live as a creepy hermit in your basement forever."

"So you don't have a plan."

"I don't need one. I can do literally anything I want, go anywhere I want. There's nothing tying me down." And it was liberating.

"I thought we agreed we were moving to Greece to live on a yacht for six months for our midlife crises when we turn forty?"

"Who says I can't have more than one?" Katie flipped the windshield wipers to a higher level. Thick, wet flakes of snow were starting to appear between the raindrops as they climbed in elevation, but the road was still clear.

"Are you sure this is safe?"

"It's barely even snowing."

"No, I meant moving to Montana. I know you love her, but—"

"You said you weren't here to talk me out of it. But I looked into it, and Montana is changing. Bozeman has a Pride parade, so that's something at least." Katie reached for the gummy bears, thinking about how she could explain to Megan in a way she could understand while she chewed. "Hate is everywhere. But so is queer love. So is queer joy. Everything I feel with Lou. If I let the possibility of hate scare me away from that love, they win."

"I really want this to work out for you. Honestly."

"So you're finally convinced she's not a serial killer?" Katie teased.

"Withholding judgment until I meet her. But if she is, she's really bad at it. She let you get away."

"You know, statistically I was way more likely to be serially killed in Seattle. Seems like all the famous ones are from there."

They lapsed into talking about Megan's favorite topic for a while, with Megan animatedly bringing Katie up to speed on all her true crime podcasts. By the time they reached the top of the first mountain pass, all traces of rain were lost to the thick fluffy snow falling around them.

Katie didn't start to get worried until they pulled over at the summit rest stop to go to the bathroom and stretch their legs. It was starting to get dark, and they were behind schedule. She checked the GPS anxiously. She had a motel reserved in Spokane, but that was at least another three hours away.

Then six more after that, and she would finally be back with Lou. The thought motivated her to keep going, even though she had underestimated how tiring the drive would be. Megan was taking selfies in the snow, and Katie called her back to the car.

"Do you care if I nap 'til we stop for dinner?" Megan asked, yawning. "Jet lag is catching up to me."

"No, go ahead."

A few minutes later, Megan was out. The snow fell harder as Katie began the long descent down the mountain pass until she could only see a few feet in front of her. It reminded her of being lost on the homestead in the blizzard, except this time Lou wasn't there to save her if anything went wrong.

Katie just wanted to get there. Her foot pressed into the accelerator a little more as she thought of the crinkle at the corner of Lou's eyes when she smiled, then more still with the deep longing to feel Lou's protective, possessive hand on her thigh again. Katie couldn't wait to see her again.

She had no idea what she was going to say to win her back. Lou was so much better at that sort of romantic stuff. She always had just the right words, and they flowed from her so easily, smooth and sweet like the honey she collected from her bees. Katie wondered if she should get Lou flowers before they got to Bozeman.

Or a ring? Should she propose to show she was really serious?

Katie didn't need Megan to tell her that was ridiculous, but her stomach fluttered excitedly at the thought. Some day. If

Lou was even open to the idea of remarrying. Either way, Katie could imagine forever with her all too easily, whatever that looked like. But they would have plenty of time to talk about all of that, if Katie ever made it to Montana.

She glanced down at the speedometer and gasped when she saw she was going almost twenty miles over the speed limit in the blinding snow. Megan jerked awake just as Katie slammed on the brakes. Time screeched to a stop but the car kept moving, hurtling across the glassy lanes. Katie glanced at Megan, looking back at her in pale-faced terror.

Katie pressed the brake pedal until she thought it was going to snap off under her foot, but it was useless. The car drifted towards the guardrail. Through the snow, she could just make out the silhouettes of mountains around them, and realized that beyond the guardrail, there was nothing. Just a sheer cliff into the bottomless valley below. The barrier loomed closer. It didn't look like it could stop a ton of metal from going over the edge, but it was the only hope they had. She was so close to finally having the life she wanted, she couldn't lose it now. And Megan. Quentin couldn't grow up without a mother.

Katie tried to steer the car away from the shoulder, but the tires weren't responding. Megan was screaming beside her, but if they were words, Katie couldn't make them out. She squeezed her eyes shut and braced for impact.

She heard a faint grinding noise as the car skidded across loose gravel, and then, miraculously, slid to a stop. Opening her eyes, she saw the nose of the vehicle pointed directly at the guardrail, inches away from hitting it. Katie let go of the steering wheel and put it in park, before lowering her shaking hands into her lap.

"What the fuck just happened?" Megan asked, breaking their stunned silence.

"I'm so sorry. I got distracted, I didn't realize how fast I was going and then when I tried to brake the car started sliding and I'm so sorry."

"This is why you should have checked the weather." Megan was pissed.

"The guy said I would be fine with all-wheel drive."

"All-wheel drive, Katie. Not all-wheel stop. It doesn't do shit if you don't have traction and start sliding."

"I'm sorry. I'll be more careful."

"Well— because we didn't die— I forgive you. But she better be fucking amazing to be worth this shit." Megan sighed. "Trade me spots, I'm driving the rest of the way to Spokane. And we are never, ever telling Rob about this."

Chapter Twenty-Two

The five-thirty alarm came way too early after a late night getting into Spokane, ordering dinner to the motel, and watching trashy reality television until they both fell asleep, but Katie had no problem waking up when it sounded. Assuming everything went according to plan, she would be seeing Lou in a few short hours.

She rolled over and tossed a pillow at Megan, so fast asleep in the other queen bed that she hadn't even flinched at Katie's screeching phone, then opened the app to check the weather. Bitter cold and blessed sun were all they faced on the last four hundred miles to Bozeman.

Katie threw another pillow at Megan. "Wake up, sleepyhead. We have to get going."

Megan groaned. "Are we on a schedule?"

"Actually, yes. I was hoping to get there by noon."

"Fine." Megan sat up and rubbed her eyes. "But you owe me a coffee. A real one, not hotel lobby coffee."

"Obviously. Now hurry up."

"Did you–"

"Check the weather?" Katie asked, heading into the bathroom to start getting ready. "Of course. What kind of idiot doesn't check the weather before driving across two states in the middle of winter?"

"A lovestruck one."

"No, but I did. Everything looks clear from here out."

"Good, now get out of there so I can pee."

Katie vacated the bathroom, finishing her morning skincare quickly at the desk instead. She got dressed and packed up her things, then flipped on the TV and scrolled through the early morning infomercials while she waited.

Lou was probably waking up, too, if she hadn't already. The little cabin would be starting to smell like grocery store coffee dripping through the paper filter to fill up the pot while Lou attended to the morning chores. She would be letting the dogs out to run behind the truck down to the red barn, climbing into the loft to throw down heavy bales of hay to distribute to the animals, collecting the hen's rich eggs, all with no idea that Katie was finally on her way.

Megan finally emerged from the bathroom, only ten minutes behind schedule. That was fine. They still had plenty of time.

"So, what's the address?" Megan asked, GPS app open on her phone as she climbed into the passenger seat.

"I don't actually know the address, but I'll know it when I see it. Just put in Bozeman for now."

"And you don't think you should call her? Maybe give her a heads up before you just turn up on her doorstep?"

"Definitely not. She would worry too much." Katie wasn't planning on telling her about their near-miss the night before, either.

"Have I told you you're insane yet today?"

"That's the first one, but I expect at least thirteen more before we get there."

They stopped at a coffee stand right next the the interstate onramp, and crossed into Idaho a few minutes later. Megan promptly fell back asleep, her half-consumed latte having no apparent effect. With no one to talk to, Katie's mind immediately drifted back to imagining the conversation she was going to have when she finally saw Lou, this time keeping a close eye on the speedometer.

Her wildest dreams told her Lou was going to sweep her into her arms without hesitation, taking her back and proclaiming her everlasting love, but Katie was more of a realist than that. She needed to be prepared for Lou's wall to be up, for her skepticism to be fully armed. Katie was ready to do whatever it would take to show Lou she was serious.

Idaho passed in the blink of an eye, and Katie found herself tearing up as the interstate sign welcomed her to Montana. It no longer bothered her that people might see her as an outsider when every fiber of her being was telling her she belonged there. Her place in Montana's arms, cradled by the mountains and nurtured by the streams, was deserved. She was home.

She rolled down the window to breathe in the crisp air, laughing at the chill. Megan woke up as cold flooded into the car, scowling at Katie.

"Are you insane?"

"That's two," Katie laughed. "Welcome to Montana."

"Pretty," Megan said, looking at the window as she sipped her cold coffee. "I can see why you'd want to look at this all the time. But can you please roll the window up? It's freezing."

Katie was happy to oblige. She grinned when she saw the first sign announcing the mileage left to Bozeman. It was starting to feel real. Her whole life was packed in the car behind her, waiting for its new beginning.

She didn't start to feel anxious until noon came and went and Bozeman was still miles away. Her window to talk to Lou was narrowing, and she had no idea if she would ever be able to find the homestead tucked off one of the side roads in Paradise Valley if she missed her on her weekly trip into town.

Finally, the Bozeman airport came into view at the very edge of town. Katie got off at the exit she remembered downtown, and turned down the main street, trying to remember exactly where the nameless bar was located.

"I think it's this one," she mused aloud as she turned down a side street, and then into an alley that ran parallel to the main one. But there was no asphalt parking lot or tattered awning anywhere along the houses.

She checked the time. 12:30. She had to find it.

"What are we looking for?" Megan asked, squirming. She'd been asking for a rest stop for the past twenty minutes, but Katie begged her to wait until they got there.

"It's a bar, but it doesn't look like one. Basically just the backside of a brick building with trucks parked outside." Katie circled back down the main street, turning at the sushi restaurant. "I know it's here somewhere."

"That?" Megan pointed to the end of the block and Katie saw it.

Lou's truck, parked two spots down from the bar's door.

"Holy shit, yes."

"Nervous?"

"Extremely."

"What are you going to say?"

"I still haven't figured it out." When Katie saw Lou, she would just have to let her heart do the speaking for her. She parked the SUV beside the truck, feeling like she was about to vomit.

"Do you want me to go in with you?"

"No, I should talk to her alone."

"Okay, good luck. I'm going to find somewhere to pee. Text me when you're ready." Megan hopped out of the car and waddled quickly down the alley, back towards the shops on the main street.

Katie pulled the visor down and checked to make sure she looked okay. Not ideal, but Lou had seen her much worse. She took a deep breath.

Now or never.

Nothing could have prepared her for what she saw entering the little bar. Out of all the scenarios she'd run through in her mind, she had somehow overlooked the idea that Lou might have moved on. The bells on the door jingled as it swung shut behind her. Maybe she should just leave again unnoticed. But then she would have to admit to Megan that she'd been wrong.

Lou was at her usual booth, laughing and leaning to look at something on the other woman's phone. Her usual chicken fried steak was on the plate in front of her, but her glass looked like it was filled with water instead of the beer Katie expected. She spoke animatedly, so engrossed in the conversation that she hadn't even looked up when Katie walked in. She looked happy, her skin glowing under the dim, stained glass bar lights and her eyes sparkling with life. Katie was frozen in place, unable to flee but equally unable to walk the ten steps over to Lou's booth say something. How could she interrupt? Should she even interrupt?

"Just take a seat wherever, hun," Claire called from behind the bar, not recognizing Katie. "I'll be right with you."

The bartender's words broke the trance, and Lou glanced up at Katie quickly before returning to her conversation. Katie watched as the blood slowly drained from her rosy cheeks, eyes widening as she slowly turned to look at Katie again. The other woman turned around and was staring at Katie as well. God, she was pretty. And younger than Katie, with a perfect body. No wonder Lou was having lunch with her.

"Seattle?" Lou whispered. She looked as nauseous as Katie felt. "What are you doing here?"

"I came to tell you I fucked up." Katie took two steps forward then stopped again, waiting for Lou to stand up and open her arms to her.

Lou closed her eyes, and her chest rose and fell as she took a deep breath. Then she opened them again, fixing Katie with a blue gaze full of questions. "Are you really here?"

"To stay. If you'll have me."

"Katie, I–"

"I know." Katie looked at the other woman. "And I'm sorry to barge in on your date like this, but the woman you're with has my whole heart. And I'm here to win her back."

"Katie–"

"Please just let me finish." Katie had to get it out before she lost her nerve. "When I left Montana, I forgot how to smile. I forgot what laughter felt like. All I could do was think about how stupid I was to throw away everything I ever wanted, this incredible life with you I never even knew I could have, because I was scared. I love you, Lou. From the moment I met you and through all the moments apart, I love you. I'm not going to run away again, and I'll do whatever it takes to prove it to you."

The color was returning to Lou's face. "I didn't think I would ever see you again." She slid out from the booth and reached for Katie's hand, pulling her closer. "And Nora is just here because I put an ad out looking for some help with that website stuff you mentioned. You were right. Once I got to thinking about it, I realized it's not a bad idea, especially with all the surplus honey from the new hives."

"Well, don't hire her. Hire me."

Nora looked awkwardly at her phone. "Lou, if I should go..."

"I'm sorry, Nora, I didn't know Katie was coming today. I'll be in touch soon." Lou shook her hand, then waved Katie into Nora's vacated seat. She sighed, and Katie ached to reach out and take her hand, but she would let Lou lead. "You said all this before, right up until the moment you decided to leave. How do I know you're serious this time?"

"Because my whole life is sitting out in that parking lot. I can't go back to Seattle this time because there's nothing to go back to."

"Because you love me?" Lou raised an eyebrow.

"More than I've ever loved another person before."

"Is that enough for you?"

"What do you mean?"

"All the same problems you had before are still here."

"Not all of them." Katie glanced at the glass of water in front of Lou.

"I've been working on it. Finding better ways to cope, sometimes. But besides that, what about your career? The whole reason you left me?"

"It was ruining my life. You showed me that. I want to be in charge of my own destiny, not bending over for other people to take advantage of until I'm so burnt out I can't function. I have an appointment this afternoon to look at an office space for lease just up the street from here. I think it will be perfect to start my own little agency to help out small businesses in the valley."

"I see." Lou looked like her mind was racing, but whatever her thoughts were, she was keeping them close. "You really hurt me, Seattle. Leaving me like that."

"I know, and I'm so sorry. And I know it will take time to get back to where we were. But I believe in us."

"I can't give you an answer right now."

"You don't have to."

"I'm going to be late to therapy."

"You should go. Text me when you're ready to talk. I'll be around." Katie knew a kiss was too much to hope for, but her heart sank anyways when Lou slid out of the booth and settled her tab without even saying goodbye.

Chapter Twenty-Three

"So what do you think?" The real estate agent asked. "Pretty perfect, isn't it?"

"I love it," Katie said. It was probably more space than she needed, but the exposed brick was gorgeous, and the wide windows let in so much natural light she didn't even need to turn on the overhead fluorescents.

"It's been vacant for three months, but if you're interested I'd move fast. Summer season is coming and at this rate, someone will be along to snap it up."

"I should be ready in a few days," Katie said. "Just have to figure things out with the bank first." And figure things out with Lou.

"What are you planning to use the space for?" The agent asked.

"A boutique marketing agency. I want to help local businesses."

"We need that. Too many corporations come in with giant budgets and push our little guys out. I'm glad to see there's still people looking out for the community. In fact, I could probably use some marketing help, myself. And I know Bruce down at Gallatin Outfitters was saying he was trying to figure out new ways to make the tourists stop in. Might give him a call."

"Gallatin Outfitters?" Katie confirmed, scribbled the note down on her phone. These were good leads, and it made the potential of the place seem all the more real. Longing gnawed so rabidly at her stomach that it hurt. It was everything she had imagined when she first started making her tentative plan.

"Look, over here you could have a little sitting area," the agent continued to sell the space, but there was no need. Katie was ready to sign the paperwork that would make it hers, at least for the next year, but there was still one missing puzzle piece. "You could put a big lamp here, maybe a cowhide rug and some leather chairs. Make it real nice and homey."

"And a coffee bar there." It was all too easy to picture. Katie needed to leave before she did something else rash. "I have to go meet up with my friend, but I'll definitely be in contact."

"Of course. And send me over a list of the marketing services you'll be offering. I have a ton of summer vacation rentals I need to get out there over the next few months."

"I will," Katie said, shaking the agent's hand before heading down the street to find Megan, who had booked a ninety minute massage at a spa she found downtown.

Lou's appointment should have been over, but she hadn't texted Katie. That was okay, as long as she didn't ghost Katie again. Katie could wait, but not forever. She was cautiously excited about all the potential she saw in Montana, but Lou was the most important piece.

It certainly felt like forever though, even though less than twenty-four hours passed before she finally heard from Lou. She and Megan had explored Bozeman together, gotten dinner and then gone for drinks as the hours of silence ticked by. They checked into a hotel and drank a full bottle of wine, ignoring the sign that declared glass bottles forbidden in the hot tub area.

The text came the next day around noon, one simple word from Lou.

"Dinner?"

They arranged to meet at the sushi restaurant downtown. Katie arrived early, waiting under the streetlamp on the corner for Lou to get there. It was snowing softly, the accumulation sparkling on the sidewalk and parked cars and Katie's breath fogged in the air, but she would stand there all night if she had to.

Lou appeared around the corner and Katie's heart skipped a beat. She was so dapper in her dark wash jeans, and her cowboy boots gleamed as if she had shined them just for the occasion. Knowing Lou, she probably had. Her crooked smile appeared as she approached, tentative but warm.

"Well, at least you figured out how to dress for the weather," Lou said, looking Katie up and down.

"I hear Montana winters are rough." The coat had cost Katie an arm and a leg, but it was supposedly rated for Arctic expeditions and worth every cent if it kept her from freezing to death in a blizzard.

"Ready to go in?" Lou offered Katie her arm.

Katie held on to her desperately until they were shown to a table and she was forced to let go. Lou pulled out her chair for her, then sat opposite. She reached across the table and took Katie's hands in hers.

"You really threw me for a loop showing up like that yesterday."

"I'm sorry."

"Just when I was starting to get you off my mind."

"I had to come."

"You really brought everything with you?"

Katie nodded. "Everything I have to my name."

The waitress dropped off glasses of water and bowls of steaming miso soup. "Do you still need a minute with the menu?"

"A few, please." Lou said. The menus both still lay untouched on the table.

Katie picked up hers, but before she opened it, there was one thing she had to know. One thing she couldn't stand another minute of wondering. "Do you still love me?"

"You brought light back into my life at a time when it was really hard to see any, and I'll always love you, Seattle."

That sounded like there was going to be a 'but' attached. Katie paged through the menu, pretending to scrutinize the list of specialty roles as she braced herself against the blow she knew was coming. "You don't have to make any decisions now," she said, offering Lou an out, a way to delay the inevitable.

"I already have. Once the shock wore off of seeing you again, I got to thinking how empty the house has been since you've been gone. And this morning when I woke up, I was cursing myself you weren't there beside me. You're the piece of me that's been missing, even before I met you. I'd be a fool to try to keep going without it."

"I was so stupid to leave."

"You had to, to figure out on your own where you belonged. And I love that about you. I'm just glad you came back, I was starting to think you wouldn't."

"But you were hoping I would?"

"Every second of every day." The corners of Lou's eyes crinkled as she smiled.

"Have a safe flight," Katie said, hugging Megan. "Thank you so much for coming. I owe you big time."

"Just be happy," Megan grinned. "And I better be your matron-of-honor."

"More like matron-of-whatever-a-higher-distinc-tion-than-honor-is. Seriously, Megs, it means so much."

"Aww, don't get sappy on me, you'll make me cry."

"No, don't, your mascara will run and you won't have time to fix it before your flight," Katie teased, so she wouldn't cry herself.

"Shut up," Megan said, pulling Katie in for one last hug. "I love you."

"Love you, too."

"Lou," Megan said, reaching out to hug her, too. "Take care of my girl."

"Always," Lou said, wrapping her arm around Katie's waist possessively.

They watched as Megan went through the security gate, turning around to wave one last time before disappearing down the long hallway that led to the gates. Katie leaned into Lou. It was surreal being back at the airport with her, where it all began.

Lou looked down at Katie, her eyes sparkling with excitement. "Ready to go home?"

"Home sounds good."

Epilogue

"Get off that thing and come join the party," Jason laughed, nodding at the cell phone in Katie's hands.

"I just need one more picture of your family by the tree for the new website," she replied. "It adds more of that human touch to your brand story."

"If you say so," he said, throwing his hands up in mock surrender. "Can't argue with all the new customers you brought in this season. You know, we had a family come out all the way from Billings for one of our trees because of that ad you did?"

"Well, they are the best Christmas trees in Montana." Katie blushed. It had taken months of convincing for Jason to give her a shot at bringing new life back into his family's tree farm. He was so skeptical that she had offered to do it for commission only just to prove that she could. And it had been the perfect project to fill her calendar during the slow season in the valley.

"Really, Katie, we can't thank you enough. I haven't seen Jay this happy in years. His grandpappy would be proud to see how his legacy is carrying on," Mandy said with a warm smile and tears shining in her eyes. She fanned her hands in front of her face. "Ugh, I swear I'm not crying, it's just the pregnancy hormones."

"No way! Congratulations!" Katie hugged her neighbor, genuinely happy for the woman who had quickly become a close friend. "Does Lou know?"

"Not yet," Mandy said. "Unless Jason told her already?" She glared at her husband, who smiled sheepishly and shrugged with mock innocence. She sighed. "We promised we weren't telling anyone but family 'til the second trimester."

"I couldn't help it, it just slipped out."

"You're lucky I love you. Go get the kids so we can get back to dancing."

Katie looked around the barn while she waited for Jason to wrangle his children. Everything had come together perfectly for the Christmas Barn Dance, and she was proud of the work she had put in to help make it perfect for everyone. It was hard to believe it had already been a year since the strange sequence of events that brought her to Montana and the valley was gathering again to celebrate the magic of winter and community and appreciation for another cycle of seasons on the homestead. Everywhere she looked, she saw smiles and laughter. The band ended their song and Katie heard the faint sound of jingling bells in the silence before they started the next one.

"Santa!" Every child in the barn yelled at the same time, rushing for the door.

Katie resisted the urge to follow them. She still needed that photo for Jason's new website. Fortunately he appeared with both kids in tow.

"One picture," he said to them. "And no funny faces. Then you can go see Santa."

The bells got louder as the sleigh made its way up Jason's drive, their peals blown in through the open barn door on a gust of cold wind. Jason's family posed by the tall tree Katie had helped pick out and decorate. Hanging somewhere deep among the boughs was a little wooden ornament she had carved under George's guidance one late summer evening. She smiled at the memory as she snapped the photo and motioned to the kids that they were finally free to go outside.

Like his daughter, George had been quick to come around to Katie once he realized she was there for the right reasons. Even though he and Katie couldn't be more dissimilar, they had bonded over a love of art. She had started teaching him watercolors, and he taught her whittling in exchange. And Diane had become her biggest cheerleader, showering her with motherly affection and effusive pride whenever Katie booked a new client or launched a new website. Lou might have found it overbearing, but it was just what Katie needed when her own mother fell short. Katie couldn't wait to see them again for Christmas dinner, planned this time.

She took one more picture of the tree with no one milling around it and sent it off to Megan.

"Gorgeous." The reply came quickly. "Hope the dance goes well, can't wait to see you next week!"

Katie was excited to see Megan and her family, though she wasn't sure how she felt about attempting to ski again for the first time since college. At least the chalet at the nearby resort looked cute and cozy. And if she did something stupid like break her leg, Lou would be there to take care of her. Embracing the adventure was so much easier when she had someone to catch her if she fell.

Kids were trickling back inside, their new presents in hand, and the band was warming up on stage for their second set. That was Katie's cue. Walking against the flow of giddy children and their laughing parents, she slipped out into the cold. Snow fell softly, and while she knew what to expect, it didn't lessen the magic of seeing the horse-drawn sleigh at all. It didn't lessen the magic of Lou.

The final present distributed, Lou hopped down from the sleigh. Katie stepped forward, and Lou finally noticed her, eyes lighting up as she opened her arms for Katie to run into. When they were sure the last kids were inside and the door was firmly closed, Lou pulled off her Santa disguise.

"How's the party inside?" Lou asked.

"Perfect," Katie sighed, warm with Lou's arms wrapped around her. "But we could always take the sleigh somewhere quieter for a little while. The horses are still hitched."

"And miss the dance?" Lou raised an eyebrow and her voice dropped to a raspy whisper. "Because once I have you in the back of that sleigh, I expect we'll be there a. Very. Long. Time."

Katie shivered, but not from the cold. "I guess I can wait a little longer." Unlike her, the barn dance only came once a year. "But I want a kiss before we go in."

"I can do that," Lou said, tilting her chin up to brush her lips over Katie's.

If Katie said the feelings were still as powerful as it was the first time they kissed, she would have been lying. They were stronger. Their love had only grown through the seasons, like the crops they had watched spring from the ground and mature through summer. The happiness she had felt in the first few weeks when everything was bright and new was nothing compared to the deep contentment with knowing she had finally found where she belonged: wrapped up in Lou's arms under the big Montana sky.

The End

Author's Note

First, let me say I love Seattle and the surrounding areas! It's a great place— no matter what Katie thinks— and one I am so fortunate to call home. I love small town holiday romances, though, and Bozeman is near and dear to my heart. When the idea for this story came to me, I knew it had to be set there. While I've taken some liberties in my descriptions of life in Paradise Valley and the surrounding areas, Chico Hot Springs is real, as are the Absaroka mountains and depictions of wildlife in the area. Lou was inspired by the many queer farmers and homesteaders who are working to uproot the heteropatriarchal norms in agriculture. Her passion for regenerative, sustainable agriculture is shared by many real people across the world working for a better future.

About the Author

Wren Taylor is a sapphic romance novelist. A passion for history and stories of empowered women serve as her primary inspiration when writing. She lives in the Pacific Northwest with her two dogs. When she's not dreaming up her next book, Wren enjoys cooking, painting, gardening, and enjoying the natural beauty of the world. Follow Wren on social media @wrentaylorwrites to stay up to date with the latest on new book releases and more!

Also by Wren Taylor

Sapphic Seas Series (Historical Romance)

Book 1: The Captain's Choice

Book 2: The Pirate's Pursuit

Book 3: The Thief's Treasure (2024)

Contemporary Romance

Homestead for the Holidays